LOVE'S
Game

LOVE'S Game

HAROLD L. TURLEY II

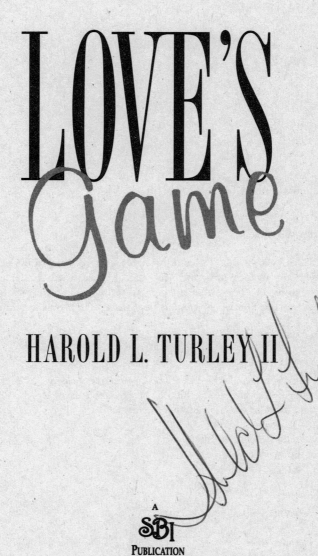

A
SBI
PUBLICATION

A STREBOR BOOKS INTERNATIONAL LLC PUBLICATION
DISTRIBUTED BY SIMON & SCHUSTER, INC.

Published by

Strebor Books International LLC
P.O. Box 1370
Bowie, MD 20718
http://www.streborbooks.com

ISBN 1-59309-029-3
LCCN 2003116852

Distributed by Simon & Schuster, Inc.
1230 Avenue of the Americas
New York, NY 10020
1-800-223-2336

Cover Design: www.mariondesigns.com

First Printing October 2004
Manufactured and Printed in the United States

10 9 8 7 6 5 4 3 2

DEDICATION

I dedicate this novel to the memory of a very close and dear friend. Big Reds,
if I had to use one word to describe you, it would be "determination."
No matter what the task, you completed it.
No matter how high the mountain was, you climbed it.
No matter what the goal was, you made sure to achieve it.
Your determination is what pushed me to complete this book.
In a way, it was my inspiration. I wish you were here with us now to read it.
Don't worry though, I'll have your copy waiting for you
when I see you again at those pearly white gates.
Always know, you are deeply missed and always loved.

Sincerely,
Your Friend

In Memory of Joshua Daniel Adams
(Big Reds)
September 10, 1981–June 4, 2002

ACKNOWLEDGMENTS

First and foremost I'd like to thank the Lord Jesus Christ, through him all things are possible.

To my mother, Anna West, we have been through a lot over the years but I wouldn't change one thing. I don't know what I would do without you in my life. You once told me I was your gift from God but I think you had it backwards. I think the gift He was giving was that of motherhood and allowing me to share your wisdom. You brought me into this world and have guided me throughout my journey. I owe everything to you, Muah!! I hope you don't expect any money though. I'm broke!!

To my heart, Candace, we have been through it all and will go through even more but as long as you continue to stay by my side, I'll ALWAYS have your back. Way Back! Just playing, words cannot express my gratitude for the hard work you do!! I guess now you'll be looking for that ring, huh? We'll see…

My children, Tre, Shawn, Malik, and Yhanae (yes, I have a handful), thank you for lighting up Daddy's life every day. All of you are my inspiration and my motivation to succeed in everything that I do. I might have a lot of titles bestowed upon me but none will ever be greater than "Daddy." Daddy loves each and every one of you.

My publisher, Strebor Books and Zane, you are my angel sent from God. You took a chance on me when no one else would. I only pray my writing backs up the faith you have in me. I won't begin to say thank you because I'd never come close to expressing my true gratitude. You've provided me the platform to turn my dream into a reality. Charmaine, thanks for all your hard work. Whenever I have a question, you make sure to have an answer. The rest of the Strebor staff, thanks for all of your hard work in making *Love's Game* what it is today. I'd also like to thank Simon & Schuster for distribution.

My family, James, JD, Ashante, Taledia, Aunt Nadine, Mark, Dytrea, Sia, Bobby, Uncle Butch and the rest of the Milner Family, I want to thank you for all the encouragement and supportive words throughout this whole process.

To Darrien, Rique, Jonathan, William, Lee, JD (not Jermaine Dupri), Allison, Nane, and the rest of my Strebor Family, thanks for all the advice. We are about to do big things in this Literary World. Strebor will be a household name soon.

Tina and Shelley, I know y'all probably thought I forgot about you, but how could I? The two of you are my Strebor Big Sisters! You both have guided me throughout this new experience. We all pretty much came to Strebor at the same time so we'll always share a bond. I love both of you and know each of you will be a HUGE success, not only with your literary careers but also in life.

My editor, L. Denise Jackson, thank you for being a part of this project. You stepped up to the plate and hit a homerun. I needed things to be done in a hurry to meet my deadline and not only did you meet it but you exceeded my expectations. You are truly a blessing and I thank you from the bottom of my heart.

To Keith from Marion Designs, the book cover is off the hook. You are truly a computer graphics genius. Thanks for all the hard work and late nights you put into my cover. Can't wait to work with you on my next project.

To Eileen and Acedro Todd, the website is off the hook!!

My Stratwood Ave family, Big Bad, Rome, Greg, Smiley, Ace, Reg, White Mike, T'won, Nino, Big Reds, Lil Dawg, Ray, June, Fat Dog, Nikki, Buck, Peanut, and Black aka Swells, y'all are my street family. I bet growing up none of you ever thought there would be a day when you'd see my name in print. Shit, half of you probably didn't believe that day would come when I first told everyone I was going to write a book. I want to let y'all know that each one of you is like a brother or a sister to me. I told you one day I'd put Stratwood on the map! I love y'all.

I know I'm missing someone and I don't want anyone to feel unappreciated. At this time, I would like to thank everyone who has given a helpful hand or stood in my corner throughout this whole process. Your encouraging words, many talks, advice and constant appreciation was much needed and will be forever treasured. I would be nothing without you. You are my friends, family, co-workers, and most importantly my biggest fans. You believed in me when I didn't believe in myself. I'm not going to name each one of you individually but know that I'm thankful and truly appreciative.

And last but definitely not least, to all the haters out there who told me that I would never get this book accomplished, I'd never amount to anything, or thought that I was lying or playing when I told you that I was going to do this—this book was for you. Your hate is what pushed me every day to make this project a reality. Without you, I wouldn't be half the man that I am. Now why you're sitting back thinking about what you can hate on next, take a bow, because in a way this book is dedicated to you. Hah! Hah!

Peace and Blessings,

Harold L. Turley II

Tyrelle
LEARNED FROM THE BEST

Every little boy has one cousin or uncle in their family they look up to and want to emulate. Mine was my older cousin Terry. I wanted to dress like him, play basketball as good as him, but most of all I wanted to have all the girls that he had.

I remember, when I was younger, he had his girl Tracy over to the house. I was staying over for the weekend because he was taking me to Triples Nightclub on Saturday to see the Junkyard Band. I saw him rush out the door, go downstairs, and then come back upstairs with a disturbed look on his face. He came into the back room with me while I was playing Nintendo.

"Go in my room and ask Tracy to show you how to work the computer," he said.

"But why? You already showed me earlier today."

"I know that but she doesn't. Just do what I said and stop askin' so many damn questions. Oh, play dumb too, so she can break it down for you. I need about a good fifteen minutes."

I didn't understand what was going on but I agreed.

"All right!" I replied.

He then went downstairs and I went into the room and asked Tracy what he had told me to ask her. Sure enough, she was more than willing to show me. About twenty minutes had passed, and in walked Terry with a slight sweat.

"Damn, boo! A nigga's missin' you. Can't I get some luvin?"

She looked at him with a smile filled with joy and was more than happy to oblige him. They both darted into the bedroom and closed the door. I knew what time it was, so Terry was going to be in there for at least two hours. Puzzled by why Terry was acting so strangely, I went over to the window and looked outside. I saw Ebony getting into her car. Ebony was the chick Terry had met about two or three weeks prior at the Safari Club.

It turns out that Terry had gotten his times mixed up with Tracy. He had forgotten that she was coming over early that day, so he had told Ebony to swing by. Terry had it that way; he never had unexpected visitors. He made sure all of his girls called him before coming over. How he did it? Hell if I knew. Later I found out that Ebony had called and said that she was up the street and on her way. Terry had me keep Tracy company while he went downstairs and had sex with Ebony in the basement. He knew that Tracy wouldn't have any problems showing me how to use the computer and that would give him the time he needed.

After he finished with Ebony he didn't just rush her out the house. No, he cuddled a little bit with her and told her that he had to pick his mother up from work so he had to get ready to go. He used the bathroom downstairs to wash off so Tracy wouldn't smell Ebony's scent on him. He told Ebony to go ahead and let herself out, like he was in a rush or running late so she wouldn't press him, came upstairs, and took Tracy right into the room so she wouldn't happen to look out the window and see Ebony getting in her car. He fucked both of them that day. The nigga was smooth, I mean *smooth!*

❖ ❖ ❖ ❖

Terry was always introducing me to all the right people. He had just been drafted by the Boston Celtics when I was in junior high school. It didn't just stop with basketball; he was much smarter than that. He made sure he knew any and everybody. He knew NFL players, club owners, and entertainers. I probably knew more people by the age of fourteen than most people would ever meet. Shit, I even knew damn doctors and lawyers. Terry knew anybody that was somebody in D.C. and, after a while, so did I.

He taught me the two most important things in life; how to manage my money and my women. I had a couple of candy scams working at school from my locker and a different girl to call my own. They all went to different schools throughout the D.C area.

"Never mess with a girl that goes to school with you because everybody will know your business," he would tell me.

When a girl has a boyfriend that goes to another school and someone wants to know about them, usually she will tell them, "*You don't know him. He goes to another school.*" Then the subject is dropped and your name is never brought up. See, this is important because you never know who knows who when it comes to girls. Everybody knows somebody! The chances of getting caught were slim to none, if you ask me.

Shit like that is what he taught me throughout my childhood; the ends and outs of how to be a playa. I only wish he'd taught me the ends and outs of how to be a man instead but like all things, you have to learn the hard way...

Jerry
REALITY SOONER OR LATER SETS IN

I sat down and carefully planned out my weekend. Everything had to be perfect. I wanted to make sure everything was airtight. Angie wasn't like any of those other chicks I dealt with; not to mention I hardly saw her. If it didn't make sense to her, she was going to ask questions. I couldn't have anything fucking the night up. She had class, cash, and an ass that just, *MADE ME WANNA HOLLA!*

I picked up the phone and called Ty (my little cousin Tyrelle) so he would know the drill. Couldn't have him not knowing what was going on. Knowing my wife, she'd probably call him first looking for me.

"Hello," he said, answering the phone.

"What's up, Ty?"

"Shit! Trying to find something to get into tonight," he replied.

"Why don't you just call up Jodi or something?" I asked.

"I would if I could 'cause I damn sure need some ass right about now, but she's in Chicago. I'll fuck around and probably call April or something. I'll explode waiting for Jodi's ass. I need some now! What's on your agenda for tonight?"

"Tonight? It's more like the weekend."

"Nigga, you do remember Tracy? You know, your wife? Sometimes I think you forget that you're a married man. How in the hell are you going to spend the whole weekend with a bitch?" he questioned.

"Don't question me. I know how to handle myself and this situation, thank you very much. That's actually why I'm calling you. If Tracy calls you tomorrow, just say that I'm with you. Say I'm asleep or something. She won't try to wake me. I doubt she'll even call, but just in case. Can't have two different stories."

"So who's the lucky lady getting all this special treatment?"

"You'll never guess. I meant to tell you the other day when I ran into her. Man..."

"Who?" Ty asked, cutting me off.

"Angie."

"Damn! For real? I haven't heard that name in a minute. Slim was tough though."

"Was? You should see her now. She's off the hook! I tell you! When they say certain things get better with age, they ain't lying!"

"So, what has she been up to?" he asked.

"Hell if I know. We weren't talking about any of that. I was just trying to set up a time to get back in that."

"Yeah, I know *you* were. I bet your ass was happy to see that some things haven't changed."

"Who are you telling? I thought she would be like naw, 'cause of how shit went down the last time, but she was game for everything. I'm talking 'bout she was telling a brotha how she misses me and shit," I said.

"So, how are you going to pull all this shit off? If I remember correctly, slim doesn't know your ass is married, so I'm sure she's going to want you to stay with her the entire weekend," he said.

"Did your ass forget who taught you what you know?"

"Here we go with this again. You taught me a lil' something," he said.

"I taught your ass more than that, so I'm pretty sure I can handle this situation."

"Okay, how?" he asked.

"First of all, Tracy isn't going to miss me. She'll probably be out with her girls or something. She does her own thing on the weekends now."

"That might be true, but I'm sure she'll recognize that her husband didn't come home that night and that's when the shit will hit the fan. Y'all may be going through this lil' beef phase now, but not coming home will put ya on a whole other level. I'm taking the Divorce Court level."

"I'm sure it would, but who said I wasn't coming home tonight?"

"What? Did you tell Angie already that you're not spending the night?" he asked.

"No, I told you I didn't tell her anything. I just set up the weekend festivities."

"Then how are you going to get out of it, 'cause you know she is going to want your ass to spend the night?" he asked.

"Look, it's simple. Usually I get home from the club around what? 3:30-4:00

a.m.? So, I'll make sure I'm home Friday and Saturday night around that time. I did tell Angie that I'm having a house built out in Fort Washington and it's not ready yet, so I'm staying with you," I explained.

"Okay, that takes care of her spending the night with you, but not you with her," he replied.

Good point! Then what do I do? I was stuck.

"Damn, good question. I didn't think about that. I see what you're saying. That just stops her from staying with me, but she'll still try to get me to stay with her. I can say I don't have any clothes or something like that? Naw, that sounds childish. If I don't stay and don't have a good excuse, she's going to question the shit out of me. I go through that enough with Tracy. I'll be damn if I'm going to put up with it from someone else."

"How 'bout this? I'll just call you on your cell round 3:00 a.m. to give you an excuse to roll. Tell her that something came up and we need you at the club. That should take care of Friday night," he said.

"What if she asks what happened?"

"Tell her I didn't tell you. All I said is we need you at the club ASAP. She'll probably still be pissed, but she'll have a good enough excuse not to trip. That way it won't fuck up any ass for you on Saturday night. As for Saturday night, I don't know how you're going to get out of that, but if you can't come up with anything, just roll. She didn't trip off the cruddy shit you did last time, so she'll eventually get over it if you roll Saturday night, too."

I liked it. His plan was perfect. I'd still be home around my usual time so Tracy wouldn't expect anything. On Saturday, I could just carry it like Ty said and just roll. It wasn't like I'd be seeing Angie anytime soon after that. Plus, I wouldn't have to hear her bitch.

"Sounds like a plan to me," I replied.

"Why didn't you call me earlier this morning or something? If you'd given me more time, I'm sure I could've thought of something, other than you just carrying her."

"Naw, don't trip. I like it. I mean, I'm not trying to carry her, but I would've already gotten the pussy, so why trip if she's beefing? She leaves Sunday morning and I won't have to hear that shit."

"Just make sure you call Jeff and let him know what's up, too. Tracy might surprise you and call him instead, then you'll really be up shit's creek," he said.

"I will. You just make sure you remind him again at the club later on tonight as well. You know how his memory is."

"You don't have to tell me. You know I know. He has fucked up many an excuse for me on several occasions. I still think it's a miracle that Jodi and I are back together in the first place."

"Hold up now; that wasn't his fault. I don't know why you keep putting that on him. I would've done the same thing if I was him. You didn't tell anybody shit. How was he supposed to know that you had that chick at your house?" I asked.

"How was I supposed to know that Jodi would pop up over the house? She hadn't said anything when she'd called earlier that day about it and she didn't leave any messages saying that she would either. I thought I'd be straight since she'd called and I didn't answer. She had to know that I wasn't home. That was supposed to give me the time to fuck Slim and get her up and out of there."

"Your first mistake was giving Jodi a key. If she has a key, she has access to surprise your ass whenever she feels like it. Your second one, your dumb ass took another chick to your house. You know better than that! You do your dirt at her house or at a mo mo," I said.

"I didn't know she was coming over," he repeated.

"Bottom line, that shit was stupid. Deep down inside you know your ass was wrong. You can't even fake! You know you can't blame Jeff. All you had to do was let us know what was up and we would've made sure she didn't come over, regardless of who she'd called."

"I don't blame him for saying that he didn't know where I was. It was when he told her, 'He should be in the house. His ass is probably sleep and doesn't want to answer the phone.' Now that was just stupid. That basically gave her the idea to come over," he said.

I could see his point.

"I see what you're saying, but what you don't see is that you usually tell us when you have something popping off. You didn't tell us anything that day. So how was he supposed to know? When your ass is sleep you don't answer the phone for shit. We all know this, so I could see why he said that. It sounded like the truth. Honestly speaking, Jodi usually leaves you alone when you're asleep. That time, she didn't. I mean, come on, Ty. Do you really think he would've told her that shit, if he'd known you had a bitch over?"

"I know he wouldn't but, still, he should've just left it at he didn't know where I was and then called me and told me she was looking for me. I mean, what if I was over Shortie's house instead? Jodi would've still come over and seen I wasn't home. Now I'm getting the shit questioned out of me when I walk through the door. And what if I'd fuck up by saying I was over Jeff's house. I would've been caught right there, and let's not forget I would've been walking up in the house smelling like pussy."

Even though he was dead wrong to blame Jeff for that situation, he'd found a way to make his point and it was valid. Even if that would've happened, he still would've been short.

"That's my point! If you have something popping off you should tell one of us in case she does call. Don't leave us in the dark 'cause I'll be damned if I'm calling you every time Jodi calls looking for you and I don't know where you are. What do I look like?"

"Whatever. I wasn't wrong. I don't care what you say."

"Weren't you the one who just told me to call Jeff and let him know the deal in case Tracy calls him?"

"That's different."

It was pointless. He was going to have his point of view and I was going to have mine. I just needed to agree to disagree.

"I'm not even going to keep going there with you. I don't feel like you can blame him. I know one thing, I bet next time your ass won't bring a chick over your house. I'll tell you that much!"

"I bet I won't either," he replied, laughing.

I heard the front door close.

"Lemme holla at you later. Tracy just walked in."

He agreed and we both hung up.

I grabbed my clothes for the night. I needed to hurry up and get out of there before she found a way to start an argument. The only way I could prevent them was by staying gone as much as possible. I'd make the dinner arrangements when I get to the club.

I went into the bathroom and turned on the shower. It would've been nice if she was asleep by the time I got out. I took a quick shower to freshen up. I walked out of the bathroom with my towel on and saw Tracy lying on the bed relaxing, watching TV.

"Where are you going this early?" she asked.

"I'm going to work."

"Can you take off tonight?" she asked.

I should've known. Every time I have something planned with another chick she wants us to do something. It's like she has ESP or something.

"Not tonight, baby. Maybe another time."

She moved over towards me and took my towel off. She began to massage my penis, teasing me.

"Come on, baby. I'm tired of all the arguing between us. I want to spend some time with you. I'll make it worth your while."

She began to give me oral pleasure that was better than usual. I couldn't believe what was going on. What had come over her? I pushed her off me. I was determined to have my night with Angie.

"Stop! Stop! I have to get out of here. Another time, baby."

"It's always another damn time when it comes to me! I'm getting sick of this shit. I had to play second to basketball in high school and college. Thank God your ass didn't make it in the pros, or we'd probably be divorced by now."

She realized what she'd just said. I remained calm.

She continued, "I'm sorry. I know how you feel about that situation. I didn't mean it like that. We hardly do anything anymore but argue. I don't care if we go to a movie or the mall; just take me somewhere. I don't care if you try to fuck me in a parking lot; just show me, in some kind of way, you're still attracted to me. Buy me an ice cream cone. I just want to spend some time with you because at the rate we're going, this marriage isn't going to last that much longer."

I had to pick and choose my words to avoid an argument, but anything short of me agreeing would've started one regardless.

"I know, baby, and I agree, but I can't tonight. It's the first of the month and I have to do the books and so forth. That's why I'm going in early. Why don't you call up Crystal tonight and do something with her and we'll spend next weekend together? I promise."

I grabbed my clothes and began to put them on. She gave me a look of frustration.

"Fine. Maybe Crystal can give me some dick," she said to aggravate me.

She got up and went downstairs. I felt bad for turning her down. It had been a while since we'd done something together. She was actually reaching out to me and I didn't grab on. But how could I? Who knew when the next opportunity to hook up with Angie would happen? I couldn't pass the chance up. I continued getting dressed.

I walked downstairs and saw Tracy sitting on the couch, watching TV in the living room.

"Baby, I promise we'll do something next weekend; just me and you."

She just nodded her head as if to say, "Whatever."

I arrived at the Cheesecake Factory fifteen minutes early. I wanted to make sure I was on time, this time, to make a good impression. Plus I wanted to see her fine ass walk through that door. I ordered a drink to take off the edge. I wasn't sure why I was so nervous, but my nerves were definitely jumping. I looked at my watch to check the time: 7:20 p.m. I feel like that was the first time we'd ever hooked up.

"Can I take your order, sir?" the waiter asked.

"Give me another ten minutes or so. I'm waiting for my date to arrive."

"Aren't you Terry Shaw? Didn't you play for Maryland?" he asked.

"Yeah," I said modestly.

He didn't look any older then twenty-one; maybe twenty-two. I was shocked that he even recognized me.

"My father talked about you all the time. He said he coached you," the waiter said.

This is interesting.

"Really, who is your father?" I asked.

"Bill Lee," he replied.

"Yeah, your old man coached me when I was fourteen. Wow, how is he doing?"

"He's fine. He just had surgery on his knee again."

"Really."

I took out one of my business cards and wrote my home number on the back of it.

"So you must be lil' Rob? He used to bring you to practice sometime. Give this to your father. Tell him to give me a call. It'll be nice to pick his brain again. Well, actually, he used to pick mine."

"Mr. Shaw, if you don't mind me asking, whatever happened to you? By the way my father talked about you; I always wondered why you aren't still in the NBA?"

"Right after I was drafted, I started to work out with the team voluntarily. You know, to show good faith. Anyhow, summer league was about to start up, and I still hadn't reached an agreement on my contract with the Celtics. All I wanted to do was play ball. It was never about the money to me. The love of the game meant everything to me. Well, I agreed to play summer league as a good faith gesture while my contract was being worked out. I tore my knee in our second game of the summer. No multi-million dollar contract, no shoe deal, and no NBA career for me."

"You couldn't catch on with another team?" he asked.

I spotted Angie standing at the door. I stood up and waved to her so she could notice me.

She did, then I continued, "Yeah, I signed a two-year deal with the Bullets about a year and a half later. They were the only team that wanted to take a chance on my knee. My knee wasn't the same afterwards. I played two years with them, then called it quits and retired. I always played at the highest level, and when I couldn't anymore, I wasn't going to embarrass myself playing just for a paycheck. Luckily for me, I got my education while I was in college and didn't just depend on basketball."

I'm not sure how old he actually was, but knowing Coach Lee, his son had to be playing somewhere. I wanted to let him know about my education and not just the NBA.

"Your father used to beat getting an education in my head all the time. He would say, '*That basketball got you into school; now let your mind get you out of it.*' I owe your father a lot," I said.

I helped Angie into her chair and sat back down.

"He tells me that every day."

Angie stood back and listened.

"So you play as well?" I asked.

"Yeah, but I didn't make it to a big-time college like you. I play at Towson; next year will be my last," he replied.

"What's your major?"

"Pre-law. I've been accepted at Georgetown Law School already."

"I see you have a plan for life after basketball as well; that's good. I usually go to Run-N-Shoot on Sunday mornings. Maybe you can show me your moves on the court sometime," I suggested.

He began to grin.

"I'd like that, Mr. Shaw. Well, don't let me interrupt your dinner any longer. Just let me know when you're ready to order," he said.

I was impressed by Angie. She never interrupted our conversation, nor did she become upset or anything. She sat back and listened, as if she was interested as well.

"I apologize for that. His father used to be my coach when I was younger," I said.

"Oh, it's no problem at all. I like how you stressed the importance of school to him. Nowadays, everybody wants to be the next Lebron," she replied. She picked up her menu. "Let's hurry up and order so we can eat, then get out of here. I want you all to myself tonight."

I was instantly turned on by what she'd said.

"Is that so? I think I can take care of that for you." I waved for the waiter to come back over to our table. "We're ready to order. I'd like a steak, medium-rare, with a baked potato and string beans."

"I'll have the barbecue chicken breast with mashed potatoes and corn," Angie said.

"And to drink?" he asked.

"Bring us a bottle of Merlot," I said.

He grabbed our menus and walked off.

"Might I ask what you have planned for us tonight?" I asked.

"All I plan to do is be with you all weekend. I should be the one asking what you have in store for me," she said.

"A night filled with fun is all I'm going to say," I replied.

We enjoyed our dinner but mostly the dinner conversation. We continuously talked dirty to each other, growing our sexual appetite for one another. I was so horny that once we'd finally finished dinner, I asked for the check and we hit the door.

We headed straight for her hotel. I'd barely gotten in the front door before she started kissing me. At that point, I knew exactly how much I had her. She couldn't wait another minute. I wanted to tease her a little longer.

"Slow down a little bit, baby. We have all night," I said.

She did.

"Would you like a drink?" she asked.

"Sure, what do you have?"

She walked over to the bar in her suite. "I have some Remy, Hennessy, and a bottle of Moët."

"I'll have some Remy."

She made me a glass and poured herself a glass of Moët. She walked over to the couch, handed me my drink, and sat down beside me. I took a sip of my drink. I placed it down on the table and stood up so I could give her a massage. She enjoyed every minute of it. My hands caressed her soft body. It became hot in the room quickly. She lunged over and started to kiss me passionately again. This time, I couldn't resist. I wanted her then. I picked her up and took her into the bedroom.

We had passionate sex but something was missing. I wasn't sure what but, once I was done, something didn't feel right. I had an empty feeling inside of me.

I went into the bathroom to wash up but I turned on the shower instead. I didn't want Tracy detecting any scents whatsoever. I got in the shower and let the warm water run over my body. I couldn't help but to question what could possibly be wrong. Angie was perfect. The night was perfect. The sex was great but something still just didn't seem right. Something wasn't hitting home. Maybe I was just tired and delusional.

I came out of the bathroom to see Angie knocked out asleep. I went back into the living room and grabbed my unfinished drink. I went out on the balcony and felt the cool breeze. I stood there staring at the midnight sky, drinking my now watered-down drink. An unpredictable question then jumped in my train of thought. *Was it all worth it? Was being with Angie that night worth turning my wife down?* The answers to my questions became a shock. No, it wasn't. No, she wasn't. Why am I shopping for milk when I have the cow at home? That, I didn't know. That, I couldn't answer.

My mind was in circles wondering what I'd done and why I'd done it for so long, if it was all for nothing. What was the point? I needed to get out of there. I went back inside the hotel room and gathered my clothes. That was definitely not the place I needed to be right then. I got dressed quietly, trying to not wake Angie. I grabbed the bottle of Remy that was left and headed out the door.

I drove around the city trying to clear my head. It was only a little after midnight so I couldn't go in the house yet. I didn't want to go to the club either because I wasn't trying to be around anybody right then. I called Ty to let him know he didn't have to call me later on since I'd already rolled. I'd hoped to get his voice mail but I wasn't that lucky.

"Hello," he said, answering the phone.

I could hardly hear him because of all the noise in the background.

"You don't have to worry about calling later on. I've already left," I said.

"Hello!" he yelled.

I could tell he couldn't hear me.

"Hello!" he yelled again.

I hung up the phone. Hopefully he'd go to his office and call back. I shouldn't have called him anyway. I should've just turned my phone off when I'd walked in the door and let him get my voice mail. My phone started ringing. I knew he'd call right back.

"Yeah," I said, answering the phone.

"What's up? You called me?" he replied.

"I was just calling to tell you that you don't have to hit my cell later on tonight because I've already left Angie's hotel."

"Why? What happened?"

"Nothing happened; I just rolled. For real, young, I really don't feel like getting into all that, so I'll just holla at you in the morning," I said.

He didn't try to force his will on me.

"Okay! Lookie here, there are a truckload of women up in here tonight, so you do you and I'll talk to you," he said.

We both hung up from one another. I continued to drive around the city. For some reason, driving calms me down when I'm upset and helps me to see things I wouldn't see otherwise. I guess I'm more at peace with myself while I'm driving. I don't have to worry about anyone asking me a rack of questions or continually wanting to know what is wrong.

I replayed the argument Tracy and I had earlier and the look on her face. All she wanted to do was spend some time with me and I'd turned her down for some ass. I just had to have my night with Angie and it wasn't even worth it. Don't get me wrong. The sex was good but it's not like being with Tracy; nothing is. The more I thought, the more things didn't make sense. Like, it didn't make sense to go out and get something you already had. The way I'd treat Tracy didn't make sense. I got on I-295 South and headed home. I needed to talk to Tracy. I needed to apologize to her.

I walked into my dark, empty house. There was no sign of Tracy. I looked around for a note but she didn't leave one. I looked to see what time it was and it was going on 2 a.m. She'd obviously gotten over not being able to spend time with me and had found something else to do. I wondered what and with whom? I stopped myself from thinking like that. I remained positive. She'd probably gone over to one of her friends' houses and would be home soon. I turned on the TV in the living and lay on the couch, waiting for her to come home.

The sound of the front door closing woke me from a deep sleep. I looked at the clock on the cable box and it read 4:48 a.m. It didn't seem like I was sleeping that long. I jumped up, pissed at what time she was strolling in the house.

"Where the hell have you been?" I asked.

She was going up the steps. She ignored my question and continued upstairs. I followed behind her. She went into the bedroom with me following close behind.

"Did you hear what I said? Where have you been?" I asked again.

"I heard you the first time you asked me, but you're not anyone to be questioning what time I come in the house," she replied.

"I'm your damn husband; that's who I am," I said.

"Really, I can't tell because you damn sure don't act like it."

"I'm going to ask once again, where have you been?" I said sternly.

"Does it matter where I've been? You made it perfectly clear earlier that you didn't want to be with me, so I just found someone that did."

I knew she didn't just say what I thought she said. She must've lost her mind.

"What do you mean, you found somebody that did?" I questioned.

"Exactly what I said," she replied.

I jumped in her face with my fist balled.

"What, are you going to hit me now?" she nonchalantly responded.

I wanted to, disrespecting me like that. I wanted to knock the shit out of her but I didn't. I continued to stand in her face looking stupid.

"So you're cheating on me now?" I asked.

It was all I could muster up. She smacked her lips and walked into the bathroom. I followed behind her.

"So what, you're not going to answer me now?" I asked.

She winced. "Get out of my face!"

"No, I asked you a question. Are you cheating on me?"

"No I'm not cheating on you but I damn sure wish I was," she replied.

"Then where the hell have you been?"

"Out!"

"Out where, damn it?"

"Not with you; I know that much," she replied sarcastically.

"You know what? Fuck it! I don't care where the fuck you've been. Fuck whoever you want! I don't give a shit!" I yelled.

"That's the damn problem right there. Your ass never gave a shit," she replied.

"Whatever!"

"I damn sure wish I was fucking someone else. That's probably the only way I'll find someone that actually cares about me," she said as tears began to come out her eyes.

I didn't care. I walked out the bathroom and in the bedroom to grab my pillows, then I went downstairs. If I'd lain in the bed with her, I would've probably killed her ass. I stretched out on the couch and got comfortable. She came downstairs.

"So, is that what you're going to do? Just run whenever we have a problem or an argument? I'm tired of you running," she said.

"Why are you talking to me? You should be telling this to the muthafucka you're cheating with. Isn't that what you told me?"

"You know what, here I am down here trying to get past this shit and you want to keep it lingering. I told your ass I'm not cheating on you. If you must know, I was out with Crystal tonight."

"Yeah, I've heard that before. I don't care who you were out with. It wasn't me; we know that much," I said, using her own words against her.

"I'm not going to keep trying to kiss your ass. If you want to stay down here and stay pissed you can do it by your damn self. I'm going to bed," she said, then stormed off. "I don't know who he thinks he's fooling. Just because he's out fucking everybody doesn't mean I am. He can kiss my damn ass," she mumbled, walking up the steps.

I thought about how my night had ended with Angie. I needed to call her. Hopefully what I'd done wouldn't affect the next night. I called on my cell phone to apologize for leaving the way I did.

"Hello," she said, answering her cell phone still half asleep.

"I'm sorry to wake you. I thought I'd be leaving you a message," I said.

"You know what? I have nothing to say to you. I can't believe your ass left like that," she said.

"I'm sorry. That's why I'm calling. I'm just getting in the house myself. Something popped off at the club and someone started shooting so I had to hurry up and get there."

I knocked on my wooden coffee table, hoping the tale I'd just told wouldn't come true.

"You should've just woken me up. I could've gone with you," she said.

"I didn't want to. You looked so peaceful sleeping, so I just let you sleep. I didn't think I'd be that long anyway. I'm sorry. Can I make it up to you tomorrow?"

I wanted to see how much of my story she'd bought.

"Yeah," she sighed, "you better, but it's going to cost you. You know I wasn't finished yet. I wanted to go again," she said.

"Really? You looked finished to me," I said jokingly.

"I was finished for that round but we were scheduled for four," she cooed.

I became turned on again.

"You better watch yourself before you find me over there now handling some business," I said.

"You don't see me stopping you, now do you?"

I thought about it but declined.

"Let's hold off until tomorrow, boo. I want to make sure we go the whole four rounds this time. I'm dead tired now."

"Well, go to sleep and call me in the morning," she said.

I agreed. We got off the phone and I went to sleep.

After what had happened, I was determined to have a blast with Angie. I'd cut shit short for no reason at all. I didn't know what I was thinking. Nothing was going to ruin things for that night. I went to Angie's, ready to get things started off the break. I didn't want to play around like I'd done the night before. I wanted to start our festivities as soon as possible.

I knocked on the door and, to my surprise, Angie was reading my mind. She answered the door with nothing on but a smile.

"I must have the wrong room. I'm sorry, ma'am," I joked.

She grabbed me. "Well, we just need to make it the right room then."

We began to kiss passionately. I picked her up, closed the front door, and took her into the bedroom. I wanted her right then. Once we made our way to the bedroom, I laid her down. I took my pants off and tried to place myself inside of her.

"Baby, wait, I'm not wet yet," she said.

I knew how to take care of that. I got on my knees and orally pleased her. I licked her vaginal walls and sucked on her clit. She became aroused and dripping wet in no time. I placed myself inside of her with ease. I wanted her to enjoy every minute of it. I took my time and paced myself like I was in a long distance race.

Our bodies met one another slowly in sync. She really began to get into it.

"Ooh!" she moaned.

She wasn't the type of woman that liked to talk during sex like Tracy. That really was starting to bother me. I like being talked to. It turned me on and helped me climax. I pictured Tracy talking to me during sex, to help guide me along. I could see all of Tracy's facial expressions as she told me to hit it harder.

I began to fuck Angie harder and harder. She still moaned with oohs and ahhs, but I couldn't hear them. All I heard was Tracy.

'Right there, baby. Yeah, I like it like that. Don't stop, Terry. I'm about to CUM!'

I'm right behind you Tracy.

"Yeah, baby, you like that, huh?" I asked.

'Yeah harder, I'm about to CUM,' I imagined Tracy replying.

"I'm going to cum along with you, baby. I'm bout to cum," I said.

I climaxed. I lay there exhausted from the sex I'd been longing for. Tracy lay on my chest, exhausted as well.

"I'm sorry, baby. I'm sorry for the way I've acted," I said.

I kissed her on the top of her forehead.

I woke up out of my deep sleep, embarrassed. Reality set in and I realized that I hadn't just make love to my wife, but Angie. The guilt started to set in. I couldn't deny my feelings any longer. It was time for my wife and me to have a long talk. There were a lot of things the two of us needed to discuss. I moved Angie off me without waking her, put my clothes on and snuck out again.

I ran in the house and upstairs. No sign of Tracy. I should've known she wouldn't be home. It was still relatively earlier. It was only 7:23 p.m. Time flew past. It went from 7:30 p.m. to 11 p.m. quickly and still, no sign of Tracy.

All of a sudden I heard a key unlocking the front door. It was her. I sat on the couch as she walked past. She went into the kitchen, then came back out into the living room where she saw me. She didn't say a word and neither did I. I didn't know what to say or how to start off the conversation. I just sat there. She went upstairs. I still didn't move. I just sat there. Quickly my guilt turned into depression. What had I done?

Tyrelle

WE PLAYIN' BASKETBALL

It was 9:30 a.m. and my phone was ringing.

"Hello!"

"What's up, nigga? You didn't call me back last night." It was my cousin Jeff.

He was just like me. We were more like brothers than cousins because our mothers were so tight. You could always catch them at a card table together playing some whisk or spades.

"I know, my bad. April came by last night and one thing led to another," I told him.

"April? I thought you were done fooling with that chickenhead. Plus, I thought you and Jodi were back together and you were going to be faithful."

"Nigga, we are back together, but there's too much pussy out here for me to be just settling down. Besides, Jodi's in Chicago for some type of medical convention. What she doesn't know won't hurt her!"

"Fine, dig your own grave. I don't know why you want to fuck wit dat bitch anyway. Only reason why April is trying to get with you is because she sees dollar signs."

"Yeah, well she ain't getting a cent so she can see what she wants as long as I keep seeing that pussy. Plus that bitch can suck a golf ball through a garden hose. You know she swallows, right? She actually gets offended if she spills one drop."

We both laughed our asses off at that. Jeff understood me. He'd been with his girl for about four years but was still messin' with skeezers behind her back. We'd run trains on a few.

"All I'm saying is that you need to watch yourself; especially with April. She's a pregnancy waiting to happen. Jodi's marriage material and furthermore..."

I cut him off. "We don't bring up those words around here. You need to go somewhere else, talking about marriage."

"Look, it's time that we start thinking about it. I'm almost thirty. I've had enough pussy for ten men. It's time that I take things seriously and you, too. Shit, Jodi's fine as hell! She has a body that can put Viagra out of business and she's a doctor. She isn't one of these dumb-ass hoodrats from the club."

I asked him, "Are you finished with the sermon? Because I'm a go 'head and get ready. We still ballin' today?"

"Oh, you know it."

"All right. I'll meet you up at the Shoot around 11:30-12."

"Bet dat!" he said.

I hung up the phone and started thinking. Was he right? Jodi and I had been together for the past three years. I started thinking about the day we'd met. She was in Med School at Howard and one of her sorors was in town. They didn't feel like sitting in the house so they swung past the club that night. Jodi said she'd been in there before but that was the first time I'd seen her in the club since we'd opened. When I saw her, I knew right then that I had to have the woman.

I sat around for a good two hours trying to figure out how to approach her. If there was one thing that Terry had taught me, it was that everything in life was like chess. Without a good approach and strategy you will lose, but if you plan correctly and make the right move, straight like checkmate! She was bad. She was 5'9", light brown, 145 pounds all in her thighs, ass and breasts, and to top it off, she had long black silky hair that was actually hers. She had on a black dress that showed every curve with black open-toed sandals. Her hair, nails, and even her toes were flawless. She had to be, if not the baddest, one of the baddest chicks in the club that night.

I decided to send her a bottle of Moët, compliments of the house, and of course I walked it over and introduced myself. When her girls finally went to the dance floor, it gave me the perfect opportunity to get better acquainted with her. We talked and talked. Before she left I slipped her my number. She called me about a couple of days later and the rest was history.

Maybe it was time for me to settle down. I didn't know. I really didn't have time to think about it right then. I mean, as far as I knew Jodi was faithful to me. She'd never strayed, but you can only trust a woman as far as you can throw one. I jumped out of the bed and started to get ready.

❖ ❖ ❖ ❖

Terry, Jeff, and I went to the Run-N-Shoot over on Marlboro Pike to play basketball every now and then. It was a way for us to release some stress. The court was our sanctuary, a place where we could just get away and enjoy ourselves. Not worry about our women or our careers. I grabbed my bag and put my long black basketball shorts, Washington Wizards cut-off T-shirt, and my Jordans inside. I put on my HOBO sweat-pants and T-shirt, a pair of Nike socks, and my flip-flops, grabbed my car keys and headed out the door. I decided to drive the Navigator today, jumped in and headed on my way.

By the time I got there, Jeff and Terry were already on the court shooting around. I went inside the locker room and put on my gear and then went out and started to warm up. The gym was packed; it usually was in the summertime. All the high school, college, and pro players were there working on their games and hanging out. Hopefully, we could pick up two good players so at least we could get in a couple of games before we left. It was at least a twenty-five-minute wait just to get on the court and after your game, if you lost you had to sign the list and wait all over again. By then you're looking at about another forty-five minutes to an hour to get back on the court.

I asked Jeff, "Did you find two more to run? I'm not trying to lose."

He looked at me and said, "Oh, I didn't tell you. Terry talked to Greg and Vic and they're running."

I became excited because I knew that with our five we wouldn't be coming off the court any time soon. Greg used to play at Cardozo High in Northwest. He then went to some Juco school and after his two years there, he'd transferred to West Virginia. Everyone talked about Tim Hardaway's killa crossover; it didn't come close to Greg's. I remembered that time at the Urbo when Penny Hardaway played and checked Greg. Greg had that man on a string. He was yanking him left and right. It was like Penny was Greg's personal yo-yo. After the game Greg had on a pair of Pennys, so he took them off and autographed them, *Greg Jones,* and handed them to him.

Vic played at Georgetown with Allen Iverson his freshman year. That was a tough backcourt. I still didn't know how John Thompson had enough balls to go around with those two. Vic still held the freshman record for most points scored by a freshman in a Big East Tournament game. He had thirty-three. He left after his sophomore year to go to the NBA but wasn't drafted. He'd been playing the last couple of years in the CBA.

Once he started knocking down the jumper on a consistent basis, he'd be in the league.

It was finally our turn to get on the court. It wasn't that long of a wait after all. The games were first to sixteen playing two's and three's or whoever had the highest after twelve minutes. We mopped up the first team we played. Greg hit three straight three's and then came down and threw an alley-oop to Vic. The score was 11-0. They then hit a bucket to pull it to 11-2. Jeff came down and threw the ball in between his defender's legs and then snatched it back. Main man fell and everybody in the gym that saw was pointing at cuz and laughing. To add insult to injury he knocked down the three ball, too. I got a quick steal once they got past half and threw a pass to Vic while he was streaking down the court. Vic sent the game home with a thunderous two-handed jam. We won the next three games fairly easy. I went to get a drink of water from the water fountain in between our next game. When I came back I realized this next game wasn't going to be easy.

Five *BALLERS* were standing on the court ready to get things started. Pep "Harlem World" Tyson, Lonnie "The L Train" Harrell, Sheik "The Freak" Pearson, Mike "The Thrill" Gill, and none other than the Houston Rockets' own Moochie Norris. I hurried up and ran to the court so we could get the game started.

Greg brought the ball down and Sheik was on him, Lonnie checked Jeff, Pep was on me, Mike matched up with Vic, and the final match-up was Moochie and Terry. Moochie and Terry had been going at one another since the boys and girls club. Had Terry not gotten locked up his second year in the league he probably would've been still playing, or at least coaching. In my opinion a reputation is harder to get rid of than anything. Greg gave Sheik a quick move to the right, pulled up and knocked down the three ball; 3-0 already.

Jeff started yelling, "Let's go!"

Sheik dribbled the ball up court with his knuckles. You could tell he was on get back. He went towards his right and crossed back to the left. Greg stumbled a little bit but recovered to play good D and forced Sheik to shoot a tough shot. Jeff skied to grab the rebound, threw the ball up to Terry and Terry lobed a pass to Vic as he was coming up the side. Poor Moochie had his back turned. "Watch your head!" Vic yelled as he caught the pass and dunked it on Moochie's back, 5-0.

Moochie threw the inbound pass into Pep and he brought the ball up the floor. As he crossed half-court, he switched the ball over to his right hand. He gave me a little stutter step, then faked like he was going to cross over to his left, so I anticipated it and jumped on his left hand. Wrong move! He snatched it back all in one motion with his right hand, stepped over, and knocked down the eighteen footer; 5-2.

As I brought the ball up the court, everyone on the side watching the game was still shouting and high-five'n each other from Pep's move. When I crossed the half I yelled out, "Penny!," and Jeff looked at me. He then came to the top of the key and caught a pass from me. I acted like I was going to set a high screen for Jeff and then spun off Pep. At the same time, Jeff lobbed a pass up towards the rim. I went and got it and dunked it; 7-2.

Jeff and I had been running that play for years. We called it Penny because we both were watching an Orlando Magic game when he played for them and he did that move.

Jeff tried to get us hyped up again and started yelling, "Let's go, come on! Let's put these niggas away!"

Moochie brought the ball up and gave Terry a quick move and went past him. Jeff stepped over to help out and Lonnie faded back behind the college three-point line. Moochie kicked it out to him and Lonnie knocked down the tre ball; 7-5.

Greg grabbed the ball out the net real quick and shot a pass down to Vic as he was standing at the half. Vic caught it and raced to the bucket for another one-handed slam; 9-5.

Moochie then decided to take over. He took the inbounds pass from Mike and brought the ball up the court. He pulled from the NBA three-point line and hit the three-pointer; 9-8.

On the next play, Jeff tried to force in a pass to Vic but Moochie was sagging off in the lane and intercepted it. He dashed up court and slipped Greg and Terry by dribbling between his legs between the two of them. He gave me a move at the free-throw line and threw a pass to Mike off the backboard for a rim-rocking dunk; 9-10.

Terry got pissed; he was not about to lose this game. He called for the ball as we crossed the half. Once he got the ball Sheik went to double him with Moochie. Terry passed it back to Greg and I guess Lonnie didn't think that Greg would shoot from the hash but he did. It hit nothing but the bottom of the net; 12-10.

Moochie came back up court again but this time pulled from deeper. *SWISH!* 12-13.

"God damn it! Terry, you gotta push up on Mooch. Don't give him another shot!" Vic yelled at Terry.

I took the ball out and passed it in to Greg. He brought it up and gave Sheik a hell of a move. He dribbled between his legs to the left and then crossed over to the right hand, then spun off him back to the left. But when he spun off Sheik, he spun right to Moochie so he didn't really go anywhere. Jeff dove down to the post. Jeff wasn't a little boy on the block either. He was 6'5" and 230 pounds. Lonnie couldn't be any more then 185 pounds tops, but he was 6'7".

Jeff caught the entry pass from Greg and had Lonnie on his hip. He backed him down a little further and then faked to the middle. Lonnie bit on the fake. Jeff then spun to the baseline with his elbows out and moved Lonnie out the way and dunked it with two hands off the drop step; 14-13.

Damn, that nigga had some sweet post moves. Moochie brought the ball up again but this time Terry was in his hip pocket.

Greg yelled, "No three's!"

We all played tight D but Greg, because if Sheik hit a three to beat us we could live with that. He couldn't hit the right side of a barn if he tried. Moochie gave Terry a move that made him slip but Greg went to help and left Sheik. Moochie passed it to Sheik and he tried to win with a three. It clanged hard off the backboard and Vic grabbed the rebound. He passed it to me and I brought the ball up the floor. There are only 56 seconds left on the clock so if it ran out or we scored another bucket, we'd win.

I said, "Let's just be smart. We're up!"

I passed it to Terry in the corner and he gave Moochie a jab step. He then put the ball behind Moochie's head and threw it up in the air. He started running towards the basket, then stopped on a dime and stepped back to where he was originally standing. Moochie was trying so hard to stop him from going to the basket that he was all the way in the lane. The ball then came down from the air right in Terry's hands and he shot it. It rolled around the rim and then fell off. The crowd couldn't believe the move Terry had given Moochie. I knew they would be talking about it for years.

Lonnie grabbed the rebound with about 45 seconds left and passed it to Moochie. He raced up the floor and found Mike standing unguarded in the corner. Mike mishandled the pass but then regained it. By then Vic was on him. He gave him a pump fake on the three and Vic bit and jumped in the air. Mike stepped over to get off a shot but Terry rotated over to him. Mike passed it to Moochie, who was still standing close to half-court. He shot it all in one motion and sure enough the damn thing went in as the buzzer sounded; 14-16. I couldn't believe it but, hey, he got paid to play the game. I went to congratulate them on a good game and headed for the locker room. I was tired as hell and ready to go.

Terry
I'M SORRY

I walked in the house, tired as hell from playing ball all day. After Ty left, Jeff and I had played a couple more games. I dropped my keys on the coffee table and checked the answering machine.

"This message is for Mr. and Mrs. Shaw. This is Ms. Keystone, John's summer school English teacher. I'm just calling to remind you that our conference is scheduled for three o'clock Tuesday, July 22nd," the first message said.

Next message. "Terry, Jamie and I are going to go to the movies after lunch so I'll be home late tonight. I don't want you thinking I'm out with some nigga or anything."

It's Tracy. She was supposed to be just having lunch with her girl and then coming home, but I didn't really feel like being bothered anyway, so I didn't mind.

I went upstairs to see if Johnny had left me a note letting me know where he was and sure enough, no note. That boy just didn't listen. I figured I'd just take a bath and let my body soak. I went into the bathroom and ran my bath water. Then the phone rang.

"Hello."

"Hey, Dad, I forgot to leave a note so I decided I'd leave you a message on the machine. I have a summer league game tonight at Georgetown. We play Oxon Hill. I should be home around eight or so."

"All right. You know that was almost your ass, boy. You better had called home. We have a conference with your summer school teacher Tuesday. There are only three more weeks left of summer school and you need to buckle down if you want to go to college and play ball. But we'll talk about it later on."

We both said goodbye to one another and I hung up the phone. I went in the bathroom and jumped in the tub. This was my moment to relax. If it wasn't me and Tracy arguing, it was something with Johnny and school. Tracy and I had had a rough year or so. She was hardly home and when she was, it seemed like all we ever did was argue. When we'd first gotten married it was all peaches and cream but that faded. Sometimes I wondered why I'd ever gotten married but then I'd just look at those beautiful brown eyes and the thought left my mind.

Johnny was probably the best basketball player in the family, at fifteen, but he was starting to smell himself. He could always play but when he'd started the past year on varsity as a freshman for Crossland, his head had grown bigger. It didn't help that he'd led them in scoring (25.3), assisting (8.6), and stealing (3.2). He'd made the first team in Prince George's County and was on the second in the Metropolitan Area. That's Maryland, D.C., and Northern Virginia. After basketball season he'd started receiving letters from Duke, North Carolina, Maryland, and Kentucky so you know that shit didn't help. That was when he'd stopped concentrating on schoolwork and just on basketball.

I sat in that tub and thought about what I was going to do to repair my relationship and get my son's head back on straight. I thought summer school would help but he was fucking up there, too. That kid had so much potential but he just didn't realize that he could throw it all away before he could ever even apply it. I decided to deal with my troubles later. This was time for me to relax and relate with myself.

I got out of the tub and went into the living room. I turned the TV on and sat down on the couch with nothing but my towel on. I started to reflect on my life and my marriage. I thought about all the problems that Tracy and I were having. Most of it was because of the way I'd treated her over the years.

"Am I finally smellin' my own shit?" I asked myself.

All the arguments I'd caused by my late nights out, cheating, and selfishness. It seemed like everything good in my life was a result of my business and everything bad was because of my marriage. We didn't even start having problems with Johnny until the arguments started increasing between us.

I thought of all the things I'd done to Tracy over the years. All the women, the drugs and, most importantly, the mental abuse I'd caused her. The only thing she'd ever given me was her love and in return, I'd given her heartache and grief.

I remembered the first time I'd laid eyes on her. I was sixteen years old. I was at the mall with my little cousin Ty, trying to pick out an outfit for the spring dance. I'd seen her walking around with her girls. Being the suave nigga I was, I'd stepped to her. I'd gotten her number, then her heart. At sixteen, you don't know shit about a relationship. It was all about going to the movies and getting some ass. I didn't even know how to hit it right back then. I remembered all the girls I was already messing with when I'd stepped to her. It didn't matter to me; I wanted her. I mean, out of the ten girls I was talking to, I was only having sex with maybe three. So it didn't bother me, getting rid of the conversationalist but never did I give up the ones giving up the ass. Not once.

That was my problem there. I started our relationship from jump cheating. Never was I honest about shit.

"Why was I such an asshole?" I said aloud.

I couldn't use that "I was young" shit as an excuse because I was still sleeping with other women.

"GOD DAMMIT!" I yelled out.

As my depression set in I grabbed my Commodores CD and played *Three Times a Lady*. The slow soft music started to play as Lionel Richie sung:

Thanks
For the times that you've given me
The memories are all in my mind

As the words kicked in, Ty entered my mind. I could see myself in him so much it scared me. The example that I'd set for him wasn't an example at all. It was indescribable. I'd taught my little cousin to play women like it wasn't anything. *'You have your main girl and then a few bitches on the side,'* I used to tell him. I'd set my ways on an innocent child, at such an early age, and that wasn't fair to him at all. He'd never asked for any of it. Now look at him. He had a sexy woman that had a good job, and a good head on her shoulders. Half the chickenheads out there couldn't even give you an intelligent conversation. This woman actually had something to offer him. But because of my traits I'd sprung upon him, he was treating her like shit. My son was even the same way. He had a nice little cutie named Vanessa but I kept catching other little girls calling the house.

My thoughts then went back to my precious wife. As the piano played in the song, the tears started rolling down my face. The woman that I loved so much, the one who meant the world to me, I treated like an old rag doll. All the women, sex, and money didn't compare to the sight of her smile. The more I thought of the pain that I'd caused her over the years the more the tears started pouring down my face. I started to sing along with Lionel:

"WHEN W-E-E ARE TO-GETHER
THE MO-O-MENTS I CHERISH
WITH EVVV-ERY B-E-E-E-A-T OF MYYY HEARR-RT"

I started to yell, "I'm sorry, baby! I'll make it up to you! I promise! Somehow, someway, I will! I love you, Tracy! You're my heart and soul and I don't know what I'd do without you! I love you!"

My emotions really started to get the best of me.

The drums started to kick, TISS, DOOM, DOOM DAT, DOOM, TISS

"YOU'RE ONCE, TWICE, THREE TI-I-IMES-S A LA-ADY-Y-Y
AND I-I-I LU-AH-AH-AH-VVE YOOOUUU"

The music faded away but the tears kept coming down. I made a vow from that point on to be the husband I should've been from the start. Be the man in her life, her best friend, and her lifelong companion. What better time to start than then? I decided to whip up a nice dinner for her. A romantic evening for two was just what we needed.

I checked the answering machine to see what time she'd left the message. She'd called at 3:38 p.m., so that meant their movie wouldn't have been any later then 4:00 or 5:00. But she did say that she'd be home late. I didn't care. I decided to call and tell her to come home. She'd been spending a lot of time over the past couple of months with her girlfriends, Jamie or Crystal, but I'd thought nothing of it. I saw that time away from her as a vacation or an opportunity to call one of my *hoes*. As the phone rang, I started to think of an excuse for her to come home. I wanted dinner to be a surprise.

"Hello," her sweet voice answered the phone.

"Hey, baby, you need to get home as soon as you can. Your son's done it again. This time I found bud in his room."

"Okay. I should be home in about an hour," she responded. That was perfect. I could have everything set up and ready for her before she got there.

I rushed into the kitchen and started preparing my meal; to romance her back and show her how much she meant to me. That was my ticket in the door, then my sweet charm would do the rest. I took some boneless chicken breast strips out of the freezer. I put the chicken in a bowl of warm water to let it thaw briefly. I started to clean the house from top to bottom. I knew that she'd be tired when she got in and would want to relax. The house wasn't real messy so it only took me twenty minutes to get everything straight. I went in the kitchen and started to prepare dinner. I didn't have time to make something extravagant but it had to make a statement. I looked in the cabinet to see what vegetables we had to go with the chicken so I could determine exactly how to make it. I noticed the rice and a thought for dinner jumped in my head. I had a can of cream of mushroom soup and a can of cream of chicken soup to make dinner complete.

"Okay, time to get started," I said aloud.

I preheated the oven to 350 degrees. I went to the sink to check on the chicken and see how it had thawed out and it was still frozen. I got a paper plate from out of the cabinet and placed the chicken on it, put it in the microwave on low and turned the timer on for one minute and thirty seconds.

While the chicken was continuing to thaw, I boiled two pots of water; one for the rice and the other to make some broccoli. I took a quick look at the clock.

"Damn, fifteen more minutes! Time sure does fly," I said.

I seasoned my chicken strips and placed them in the oven. I got another pot from the cabinet and started to cook both soups together. I started to rush because I wanted dinner to be at least cooking before she got home. I poured the rice into the pot of boiling water to cook and the broccoli into the other one. I took the chicken out of the oven and poured the boiled soup over it. I placed it back into the oven and let it finish cooking. Within thirty minutes, everything would be ready.

I went upstairs to run some bath water. I added some bubble bath; just like Tracy liked it. I lit some scented candles alongside the tub—French Vanilla aromatherapy —and turned the lights off in the bathroom. I had to step out of the bathroom and look at it from the bedroom to confirm. Yes, it was a beautiful sight.

I peeked out the window and saw Tracy's car pulling up.

"Right on time," I said.

I ran downstairs and out the door with my hands behind my back. When I got to the car I leaned over and kissed her on her cheek. I handed her the rose hidden behind my back.

"Welcome home, boo! Don't worry about the bags. I'll get them. Go ahead in the house and sit down on the couch," I said.

She proceeded in the house while I grabbed the bags from the back seat. When I got in the house she was sitting on the couch.

She asked, "Terry, what's this all about? I mean, where's Johnny? I thought you said he was smoking."

"Don't worry about that right now. Just enjoy tonight and we'll talk about it in the morning. I know you're tired so go upstairs and get out of those clothes and relax."

"Boy, I'm not in the mood for that now," she said.

"Tracy, come on."

She followed me upstairs into the bedroom. I pointed into the bathroom at the tub.

"Your water's waiting for you, my dear," I said.

She looked at me with a shocked expression, as if to wonder what it was all for. But her body was aching. I guess walking around in the mall all day and then sitting in that theater had really worn her out. She took her clothes off and jumped in the tub. I turned on the stereo in the bedroom and played some smooth jazz for her: Boney James' *Seduction*. I handed her a bowl of fresh strawberry and pineapple slices and a glass of chilled white Zinfandel.

While she was enjoying her bath, I ran downstairs to get everything set-up for dinner. I got the dinner candles and dimmed the lights. I went and checked on the food and everything was ready. I took the chicken out of the oven and turned off the rice and broccoli. I set the table and made a cozy fire in the living room.

I ran back upstairs and grabbed her washcloth along with some soap. I washed her body from head to toe. I wanted to jump in the tub and fulfill every sexy fantasy that was running through my mind. But that was for later so I stuck with my plan. After I finished washing and rinsing her body, I asked her to go in the bedroom and sit down on the bed. I went to get the lotion from the dresser.

"Baby, lie on your stomach for me," I said.

She did. I began to lotion her body with Victoria's Secret Garden Vanilla Lace.

As I lotioned and caressed her soft silky skin she began to become aroused. I grabbed her silk robe and helped her into it. I showed her down the steps to the meal I'd prepared for her.

"Don't get my wrong. I'm enjoying every minute of this, but what's all of this about? I mean, why are you doing all of this? Is there something you want to tell me?" she asked.

"Sweetheart, I'll explain everything in due time. Just be patient; its nothing bad," I replied.

I turned on our dinner music, Anita Baker's *Rhythm of Love* CD. I started our dinner off with a garden salad, then served the main course. As the CD went around for the second time, we were just enjoying one another's company and conversation. In the middle of "Body and Soul" I asked her to dance. She accepted. We danced in the candlelight and it was as if I was falling in love with her all over again.

"I know you're wondering why I'm doing all of this and where it came from. You're my queen but I've been treating you like a pauper. I need to appreciate you more than I do. Through everything, you've been there. My career, the times I've cheated on you, and even the false paternity suits."

The next song started to play.

"Sweetie, I just want to say that I apologize."

The song "I Apologize" began to play. I couldn't have planned it better if I'd tried to.

"Baby, I just want you to know, from this moment forward, things will be changed. I'm going to be the man you fell in love with, the man you deserve, a man who cherishes your every move, thought, and feeling. What I'm trying to say is, Tracy, will you marry me?"

She looked at me with tears in her eyes but still with confusion.

"I know we're already married but the man you married was a complete fool. A man who didn't know what a good thing was and it was right in front of his face. I want to renew our vows to one another. Do things the right way before the eyes of God."

The tears kept coming down her face.

"You don't know how much I've wanted to hear those words come out of your mouth. But..."

I cut her off. "Tracy, you don't have to say a word. I love you and, from this day forward, I want to make sure you recognize that each and every day of our lives."

I leaned over and started kissing her. Her lips felt so good on mine. I picked her up and took her upstairs to the bedroom and laid her on the bed. I restarted the *Seduction* CD over again and undid her robe. I started kissing on her neck and worked my way down her body. Once I reached one of her succulent breasts I started to lick her nipple and around it. I sucked on her breast and gently bit her nipple to stimulate her. I worked my tongue back down her body until I reached her belly button. I began to suck on her belly button slightly.

"Turn over, baby, and lay on your stomach."

I reached on the side of the bed and grabbed the strawberry motion lotion that I'd planted there to give her an exotic feel. I poured it on her back and started to blow on the lotion to heat it up. I proceeded to lick it off her back. I heard her moaning softly.

"Ummh! SSS! Ahhh!"

I knew she was enjoying every minute of it. I reached her butt cheeks and licked them, too. I poured some more on her butt and continued.

I said, "Wait one minute, I'll be right back!"

I don't even think she heard me. I ran downstairs, got a small bowl and filled it with ice, and darted back upstairs. There she was, lying on her side, gazing at me with such innocence in her eyes. I took an ice cube and rubbed it up and down her body. As she became even more aroused, I placed a piece of ice in my mouth and turned her over on her back. I started kissing her belly button again with the cube of ice in my mouth. I took it out and rubbed it on her vagina, around her clit, and in and out of her. I licked after the cube and started sucking on her clit.

"Yeah, baby, right there! Don't stop," she moaned.

I spread her lips and continued to lick and suck her clit. While doing so I was still moving the cube in and out of her as if I was fingering her. After a good five minutes she'd already climaxed but I wasn't done yet. I was in a freaky mood. I drank all of her juices and continued to suck on her clit some more.

"Umm! Oh, baby! Yeah!"

As I continued to please her with my tongue, reaching her deeply, she became more excited and started to moan.

"Umm, baby, yes! Ohhhh! Baby, I'm cummin' again! Ooh, Terry! I'm cummin'!"

She tightened her thighs around my head so I couldn't move if I tried. I was getting excited myself. I continued to suck on her clit harder and faster until she was finished.

I worked my way back up her body and positioned myself inside her. It was nice and wet and felt better than ever. I began to stroke her with long, smooth, slow strokes. After every stroke, it felt as if I was going deeper and deeper. About fifteen minutes had passed while I was on top of her, so it was time for a little change. I flipped her over and let her show her stuff. I wasn't disappointed either. She began to move back and forth while tightening and holding onto my dick with her vaginal muscles.

"Ummh," I moaned as if I was her bitch.

She began to move faster and faster until she came again. She stopped to gasp for air and lay on my chest.

"We aren't done yet," I told her.

"You haven't cum already?" she asked, sitting up slowly.

"Turn over," I whispered.

She turned over on her knees and I started to hit it from the back. I started off as usual, nice and slow, so she could get back into the flow. The more she moaned and grabbed the pillow the faster I went and the harder I hit it. I smacked her ass.

"Yeah, baby, harder!" she yelled.

The faster I moved the more excited she got.

"You like that, baby?! Huh, you like it?!"

"Yeah! Harder, baby, harder!" she screamed.

I just kept hitting that ass harder and harder and spanking it at the same time; making her reach her climax.

"Baby, I'm cummin'!"

I could feel myself starting to explode as well.

"I'm cummin' with you, baby."

We both climaxed. It felt like I'd just nutted a gallon of semen. I pulled out of her and lay on the bed. She started to shake uncontrollably. She was having an orgasm. Once she finished, I grabbed her and held her for the rest of the night and thought about what a lucky man I actually was.

Jeff
READY OR NOT

Michelle, Chelle as I called her, was up early in the morning and loud as usual. I was tired as hell from a rough night at the club. It had been packed, like always on a Saturday night, and DJ Rico was rippin' the one and two's. Chelle was up rushing, trying to get ready for church. I was shocked she wasn't trying to get me to go with her.

"Jeff!" I heard her yell from the bathroom. I'd spoken too soon.

She continued, "Get up and answer the phone."

Who in the hell would be calling me early on a Sunday? I got up and answered the phone.

"Hello," I said, still half asleep.

"What's up, J? How was business last night?"

It was Terry's loud ass waking somebody up. I should've known.

"Don't you know people are usually asleep around this time? To answer your question, it was packed as usual," I told him. "What happened to you last night? I thought you were coming to the club?"

"I was but Tracy and I spent some quality time together."

"What!" I replied, excited.

"I mean, dawg, I was just sitting around thinking last night about half the shit that I've put her through. I've been cheating on her for a long, long time now and she doesn't deserve that shit. She doesn't deserve this treatment; nobody does. It's time for me to grow up and do right by her. I'm trying to teach my son to be a man, but I'm not acting like one. What kind of shit is that? It's time to change. Last night I expressed all those feelings and thoughts to her and let her know that I'm going to be the man that she fell in love with."

"She fell in love with a cheating bastard," I said, laughing my ass off.

Terry started laughing with me.

"Off the no bullshit, though, I proposed to her again and everything. I want us to renew our vows. You know, start off on the right foot," Terry continued.

I was shocked and couldn't believe what I was hearing. All of this coming from the same man who'd once fucked three girls at the same time while I taped it for him. He'd showed me the ins and outs when it came to women. Shit, the first girl I had sex with was a chick that he'd gotten for me. The funny part was after I finished, he'd hit her also. I didn't even think he knew how to spell monogamy, but he was now trying to live that life with his wife. What could I really say?

"I'm proud of you!" I paused. "You know, it's funny that you're actually saying this because I've been thinking about asking Chelle to marry me a lot lately."

"No bullshit?"

"Straight up! I think it's time that I settle down."

"That's all right, young. Y'all should go ahead and tie that knot."

While Terry changed the subject and started talking about business again, my mind drifted towards Chelle and me. I loved her and wanted to be with her, but forever was a long time. I'd been with her for three years and I thought it was time we took our relationship to the next level. I was unsure if that level was marriage, though. She'd been there for me through thick and thin. That word *forever* scared the shit out of me. I became even more confused about my situation. I started thinking about Terry's marriage. He'd been with his wife for a long time. He'd also cheated on Tracy during 99 percent of their relationship; not just their marriage. If there was one thing I was certain about, it was that I didn't want to be one of those men who cheated on his wife. I wanted to be bigger than that and if I felt that I was going to stray away from her, maybe that proved I wasn't ready.

"Jeff!" I heard Terry yell, breaking me out of my daze.

"Huh?" I replied.

"Nigga, you ain't heard a word I said, have you?"

"My bad, I've got a lot on my mind. Let me call you back later on and we can discuss the possible sites for the new club."

That was the last thing that I heard him say. God knows what he was talking about after that.

"Okay, bet," he said.

I needed advice and I needed it bad. I was at a point in my life where I wasn't sure whether to move forward, stay where I was, or take a step back. There was no one better to call than my mother. I picked the phone back up and dialed her number. Hopefully she wasn't at church.

"Good morning, Blackwell residence," my mother said.

"Well, good morning to you, Mrs. Blackwell. How are you doing this morning?"

"I'm fine. Your ears must've been burning 'cause I was just talking about you to Ms. Thompson across the street."

"Oh Lord, what did I do now?"

"Well, you know her daughter's getting married next year. That Marcus finally decided to propose to her," my mother insinuated.

"Finally? What do you mean finally? They've only been together, what, a little over a year? They're still getting to know one another. The only reason why y'all were pushin' it was because he got her pregnant," I shot back at her.

"Nobody made that man propose to her. As for him getting her pregnant, he should've kept his little man in his pants. What I find funny is that she's younger than you and hasn't been with Marcus as long as you've been with Michelle but she's engaged before you. Maybe I need to be having this conversation with Michelle. Put her on the phone," my mother said.

I knew what she really wanted to say to me but that time it was more a funnier situation than annoying because I was actually calling her for advice concerning marrying Chelle for a change.

"Ma, Chelle's gone to church already but I do have a question that I need to ask you. When did you know you were ready to get married? I mean, how did you know Dad was the one you wanted to spend the rest of your life with?"

"Why?" she asked.

"Cuz, I want to know," I said.

"I'm going to ask you one more time, child," she said.

"I've been thinking about marriage a lot lately but I'm not sure if I'm ready. I don't hear that little voice everybody talks about saying, *'Marry, Chelle.'* I'm just not sure," I told her.

I guess my mother was shocked or surprised by my response because there was a long delay.

"Well…when your father and I were getting married, I was scared to death. At first I just thought it was nerves and I'd get over them, but then, as the time kept getting closer and closer, I knew I was frightened. I wasn't sure if I was making a mistake or not. I needed some fresh air badly so I walked over to the window and stuck my head out. All of a sudden I heard your father and his ex-girlfriend, Nadine, talking. She was telling him how much of a mistake he was making by marrying me. That's when he told her, *'The only mistake I made was sleeping with you. My mistake was cheating on her with you but that's long over. I told you the day I knew she was the one, that it was over between us. From that point, I haven't looked back and don't plan on it now. That was my mistake right there; being with you and not telling her. Not being honest with her was a mistake but my marrying her is the only thing right out of all of this. I'm through making mistakes.'* Then he walked away.

"I didn't know what to think at that point. I'd trusted him and he'd betrayed that trust by cheating on me. The trust I had in him was just flushed down the toilet. I started wondering how could I not see him cheating. When did he have time? There was no way possible I could be with a man that I didn't trust. I was ready to call the wedding off, then I heard a knock at the door.

It was your father. He said, *'Liz, please do not open the door because we can't see each other before the wedding, if there is a wedding. I'm not sure you will want to marry me after I tell you what I have to say but the truth needs to be told. You deserve it. This is supposed to be the happiest day of my life but I'm far from happy. Today we start our lives together as man and wife, before the eyes of God. What kind of man would I be to start it with deceit? Liz, I cheated on you about a year ago. It was with Nadine. It was a mistake. I know that now. I haven't looked at another woman other than you since that day. I can't even explain why I did it because I don't know. What I do know is that it was stupid and will never happen again. You're the only woman I need and want. Liz, I love you and even if you choose not to marry me I'll still love you. I want you to know that. You need to know that. I want to spend the rest of my life with you and only you. I want to grow old with you, take long walks with you but, most of all, be with you. Hopefully you'll still want to be with me. All I can say is I'm sorry but I know that sometimes that's not enough. In time, I will restore the trust and faith that you once had in me.'* That's when I knew that I loved that man with all my heart and wanted to spend the rest of my life with him.

"He was man enough to fess up to his mistakes. He was willing to risk losing me to tell me the truth. He didn't know that I knew; he just wanted to be honest. He wanted to be the trustworthy man that I loved. Even though I was hurt by his actions, I couldn't have loved him more than I did at that point. He told me. I still, to this day, can't believe he did that."

I couldn't believe it. My father had actually cheated on my moms. He'd even had the balls to tell her that on their wedding day. That was love.

"I hope I was able to be of some help, son," my mother said.

"Believe me, you were a lot of help but I'm still not sure."

She paused and then asked, "What exactly aren't you sure about?"

"I don't know. Don't get me wrong. I love Chelle and she's all that I think about. It's just this forever thing. Plus your situation is totally different than mine. How could you not know after what Daddy did? That was a clear-cut sign of how much he loved you. I don't have that in this instance. I'm not trying to be one of those people getting married three or four times before I actually find *Miss Right*. When I get married I want to be like you and Pop and stay married."

"Okay, just ask yourself two questions. Is there any other woman in this world that you want to spend your life with? Can you see yourself with any other woman? Your answers will tell you if you're ready or not."

Once again my mother had a solution to my problems.

"Thanks, Ma. You've just helped me enormously!" I told her.

"That's what mothers are for. You just make sure I get the first phone call when she says yes. You hear me?"

"I hear you, woman. I'll call you later."

That was just like my mother to know exactly what I was thinking before I even said a word. She already knew I'd decided to propose to Chelle.

Tyrelle
WRONG STATE OF MIND

Last night was pretty slow since it was a Tuesday. We made some money off happy hour but there weren't too many people at the club partying afterwards. I needed to get up early to take care of some business. I glanced over to see what time it was on the alarm clock. It was 8:37 a.m. I'd get up at 9:00. I'd just rolled back over to get comfortable when the phone rang.

"Hello," I answered.

"Hey there, sexy. You miss me?" I heard a sweet voice say. It was Jodi. I damn sure did miss her. I could've used her fine sexy ass next to me right then.

"You know I miss your ass," I shot back at her.

"Watch your mouth! Well, don't worry; I'll be home in two more days," she said.

I wished that day was Friday. "I know. So how's the conference going?"

"I didn't call you to talk about work. I called to see how your behind is doing and if you've been behaving yourself," she said.

"I'm fine. I'm a little bit tired right now. You know, Tuesday's my night at the club. I didn't leave until 3:30 this morning and it's what now, going on nine? I think that should speak for itself."

"I'm sorry, boo! I forgot last night was your night at the club. Did I wake you?"

"No, not really. I was about to get up anyway. I have to go to the bank and deposit the money from last night and then meet Terry to check out this possible site for the new club."

I realized that she wasn't at the conference. "What are you doing on the phone? Shouldn't you be at the conference?"

"We're on break until nine-thirty," she responded.

"Oh, I see."

"Well, I just called to check up on you. Go ahead and get ready for your day. I have to get my presentation ready. I'm speaking at ten."

"Presentation! Go head wit' your bad self!"

"Boy, hush. I'll call you later on to check on you," she told me.

"Just make sure it's before seven-thirty because..."

She cut me off. "I know, I know. It's Wednesday night. I forgot that you worked yesterday because I wasn't thinking but I do know my man's schedule. Talk to you later. Bye, boo," she said.

I hung up the phone, feeling on cloud nine. I got up and headed straight for the kitchen. I placed two Pop Tarts in the toaster and a cup of water into the microwave. I went outside to get *The Washington Post*. My water was done boiling, so I grabbed my instant coffee mix and made a cup of coffee. I grabbed my Pop Tarts and took my mini-breakfast into the living room. I laid my food down on the coffee table, sat on the couch, and started to read the paper. I wanted to check out the Style section to see the promotional ad we'd placed for that night's events at the club.

Wednesday's Ladies Night at Club Mystic featuring the DC Bad Boys; Texas Pete, Midnight, Chocolate Deluxe, and many more. Ladies are free before 8 p.m. with a free soul food buffet. DJ Rico will be on the 1's and 2's.

I loved it. When we'd first started ladies night at the club, I thought we'd lose money because we were letting all those women get in for free, but the free advertisement was just to get them in the door. They had to rush to get there before 8 p.m. and the show didn't start until 11 p.m. That meant three hours of them just sitting around and talking. The women that made it in early spent at least $25 each buying drinks, waiting for the show. Liquor was the liquid courage women needed to do and say the things they did to strippers. The women that came after 8 p.m. had to pay the $10 cover charge. The first night we'd started it, we'd cleared over $6,000. Now, it was more like $15,000 and that's after we paid the strippers their $2,000 charge to strip. Business was definitely good on Wednesdays.

At first we all wanted to see all the freaky women that come to the show; that's why we'd all decided to work on Wednesdays. But it had become a necessity because women got out of control at times. The whole male stripper thing was overrated to me. Half the strippers were gay, in my opinion, and the other half? Lord knows.

I got up off the couch after reading the rest of my paper and got in the shower. I put on my beige linen short set with my sandals and Armani glasses. I didn't want to dress down because we were going to conduct business but I didn't want to wear a suit either. I squirted on my cologne, grabbed my car keys, and headed out the door. I called Terry on my cell phone once I got in the car to tell him that I was stopping at the bank to deposit the check, then I would be at the club to meet him. I stressed for him to be there in an hour. It was a 30-minute drive into the city from my townhouse in Mitchellville, Maryland, so I had enough time to hit the bank and meet him. The bank and club coincided with each other on Seventh Street in Northwest. I deposited the $4,800 that we'd made into our account and then walked across the street to the club.

Terry was already waiting for me inside. He was always early for everything. He had on a pair of black casual shorts with a matching black top, some sandals as well, and his Gucci sunglasses. I went and placed the bank slips on our accountant's desk and was ready to go. I decided to follow him on our 20-minute trek to Oxon Hill, Maryland. We went to a shopping center down the street from Rivertowne Commons. There were a lot of places to choose from for the new club in the complex but I had my eyes on the old Rite Aid or McGregor's. Both had enough room for a huge club and Oxon Hill was an up-and-coming suburb. I liked it. Everybody went to Rivertowne Commons to go to the movies, so it was a familiar and convenient location. Plus it was only five minutes from both the D.C. and Virginia lines and right off the Capital Beltway. It was perfect.

We toured both sites and liked the former Rite Aid a little bit more. The former McGregor's was right next to where they were building a Shoppers Food Warehouse. The Rite Aid was on the other end so it had some distance. It just didn't seem right having a club next door to a grocery store. I was sold on the place. The only thing that mattered was the selling price. Terry had taught me a long time ago to never show your true feelings in business. If people felt you wanted something badly they would dick you in a heartbeat to get over. Terry told the agent that we had other sites to look at and we'd contact him by the following Friday at the latest. Friday? We could call up our attorneys and have the matter settled by the end of the week. We all shook hands and we both walked away.

"Terry, why did you tell him next Friday?" I asked.

"Because, I could tell you liked the place and I didn't want him to know that both of us did. Plus, Jeff has to see the place, too," he replied.

"But if you like it and I like it then Jeff's short. We vote on everything. Majority wins."

"Yeah but you at least give him the courtesy to check the place out and form his own opinion. He might see flaws in the place neither of us saw that would change our minds. It's just smart business," he told me.

I guess I still had a few things to learn. I don't know how he knew I liked the place. I wasn't showing any facial expressions. Or was I?

"Have you thought about settling down with Jodi?" he asked.

"What?" I responded.

"Nigga, don't play dumb. You heard me. Have you started thinking about settling down with her?"

"I have settled down with her; in a way. That's my girl. I'm about to ask her to move in with me and all."

Hopefully he'd buy that and leave me alone about the situation.

"Okay, that's good and all, but what about the other women?"

"What about them?" I responded.

"Since you've decided to take things to another level, are you going to cut all the other girls back and be about only Jodi?"

That was an easy answer.

"Hell, no! For what! What Jodi doesn't know won't hurt her."

"Do you know who you sound like? Me! That was my fucked-up attitude about cheating but let me tell you something, when she finds out it will, and believe me she will find out. Women have a way to find out anything. I was wrong then. If you're not going to commit to her, then show her the respect enough to tell her. Let her know everything upfront so she can make her decision on whether she wants to be with you or move on with her life," he told me.

The man must've been out of his mind; asking me to tell her. Why would any man in their right mind do something so stupid? I might as well tell her about the women that I'd already been with since we'd gotten together.

"Man, I think you've lost your mind. Tell her? Come on now. What am I supposed to say? Jodi, I want to be with you and fuck other women, too? Huh? Is that what I'm supposed to say?" I asked sarcastically.

"Actually, yeah. You'd be honest with her and she'd know where the two of you stand. Selfish. That's all you're being by not telling her: selfish. If you care about her, tell her the truth. You can't love her and not tell her. It'll only hurt her in the long run." He paused. "I just realized how much pain I've caused Tracy over the years. The same way I've treated her is the way I've taught you to treat women. So you will only put Jodi through that same pain. You had no problem letting me teach you to be a womanizer; let me teach you now how to be a man."

"Nigga, I am a man!" I responded.

"If you can cheat on your girl and don't even have the balls to tell her, no, you're not. Don't get me wrong; I'm not trying to put you down. Not at all, dawg. I'm far from being a complete man myself. My shit still stinks! I'm just trying to do right by *my lady*!"

I started to laugh my ass off as he said that like his father used to. He always had a way to get his point across and still make you laugh. That was my cousin.

"Well, I'll see but I can't promise you anything," I told him. I got in my car. "I'll see you tonight. Holla."

I headed home. I was tired from a long morning and it was already past two in the afternoon. I decided to take a nap once I got in the house, to rest for that night.

❖ ❖ ❖ ❖

I got to the club around 6:30 p.m. with some black Britches of Georgetown slacks and a short-sleeve black Armani shirt. I had on my black Kenneth Cole boots to complete my outfit. I was definitely dressed to impress. It was a considerably long line outside already.

"Tonight is going to be a good night," I said.

I stopped at the bar to speak to the bartender and get a rum and Coke. I got my drink and went to my office to sit back and enjoy my cocktail in peace. I plopped my feet up on my desk and lounged. Jeff walked in about five minutes later and dropped a bombshell on me.

"Ty, guess what?" Jeff said as he walked in the office.

I really didn't even want to know. I wasn't in the mood. It had to be something between him and his damn girl or about Jodi and me. Either way I didn't want to here it.

"Can we talk about this later on, or tomorrow? My mind is in fifty other places right now."

"I just wanted to tell you real quick that I proposed to Chelle Sunday night and she accepted," he said.

My mouth dropped and I'm not saying that to be funny; it literally dropped.

"God damn it!" I said out of frustration.

I was tired of this shit. First Terry goes and gets married, but at least it was mostly because of little Johnny, then Jeff starts talking this settle down crap, then Terry has a bad slice of pizza and decides that he doesn't want to fuck other chicks and I need to do the same, and now outta the blue Jeff proposes to Michelle.

"I can't believe you just up and proposed to her. When were you going to talk to the fellas about it? Don't get me wrong, I like Michelle. She's all right by me, but marriage? Why do you feel you need to marry her? Is there a specific reason? I just don't understand. I mean, for what? Are you even sure you're ready for a commitment like that?" I interrogated.

"I'm more than ready. I really don't want to argue with you tonight, Ty. I just wanted to know how you'd react if I did propose to her. I haven't actually proposed yet but I'm going to; just so you know. I've thought about it long and hard and I'm ready to be with her and *only* her from this point on."

I'd had enough. I'd heard all I wanted to hear and then some. Both of my boys had decided to be with one woman in a couple of days. Who was I supposed to hang with from then on? I'd be damned if I was going to follow in their footsteps. I didn't care how much I loved Jodi. I stormed out the room and went straight to the bar.

"Hand me the bottle of Bacardi," I told Darin. "It's going to be me and Ron B tonight," I professed.

By the time I was halfway finished with the bottle the place was packed from front to back with nothing but eager and horny women. I started to mingle as usual, with different intentions this time. I was looking for the lucky winner of the fuck my brains out contest. I walked through the crowd of women, searching for a couple of prospects when I stumbled into April.

She was a regular on Wednesdays, and in my bedroom. I looked her up and down slowly. I couldn't tell if she was wearing that dress or if the dress was wearing her. She looked good and the alcohol was intensifying it. She had on a silver strapless dress with a long slit up both legs, showing nothing but thigh. I didn't even realize that she'd spoken because I was staring so hard.

"Tyrelle!" she yelled to get my attention.

"Yeah, what's up, baby?" I said, trying to play it off. "Getting ready for the show, as usual?"

"Yeah, of course!"

"What are you doing later on tonight?" I figured there was no reason to beat around the bush when she already knew what I wanted.

"Coming over your house, I hope. I'm going to need some after seeing these men," she said.

That was music to my ears. "I have a couple of things I need to take care of. I'll make sure I see you before I leave or, should I say, before we leave."

She leaned over and kissed me. "I'll make sure you can find me."

I walked back into the crowd of women with a dick harder than a rock. I sat down at the barstool and covered up for a moment until my soldier was at ease, then continued to mingle with other women. I was working on my third number when the DJ started playing Luke and getting the crowd ready for the strip show. That was my cue to exit stage left. I headed back to my office.

After the show the women stayed around hoping to be the lucky one to spend the night with one of the strippers. I headed toward the door to collect the money from the register. Usually I waited until the club was clear but I was ready to go and get my *freak* on. We probably didn't make that much off the door anyway. I was making my way towards the office when April jumped in front of me.

"Let's go now! I'm wet and horny as hell. How long do you think you'll be?"

Now I knew exactly why I liked her. She played no games. When she was ready, you knew. I started to have second thoughts about the entire thing, thinking about Jodi, but I needed some badly. Jodi wasn't home so I couldn't just go over her house and get it.

"Give me twenty minutes," I told her.

I headed for the office while she waited for me at the bar. I counted the money from the door and we made nearly $1,500. Damn, we actually made a killing. I went and looked for Terry or Jeff, whichever I could find first. I wanted to let them know I was gone. I saw Terry over by the stage.

"Hey, I'm bout to bounce. I'll holla at you later. The money from the door is already in the safe."

"Okay. I'll call you tomorrow. Maybe we can do lunch or something," he said.

"Just don't call me early in the morning!" I said while I was walking away.

I headed toward the bar, told April let's go, and was out the door.

❖ ❖ ❖ ❖

I told April to make herself comfortable in the bedroom while I took a shower. We went upstairs and I jumped in the shower. I let the hot water massage my tensed body. All of a sudden the light in the bathroom went out. The shower curtain opened with April getting in. She started kissing my back and then turned me around and started kissing my chest. It felt so good, the combination of the water on my back and her on my chest. She made her way further down my body to my dick and started lickin' and suckin' it as if her life depended on it. I closed my eyes and grabbed the shower curtain rod for support.

She stopped, stood up and propped her leg up on the tub, then placed me inside of her. I wanted to stop because I didn't have on protection but my little head was running things. I picked her up and started stroking her harder. She began to moan and scream while I became fully aroused. I started moving faster and pumped harder. She grabbed hold, as she was about to cum. I was right behind her and there was no stopping me now. I finally came inside of her.

I put her down and she started to suck it again. I shook and quivered like a little bitch. After ten minutes of her arousing me with her mouth, I became hard again. I picked her wet body up and took her into my bedroom. I laid her on the bed and opened her legs. I started licking and sucking her body from her firm breasts all the way down to her nicely shaven vagina. The faster I moved my tongue on her clit the more she moaned.

"Ohh!"

I reached my hand into the drawer of my nightstand and grabbed a Magnum condom. I put it on and placed myself back inside of her. I stroked her slowly and smoother this time, taking my time, wanting to enjoy every minute of it.

"Let me get on top?" she asked.

I rolled over and she started to move back and forth, up and down, harder and harder. She came after a good thirty minutes and I placed her on her knees so I could climax. I started smacking her on her ass and grabbing her hair.

"Whose is it? You like that!"

SMACK!

She responded, "It's yours, baby. It's yours!"

I became excited and started to go faster and harder. You could hear the echo of my body smacking up against her butt.

"Harder, Ty! Harder!" she yelled.

I was there. I came. She came for her third and final time of the night. She got up and went into the bathroom. I rolled over and dozed off while she was in the bathroom washing up. She came out the bathroom fully dressed.

"Thanks for a hell of a night. I have to get up early in the morning, but I'll call you later," she said.

I was half-asleep and really didn't care what she said. She'd drained me to the fullest. I heard the door close and moved to the middle of the bed.

"And those niggas want me to settle down."

Tracy

WEEKEND GETAWAY

"**D**amn, I wish I could be you! Not only do you have a husband who's successful and owns his own club, but you're also fucking one of the finest strippers that works for him. Talk about having your cake and eating it too," my friend Crystal said.

I'd been secretly seeing Renard for the past year. I'd finally become tired of all the women, the lies and, most importantly, the deceit. I'd needed someone, who wanted to be with me and give me a little R&R. He'd tried to be there for me emotionally as well but all I was really interested in was the sex.

I'd first noticed him at the club stripping, but we'd just played eye tag with one another. I guess he was trying to hide his true feelings for me, out of respect for Terry. Then one Sunday morning I'd seen him at Crystal's church. I'd never heard of a God-fearing Christian who made a living providing sexual fantasies for women. It had never really dawned on me that half the outrageous things the other strippers did, he didn't do. He provided you with a show and that was it. All that putting his dick in women's faces or getting them to suck it while he was on stage; he never did anything like that. I guess you could say he was a gentleman on stage.

Crystal continued talking, saying, "If I were you, I'd keep them both or get rid of Terry's ass. Shit, that nigga's treated you like shit from day one. It's time to trade his ass in for a better model. I hear that new color Midnight is the shit!" she said, laughing, mocking Renard's stage name. "As a matter of fact, you need to be hooking me up with one of his co-workers," she continued.

"You'd actually be with one of them trifling ass niggas. They stick their stuff in a different girl after every show."

"Well, I could be one of them. My body needs some damn maintenance. I'm tired of having to do the job myself. What's wrong with a man with a big dick that can put my back out? I don't want a relationship with any of them. Just do your job and go the hell home!" she said.

I heard that, but I was looking for more than some one-night stands.

"Girl, you're out of control. Is that all you think about, is a big dick and some good sex?"

"When you're not getting any, you damn right! But I do think about other things as well. I think about his wallet, too!" she responded.

We both laughed at that one.

"Sike, naw," she continued, "I want to fall in love like the next woman but it's not like there are a lot of good men out here to choose from. Half of them just want to get in my pants and the other half aren't about shit. I'd even settle for someone who has a little dick as long as he treats me like a queen. He just has to know how to work that tongue, though. Look at your husband; he's a perfect example of what I'm talking about. I won't allow myself to go through half the shit you have. He might provide good for the family and all but the nigga is flat out trifling."

My girl didn't always know what to say out of her mouth, but I was used to it. She wasn't intentionally trying to hurt my feelings. She was just speaking her mind and trying to get me to see how she felt. But she could never see what I saw.

"I actually think he's changed. Since he's rediscovered himself and vowed to change, we talk now. And I don't mean the usual hellos and goodbyes; we hold conversations. After we'd made love the other night, he sat there and held me. He wanted to talk about my day at work and how I felt. He didn't just roll over and go to sleep. When he isn't at the club he's spending time with Johnny, helping him with his schoolwork, or cooking dinner, or cleaning the house. He's just much more considerate now of my feelings and the well-being of his son. It's like I'm falling in love with him all over again."

"Child, you're a damn fool if you give that man another chance. Throw some new pussy in front of his ass and he'll go back to being the same dog he was before. It doesn't matter how good the nigga treats you if he can't be faithful to you. Come on, Tracy, one month doesn't make up for fifteen years," she said.

Crystal was right. Terry had acted that way when we'd first met. He was all nice and sweet, then after we'd been together for a while, I'd finally met the real asshole. He'd pulled the same stunt to get me back when I'd first caught him cheating and, once again, I'd fallen for it. I'd been his fool long enough. I wasn't going to put myself through that again. I'd be damned! I was going to continue to see Renard. I wasn't really convinced Terry had changed and I wasn't going to risk losing Renard for any uncertainties.

"I need to get ready to go, girl. Renard's taking me to Ocean City for the weekend," I told her.

"I knew your ass wasn't going to give up that god of a man. Just don't forget to hook me up with one of his co-workers," she said.

❖ ❖ ❖ ❖

I came home to an empty house. Terry had gone with Jeff to the new site for the club and then he was supposed to be going to Johnny's game. He'd really been spending a lot of time with his son, and not just playing basketball. He'd taken him fishing, bowling, skating, you name it. He just wanted to be around his son more than he was before. I guess he thought a lot of Johnny's problems in school were because he hadn't been around a lot. I had to stop thinking about him. I was headed upstairs to get ready when the phone rang. I ran up the rest of the stairs and into the bedroom to answer the phone.

"Hello," I said, out of breath.

"Hey, baby. What are you doing, working out?" Terry asked.

"No. I ran up the steps to answer the phone."

"Oh. What are you about to do?"

"Take a shower so I can hurry up and get out of here."

"Where are you going?" he asked, puzzled.

"Dover," I told him.

"Is that this weekend?"

"Yes, Terry. I told you the other night that the girls and I were taking a trip to Dover Downs to do a little gambling."

"You sure did. Do you think you have time to go to the movies with me and Johnny before you go?" he asked.

"Not this time. Let's do something together next weekend instead."

"Okay, but it'll only be the two of us. Johnny finishes summer school on Wednesday and Saturday he leaves for Nike Camp for the week."

"Well, it's a date then, but let me get in the shower so I can get out of here," I said hurriedly.

"Okay, call me when you get there so I know you made it safely. I love you!"

See, this was what I was talking about. I'd been on I don't know how many trips, with either my girls or Renard, and he'd never asked me to call him when I'd gotten there. He definitely wasn't expressing his love for me either, before I got off the phone. He'd always just say okay and go on about his business. Half the time he didn't even say bye.

"I love you, too," I said, hoping he didn't hear the shock in my voice.

After I hung up the phone, my mind wondered again. Had he really changed? I wanted to believe him so badly because deep down inside I was still in love with him. Now he was doing the little things that he wasn't before. The occasional "I love you" or planning the family outings. My fear for playing his fool yet again brought me back to reality.

I zapped out of the daze I was in and got in the shower. I had to meet Renard in a little under an hour at his place. I got out of the shower, put on my clothes, and began to pack. I packed lightly because we hardly went out while going on one of our sexual adventures. Once I finished packing, I grabbed my keys and headed out the door.

Renard was outside putting his bags in the back of his black Expedition when I pulled up at his townhouse. He was 6'2" and 245 pounds of muscle. His stage name was Midnight because of his deep dark chocolate complexion. He had brown eyes and the sexiest bald head. Crystal was right; the man was definitely a god. I pulled up past his truck and into the garage. He walked over and opened my driver's side door.

"Hey, baby! How are you feelin'?" he asked.

"I'm fine. Are you finished with your stuff?"

"Yeah, why? Are you in a rush?"

I replied, "I just wanted to know so I could start putting my stuff in the car."

"Sweetie, I have this. Just take your sexy self in the house and relax," he told me.

I walked into his house. As you came through the front door, the washroom was on your left and then there were a couple of steps. The kitchen was on your right side with the living room in front of you. I kept straight; past the steps leading upstairs and downstairs, into his living room. There was no TV or anything like that in the living room; just a nice Italian sofa with a matching loveseat. Throughout the living room he had fine oil paintings and a unique floral arrangement. The way the house was decorated you just knew he had someone decorate it for him. A man couldn't have taste that impeccable—at least not a straight man.

I began to think about my first time in his house. It was about ten months prior. Before I could get deep in thought Renard walked in.

"You ready to go, baby?"

"I'm ready when you are," I told him.

We headed out to the truck and got in. He closed the garage door so no one would notice my car and we went on our way.

"Hey, I've been thinking lately. Why don't you move in with me? I love you and want to spend every possible day with you," he said. He looked me into my eyes and continued, "I'm tired of having to hide our relationship and our feelings from everybody. I'm not ashamed of you, or this relationship. I want to be more than just someone you're having an affair with. I want to be your man."

I couldn't believe my ears. It was bad enough that Terry was making things difficult with the way he was acting but this was taking things overboard. I didn't even look at Renard in that way.

He was just a big dick for some good sex in my eyes. I was tired of being run over by Terry so I'd gone after Renard. And like Crystal would've said, he was giving my body some much-needed maintenance. Having a relationship outside of sex was out of the question, or was it? I began to wonder.

He did know how to treat me; physically and emotionally. I didn't love him, but I could always learn to love him with time. I began to stress over the situation. I didn't want to hurt him but I wasn't going to live a lie either. I definitely needed the weekend as an anxiety reliever but it would probably complicate things even more. If I had sex with him he'd probably take it as my wanting to be with him. Since I wasn't sure if I did, then I shouldn't. I tried to get out of the question for then.

"Can we talk about this later?"

He disregarded what I'd asked and said, "Why put it off for later when we can talk about it now? It should be an easy question for you to answer; unless you have a problem with living with me. Do you?"

I wanted to tell him that I did have a problem with it but it would just hurt his feelings. He'd want to know why, then I'd tell him that I was unsure. Then somehow we'd get on Terry and that's when the shit really would hit the fan. If he knew that I still loved my husband and not him, he might pull an Ike on me.

"Boo, it's not that I don't want to live with you or even be with you. It's just that right now I need to be by myself. If I were to make any moves it would be out and on my own. I'm not going to go from one situation into another one. That's just not smart."

"Yeah, I guess you're right," he said.

I thought I was out of the woods but, boy, was I wrong.

"So when are you filing for the divorce?"

God damn! When it rains it pours and I didn't have an umbrella.

"I really don't want to have this discussion now. I just want to enjoy my weekend. Didn't we both agree to not discuss things between me and Terry anyway?" I asked him.

"I didn't agree to anything!" he said, raising his voice. He tried to calm himself down and continued, "You came up with that stuff. I just didn't say anything. I thought it would be best if we didn't talk about it at that time. I want to know now because it affects me. Like I said, I want us to be together but we can't take our relationship to the next level because you're married."

I became irritated by his persistency. He just wouldn't let up. *Ring Ring Ring,* my cell phone started to go off. Thank God!

"Hello."

"Hey, baby, I just wanted to tell you that since you're not home I'm going to work tonight. The club is really starting to get packed on Saturdays so at least two of us need to be there. You know Ty will be there with Jeff but I don't have anything to do so I'm going to hang with them."

"I thought you and Johnny were going to the movies tonight?" I asked him.

"We were but his lil' girlfriend called and Pops got put on the backburner," he said, then paused. "Well, don't let me hold you up. Have fun this weekend, baby. I'll see you when you get home. I love you!"

I didn't know what to do. I hung up the phone and turned it off. If he called back then the call would roll straight to my voicemail and he'd think that I was in an area with a bad connection. Crystal had taught me a thing or two about the cheating game.

"What did he want?" Renard asked, sounding disturbed.

"Nothing much. He just called to tell me that he's going to work tonight and that Johnny went out with his girlfriend."

"Yeah, right, he's going to work all right. Workin' on another chick," he said with a smirk on his face.

I didn't find that shit funny at all. How dare he talk about another man when he's fucking a damn married woman? I was ready to tell his ass to take me the hell home. I guess he could detect that I was pissed but I was beyond that.

"Why's your face all frowned up?" he asked.

"Look, right now I'm not in the mood to play 20/20," I warned him.

"I know you're not getting pissed over what I said about his ass."

"It's not even about him. It's the point of you throwing him cheating on me in my face. I don't need to hear that shit from you. I know what's going on in my *fucking* life!" I yelled at him.

I'd reached that point and then some now. I just wanted to get to the condo, take my clothes off and sit in the Jacuzzi. We sat in silence for the remainder of the ride.

Why do men always have to mess things up because of their egos? I had a perfectly good weekend planned and this nigga had to ruin it. But he did show me that he actually cared about me. I just didn't like the immature way he'd done so. I really didn't know what to do because I'd been happy with Renard and the relationship we'd had. We'd hardly argue; plus the sex was great. Terry had my heart, though, and I really did think he had changed his ways. No one could make me feel as special as Terry, nor could anyone hurt me as much. That was the feeling that scared me the most; being hurt again. I really had a dilemma on my hands.

When we arrived at the oceanside condo I headed straight in the house and to the bedroom. My ass didn't say a word and damn sure didn't grab any bags. I went into the bathroom and ran some water, took my clothes off and got in the tub. The water was still running but I didn't care. I let it run over my body until it filled the tub. I closed my eyes and let the sizzling hot water massage my body. It felt like little needles sticking me all over and it was so soothing. I put my mind at ease and my body at rest.

I thought about my situation again. How in the hell was I going to tell him about Terry? Cheating on Terry was one thing because he'd never been honest with me about his dirt. Plus, what goes around comes around. Renard, on the other hand, had been honest with me about everything. At least as far as I knew he had been. Damn, the more I thought the more confused I became. If Terry did really change and could be with only me, then it would be easier to solve. I just didn't have any way of knowing if he had or not. How could I trust him? The whole reason for making mistakes is to learn from them. If I ran back to him, then I obviously hadn't learned a thing; unless he really had changed. It was pointless. I wasn't getting anywhere. I couldn't take it anymore. I was driving myself insane. I tried to direct my attention towards something else but couldn't. I was emotionally drained. I finally dozed off in the tub with my issues still unresolved.

I woke up around 9:30 p.m. I'd slept for about four hours. We'd gotten there around 5 p.m. so it had probably been more than four hours and my wrinkled body showed it. The water still felt nice; until I made that first move to get out of the tub. Then I found out how freezing the water really was. I turned the shower on and took the stopper out of the tub and washed my body.

My satin robe was waiting for me when I came out of the bathroom. I hadn't put it there so I knew that Renard was up to something. On top of the robe was a bra and panties set from my bag, the lotion, a single rose and a note. I put the lotion on my body and slipped on my bra and panties. I then picked up the note and began to read.

Tracy,

I'm sorry for the way I acted. Sometimes I let my emotions take over before I think about the situation. I just feel threatened by your husband. At any time he could start acting like he has changed just to get you back and probably would succeed. I don't want to lose you. You really mean a lot to me and I want to be with you and only you. I want us to be together so much that my pursuing only pushes you away. I don't want to push you away. I only want to bring you closer to my heart. So from now on, whenever you're ready you know where I stand. Until then we can still go about things the way we have. Any time spent with you is the best time of my life. Tracy, I guess what I'm trying to say is that I love you. Don't think that because I wrote that you have to tell me you love me as well. If you don't that's fine; one day you will. I just wanted you to know my thoughts and feelings. So from here on out I promise to take things slow and let them develop; instead of trying to develop them myself.

With Love,

Renard

I didn't know how to respond. This man really loved me. I put on my robe and looked for him. There was a fire blazing in the living room but still no sign of him. I walked out on the deck and saw him sitting on the beach. He was sitting there with his robe on and a bottle of wine in his hand. He grabbed my hand and guided me to sit down in between his legs, facing him. He poured me a glass of wine and handed it to me. I took a sip from the glass to calm my nerves. I wasn't planning on having sex with him because of the incident in the car. I definitely couldn't do anything now; it would only make matters worse after he'd poured his feelings out to me.

He really was sweet. I leaned over to thank him with a kiss. The sensuous kiss had my juices flowing like a waterfall. When I got out of the tub my body was bone dry but that was no more. I was past wet. My panties were soaked. We lay on the beach and began to kiss passionately. I felt his ten-inch dick poking my inner thigh, trying to find its way inside of me. My emotions got the best of me and I tried to guide it home.

He stopped me and said, "No, No, No, stop. I want this night to be special."

He grabbed hold of me and we cuddled on the beach for the remainder of the night.

❖ ❖ ❖ ❖

I woke up and couldn't believe it. I felt so special by just being held and touched without having sex. He made love to my mind this time, instead of my body.

I rolled over and noticed Renard wasn't next to me. I walked into the house and saw him making breakfast in the kitchen. I walked right by him and into the bedroom to check and see if I had any messages.

"You have three new messages," my voicemail said.

"First message, 'Hey, baby, it's me. I'm at the club and want to know if you made it there safely. I haven't heard from you yet. I guess you're stuck in traffic. Call me and let me know you made it there safely. Either leave a message at home or at the office. Love you, and have fun,'" Terry's voice said.

"Next message, 'Damn, girl, what's going on? I haven't heard from you yet. You should be there by now. Please call and let me know that you made it there safely. Call the office. Better yet, I have my cell on vibrate. Call my cell phone. Love you!'"

"Next message, 'Baby, I'm really worried now. Your mother hasn't heard from you yet either. This isn't like you. Hopefully you'll hear this message. Please call me and let me know that you're okay. I'm home now. Please call *as soon as you get this*. Love you!'"

The boy was really worried about me. I immediately called him to explain.

"Hello," I heard his voice say.

"Hey, baby, I'm so sorry I didn't call you back last night. I didn't get your messages until just now. When we got here last night..."

He cut me off. "Do you know how worried I was about you? I called the hospitals, your mother, and the police. I called everybody! I called Crystal's house hoping she had her cell phone number on her answering machine but that hussy doesn't even have an answering machine."

"I don't know what to say, but I'm sorry. It wasn't intentional, baby. When we got back from the casino, I was dead tired so I just went to sleep. I didn't even bother to check my message. Plus I didn't think you'd mind if I didn't call you."

Why should he? He didn't care any other time whether I made it there safely. All he cared about was what bitch he was going to bring home that night.

"Well, I mind. I worry about you, baby; especially when you go on your lil' trips. Anything can happen out on these streets. I just want to make sure you get wherever safely. I don't care if you're going to work. I still want to know. Next time please call me, boo," he said.

"Okay, baby! You sound tired. What time did you go to sleep last night?" I asked.

"I just started to doze off not too long ago. Other than that I've been up all night. I couldn't go to sleep; not until I knew you were all right," he said.

"I'm sorry, baby. I didn't mean to worry you like that. I promise to make it up to you when I get back home. Go ahead and get some sleep and I'll see you later on tonight."

"You don't have to tell me twice. I'll talk to you later, baby. I love you!"

"I love you, too. Good night!"

I hung up the phone finally feeling loved from the man of my dreams, and my mind was clear. I knew exactly what I was going to do and whom I was going to be with. My husband really had changed over the past month or so. I had to give it another chance. I just had to. There was no other man that could make me feel the way he did.

"Tracy, breakfast is ready!" Renard yelled from the kitchen.

For a split second I'd forgotten that I was even with him. I walked out of the bedroom and sat down at the table. We had Belgian waffles with maple syrup, bacon, sausage, and fried diced potatoes. I said my grace and dug in. I spent the rest of our day reading and relaxing. Renard gave me my space, so it really wasn't that big of a deal. We'd said earlier in the day that we'd leave around 8 or 8:30 p.m. because he had a show to do. He didn't bother me all day; until about 6:30 p.m. I was lying on the couch reading an *Ebony* magazine. Renard walked out of the bedroom with nothing on but his birthday suit.

"That's enough reading. I need some personal attention," he said.

He stood there nicely oiled, like he was about to perform for me, with his dick rock hard just calling my name. *"Tracy! Tracy!"* I just had to answer it this one last time.

After we finished having sex, I realized what a mistake I'd just made. The whole time he was touching me I was thinking about my husband. When he touched me, I pictured Terry touching me. When he kissed me, in my mind it was Terry kissing me. I regretted having sex with him. I regretted having a fling with him. My mind was made. It was definitely over between the two of us. Terry had had my heart since I was fourteen years old and he still did. I'd tell Renard after we got back. There was no sense in telling him then, and him leaving my trifling ass out here.

I'd once hated Terry for playing me all of those years. I now hated myself for stooping down to the same level. I was going to end up hurting a perfectly kind and sweet man because of my selfishness. Cheating doesn't benefit anyone because you end up hurting everyone.

SHOPPING CONFUSION

I walked inside the jewelry store looking for the perfect engagement ring for Chelle. If there was such a thing. It would be even better if I could get it within my price range. I wasn't cheap; just an overprotective shopper so to speak. I'd seen a couple of rings earlier with diamonds that weren't even that big for a grand. That just didn't make any sense to me.

I went to Pentagon City thinking I'd get a good deal but same old same old. I kept running into salespeople on commission who'd suggest things in the best interest of their pockets and not my girl. I went to Kay Jewelers first to look. They had a pretty nice selection but none of the rings I liked had price tags on them. That couldn't mean anything but trouble. There were two rings in particular that caught my eye. I went over to the saleswoman to find out how much they were. She told me one ring was $835 and the second one was $999.99. They both were one-half carat, two-tone engagement rings in 14kt gold. They couldn't have been worth any more than $500, $600 at the most. She had to be out of her mind. I headed out of that store as fast as I walked in it.

I went to J.B. Jewelers next. I figured I needed a different strategy this time. I decided to act like a big spender. I was going to look at higher-priced rings so that the salesman would assume that I had money to spend. Then I would ask about a cheaper ring that I liked and compare the two of them. Either he would bring down the price a bit on the more expensive ring to kind of balance it out or he would give me a lower price on the less expensive one. Either way it would be a win-win situation.

When I walked in the store there were three salesmen inside, two white guys and one black guy. Both of the white guys were already helping other customers. Even better. The black guy had no choice but to help me. This man tried to sell me a 2-carat 14kt ring for $6,000 and a nice half-carat ring for $1,500. I couldn't believe my damn ears. I wanted to punch him in his face when those prices came out his mouth. He was trying to rob me, just without the gun. After that, I decided to call it a day and head home.

During the car ride home I started thinking about the possibility of proposing to Michelle without a ring. I was going to get her a different wedding band anyway. Why not just get the wedding band and not the engagement ring? I could still make the proposal memorable without a ring. What does the engagement ring actually symbolize, besides something for her to show off to her girlfriends?

I started to picture her reaction to me proposing without a ring. It didn't seem like a good idea anymore. I started to call Terry and ask him to hook a nigga up with a ring. He knew everybody so I was pretty sure he knew somebody who sold engagement rings. Then I thought about Jodi. Chelle was forever complimenting Jodi on her taste in fashion. I looked for her number. It was in my phone book somewhere around the house because Ty was usually over there anyway. Finally, I located my phone book in my nightstand, found her number, and dialed.

"Hey, Jodi. How are you doing?"

She recognized my voice. "I'm fine. Your boy isn't here. He should be at his house," she said.

"I know. I talked to him earlier. I wanted to talk to you about something," I told her.

I knew her mind was wondering why because there was a long pause. I didn't talk to Jodi much like that. We were friends more by association. The only time we really held a conversation was if I was visiting Ty or calling him and I spoke in passing.

"So what did you want to talk about?" she asked me.

"I have a problem." I paused. "I've decided to finally propose to Michelle but I'm having the hardest time buying a engagement ring for her. It seems like every store I go to they try to dick me."

She let out a sigh of relief. "Boy, you scared me there for a minute. I thought you were going to tell me one of those Jerry Springer confusions or something."

I couldn't help but laugh. I understood exactly where she was coming from.

"Naw," I said to calm her nerves. "I just want you to go shopping with me."

It was better for her to go with me than me by myself. Jodi and Chelle weren't real close friends where they called one another every day. Basically they didn't call each other at all. They just talked at group functions, cookouts, and dinners; things like that. I didn't have to worry about Chelle finding out that I was thinking about buying a ring or proposing. Plus, women are more into jewelry than men so they get better prices because they know their shit.

It's the same way with a mechanic for a woman; if she goes by herself the mechanic will generally try to get over on her because women tend to know nothing about cars. But if she brings a man with her then the mechanic will give a reasonable price. Don't get me wrong. Mechanics get over on men, too, but they'll try a woman first.

"Sure," she responded. "When are you trying to go?"

"It's up to you. I'm on your time. Whatever time is best for you, I will make work for me," I said.

As far as I was concerned we could've left right then and there. I wanted to propose like yesterday, so the sooner we found a ring the better. I don't know why I was in a rush but I just was. The faster I proposed the faster we could get married.

"Well, let me look at my schedule," she said. She put the phone down to get her calendar. "Next Saturday's good for me."

I didn't care. Any date was good for me. If it wasn't I would've made it good.

"It's a date then. Make sure you bring some champagne because you know I'm trying to get with you," I said, laughing.

"No problem. Just make sure you have some rubbers. I like to use Visas."

I cracked up laughing at her joke. I never knew she even had a sense of humor. I guess being in a relationship with Ty made you have one because he made fun about everything. Jodi and I always had intelligent conversations about different world issues. This boy really had a gem in his life. Hopefully he'd realize it before he lost her.

We said our goodbyes and hung up. I felt a little better about the whole situation. My phone started ringing, not even a half an hour after I'd gotten off the phone with Jodi.

"Why would you ask Jodi to go ring shopping with you? Now I'm going to have to hear this marriage shit," Ty said to me.

"Dawg, it ain't even like that. Women get better deals on rings than men. I wasn't getting any love when I tried to get one on my own. They just kept trying to dick me like I was a sucker or something," I told him.

"But still you didn't have to put Jodi in it. Michelle's got friends."

"Friends with big mouths, plus those bitches don't even know how to match their socks. Why the hell would I let them help me pick out Michelle's engagement ring?" I tried to explain.

"Why Jodi?" he asked.

"She's perfect. Chelle's always saying she has good taste. Plus they don't talk like that, so I don't have to worry about her slipping up and giving it away."

"I just wish you'd asked someone else to go with you. I like our relationship the way it is and now I'm going to have to hear this shit," he told me.

I caught slack from Ty the rest of the week about me asking Jodi to help me find a ring. I saw his point of view but he just didn't see mine. I wasn't trying to put any thoughts in her head. I was just trying to get a ring. If she materialized any thoughts about marriage on her own, well, good for her, but it wouldn't be because of me. All I could say to her was, "Good luck!"

❖ ❖ ❖ ❖

I picked Jodi up early in the morning. We headed to Wheaton Plaza first. We went to four different stores there. I spotted a couple of really nice rings but none of them really grabbed Jodi's attention. Since I'd asked her to come for her opinion, I had to trust her instincts.

She wanted to go to Pentagon City next. I told her about my experience there but she didn't care. She was determined. We got there around 2:30 p.m. I was hungry by then so i headed to the food court while she window-shopped for a ring. We both agreed to meet up at Kay Jewelers in fifteen minutes.

I went to Boardwalk to get an order of large fries. That was enough to hold me over until I got home and made myself some dinner. I had to stay downstairs to eat them because you can't walk around the mall and eat food. I even saw security once stop someone walking around the mall with some McDonald's from downstairs. They made him wrap his burger up and put it back in the bag. *Was that...?*

I got up from my table to get a better look. It was Tammy, all right. She was one of Chelle's friends. She and some dude were going to the movies. The movie theater was in the food court area as well. She looked right at me and started waving. She'd spotted me. Now I had to think of a reason for being at the mall to cover myself because I know she'd tell Chelle she'd seen me. I didn't want Chelle to have any suspicions about anything. I decided to buy something to cover my reason for being here.

I headed back upstairs to Kay Jewelers to meet Jodi. When I got to the store, I looked around to see if any of the salesmen that I'd dealt with the prior week were there. Of course they weren't. There were two totally different employees there this time, a guy about 5'8" who looked a little bit on the feminine side if you asked me, and a sexy woman. She was light-skinned, slim with a cute Coke-bottle shape, and had the fullest lips. She looked like she was around twenty-four; maybe twenty-five. I figured she was pretty good at her job by the way she looked. She had on a black Donna Karan pantsuit with Gucci boots to match.

She was talking to Jodi at the far counter. I walked over to them. They were sitting there carrying on a conversation like they were girlfriends from way back or something.

"There you are!" Jodi said. "Rhonda, this is Jeff. He's the lucky groom looking to buy an engagement ring."

Rhonda put her hand out to shake mine.

"Pleased to meet you. Why don't you look around the store and let me know if you see something you like."

Jodi went back to continuing her conversation with Rhonda about how her boyfriend wouldn't commit to her. Damn, Ty was right!

Her finding out that I was going to propose to Chelle played a part in her evaluating her own relationship. But that was human nature. When something good happens to someone you know you put yourself in their shoes. The bottom line was Jodi would've found out that I'd proposed, even if I didn't ask her to go ring shopping with me. So whatever thoughts she formed would've materialized sooner or later. It was time he took his relationship with her serious anyway.

I decided to test Rhonda and see if she was like the rest of the salespeople. I went to the counter where the same two half-carat rings were.

"These are nice. How much are these?" I asked.

They both walked over to the counter.

"Those are a good selection," Rhonda said.

"They're all right but I saw another one in here that's bad. It's back over where we were standing," Jodi said.

"Yeah, I liked that one better too, girl," Rhonda agreed.

"Okay, but how much are these two?"

"Well one is $499.99. Hold up, I'm sorry," she corrected herself. "They're both $499.99."

I couldn't believe my damn ears.

"Are they on sale or something? That seems mighty cheap," I asked.

"No, that's how much they are. The retail price for this one is listed at $835 and the other is $999.99. We sell them for $500 because it gives us an edge on the competition."

I double-checked to make sure the bitch from last week wasn't there again. It was a good thing she wasn't. Her ass would've been grass. Trying to sell me a ring at retail price so she could pocket my money. What pissed me off the most was the white dude had heard her ass trying to get over and didn't say a word. I probably would've gotten locked up if either one of them had worked that day. I wasn't going to spend a dime of my money in that store. I didn't care if she was selling the rings for a dollar.

"Well, I want to shop around and compare prices with other stores," I told Rhonda.

"You haven't seen the other ring yet," she replied.

"I know. We'll be back. There's another mall I want to take Jodi to before the store closes. She picked out the ring she liked here. I want her to look there as well and compare the two."

"I understand," she said as she looked at Jodi. "Girl, if you see something there you like and we have it or something similar, I'll beat their price," she said.

She was making it hard for me to turn her down. Kay Jewelers was usually good to me. I just couldn't get past the fact that the bitch had really tried to get over on me before. I had a whole new look at customer service. My mind went straight to how we did business at our club. I prayed that we hadn't treated our customers that way and I was going to see to it that we didn't from that point on. Jodi and Rhonda exchanged numbers to keep in touch and then we went on our way.

"So where do you know her from?" I asked Jodi.

"Who? Rhonda? I just met her today. We started talking while I was waiting for you. She's nice. She said she's been to the club a couple of times, too."

That's interesting. I'd never seen her there. I wondered if Jodi told her I was the manager of the club. Knowing her, she had and that was probably why I'd gotten such a good price. She was trying to position herself to get special privileges at the club. Women were smart like that; always thinking ahead.

"Let's go check out the store upstairs," I said.

"Okay, but I want to go to Victoria's Secret first."

I had no problem with that. I could pick up some lotion or a gift for Chelle. I had to have a reason for going to the mall anyway. I forgot I was at the mall with a woman, though. Victoria's Secret turned into the Limited, the Gap, Liz Claiborne, and Express real quick. I didn't even realize it. Before I knew it, I was giving Jodi constructive criticism on the outfits she was trying on. Out of all the stores we went to Jodi didn't buy a single thing she'd tried on. She ended up buying a bra and panty set from the first store we'd gone to. I had to admit it; they were sexy. Ty would love watching Jodi model them for him.

"Oh my God!" Jodi said, looking at her watch. "It's almost four-thirty. I have to work tonight. I'm covering for someone in the ER."

We still hadn't picked out a ring. We'd gotten sidetracked shopping.

"Well, when's the next time you can go with me?" I asked her.

"I'm not sure because I'll be covering for her for the next two weeks. Probably in like three weeks. I get a week off after I finish her shift," she responded.

That was fine with me. I hadn't made up my mind what I was going to say to Chelle when I proposed nor did I have a place to do it. I needed some time to have everything set-up perfectly. I took Jodi home so she could get ready for her shift. I headed straight home myself so I could get ready for work.

❖ ❖ ❖ ❖

I walked inside the house and went upstairs. Chelle was sitting up on the bed, looking pissed. I went into the bathroom to sit on the toilet and think back to what I might've done or forgotten to do. I always faked like I had to shit to buy me some time to think. Usually she wouldn't come in the bathroom, but not this time. She rushed in the bathroom and just stared at me, as if I had something to tell her. I couldn't think of a damn thing I could've done. I just ignored her like she wasn't even in here.

"Don't try and act like you don't see me standing here," she said.

"I see you. I'm trying to use the bathroom. Whatever it is it can wait until I get out."

She ignored my response. "Please don't lie to me. Just tell me the truth because I already know."

She walked over to the tub and sat down. She looked me in my eyes and I could see that she was in pain. She was trying to fight back her tears.

"Who is she?" she asked.

Who is she? What the hell was she talking about? Who is who?

"What are you talking about, boo? Who is who?" I questioned her.

"You know who the fuck I'm talking about! I told you; don't lie to me! Is she one of those bitches from the club? Who the hell is she?" she said hysterically.

I had no idea who or what she was talking about. I knew she knew exactly who "She" was, though. I wasn't saying shit. She wasn't going to get me to confess to anything I'd done in the past. I'd fuck around and tell her some shit that she wasn't even talking about. I know they say what's done in the dark always finds its way into the light, but damn. I hadn't cheated on her in almost six months. And that was in Atlanta. There was no way she could've found out about that unless...unless Ty had told her. It was all starting to make sense. I couldn't believe my boy had sold me out to stop me from getting married. I was pissed.

"I don't know what the fuck you're talking about, Chelle. I know one thing though; you better get the hell out of my damn face with this bullshit," I told her.

I wiped my ass like I'd actually used the bathroom and walked out to my bedroom. I couldn't believe that nigga had snitched on me. I still wasn't giving myself up; caught or not. She was going to have to make specific accusations. She was trying to give me enough rope to let me hang myself; like I was a kid or something. I wasn't going to hang myself. If anything, I was going to widen the grip around my neck and get out of it.

"So you don't know what I'm talking about, huh?" she asked me, trying to set me up for the kill.

"I told you I didn't."

"Then who the hell were you walking around Pentagon City with all day long, bunned up?" she finally asked.

I calmed myself down. Tammy must've seen me walking around with Jodi after her movie. She didn't waste any time calling Chelle, did she? I giggled.

"Is that what this is all about? I was at the mall with Jodi," I told her.

She sucked her teeth, like she didn't believe me.

"I told you don't lie to me and you're still going to sit there and lie to me in my face. I just want to know who the bitch was. You know what? It doesn't even matter. How long have you been cheating on me with this bitch?"

I walked over to the phone and started to dial Jodi's number. That was all I could think of. No matter what I said she wasn't going to believe me.

"Who the fuck are you calling?" she yelled at me.

"I'm calling Jodi. She can tell you; since you don't believe me."

"Don't be calling…"

I cut her off when Jodi answered the phone. "Hey, Jodi, this is Jeff. Chelle wanted me to call you because she has something to ask you."

"Okay," she said.

I handed Chelle the phone.

"Hello. How are you doing, Jodi? This is Michelle."

"I'm sorry to bother you with this but were you with Jeff today?"

"You were."

"Oh, y'all went to Pentagon City. Well, thanks, girl. You cleared everything up for me. My girlfriend told me that she saw him at the mall today with some broad and that was about to be his ass. Child, you know how these niggas be lying, so I wanted to check with you first before I got to cuttin' his ass up in here."

I looked at her like she was crazy; knowing damn well she wasn't going to do shit.

"Well, I'll talk to you later, girl. Thanks."

She hung up the phone and looked at me, embarrassed.

"I'm sorry, boo, I acted like that, but what would you think if Ty saw me at the mall with some boy and told you?" she asked in her defense.

"You don't have to defend yourself. I would've reacted the same way you did, if the shoe were on the other foot," I told her.

"So why were y'all at the mall together? Did you run into her there?"

I didn't know when Tammy had first seen me, so I didn't want to say something that would make Chelle question my response.

"No, I went to pick her up. Their anniversary is coming up and she wanted me to help her pick out a surprise gift for Ty."

I started to tell her that Ty was thinking about proposing to her and she wanted to show me the ring she wanted, in case Tammy had seen us in a jewelry store, but I didn't want Chelle to have any thoughts in her head about marriage. I wanted everything to be a total surprise when I proposed.

She lunged over at me with both arms extended to hug me. "I guess I have to put more trust in you that you won't cheat on me. Sometimes it's hard but that's still no excuse."

I wanted to punch Tammy in her gossiping mouth but she was just being a good friend. I couldn't fault her for that.

"At least she asked me to help pick out his gift. I remember when he got her that ring last year with her birthstone in it and it was too big."

"I remember," she said, agreeing with me. "He tried to blame me for it. I told him that he should've asked me. I wear a six and her fingers are about the same size as mine," she said.

That was just what I needed; her ring size. I had to admit I was definitely good. "I know, boo. I know!"

Tyrelle
IT'S JUST NOT WORTH LOSING

have nothing to do one night. Jodi was working nights then and I wasn't trying to just sit in the house; at least not by myself. I needed some pussy. I just had to have her out by the morning. Knowing Jodi she'd just pop up over my house unannounced and sleep there when she got off. I looked through my phonebook for who I wanted to be with. I should've just called April but I was getting a lil' tired of her. It was time to try someone new.

I came across Nakia's number. I'd met her about two weeks ago; at the club, of course. She was dark-skinned with a seductive body. Usually I only stepped to light-skinned or brown-skinned girls but I couldn't help myself with her. She was so beautiful that she could stop traffic. I felt like R. Kelly.

My mind's telling me no.

But her body, her body's telling me yes.

She had a body that was definitely calling me. She had long black hair with brown eyes. The woman was way beyond sexy. It was finally time to hook-up with her.

"Hello. Can I speak to Nakia?"

"This is she," her soft voice said.

"Well, hello there, sexy. How are you?" I asked.

"I'm fine, but I'd be better if I knew who I was talking to."

"It's Tyrelle. I met you a couple of weeks ago at my club."

She paused, probably trying to remember who I was.

"Oh yeah. I remember you. How are you doing?" she asked.

"Not too bad. I was wondering if I was going to see you tonight at the club, or did you make other plans?"

75

We were two consenting adults. There was no need to beat around the bush; plus that wasn't my style. I was straightforward and I liked my women to be the same.

"I didn't plan on doing anything tonight. I'm kind of tired. I was going to stay in the house and watch a movie," she said.

"Well, how 'bout I come and see you? Maybe for an hour or two? We can watch the movie together," I suggested.

"I don't know. We only really talked one time. I'll just meet you at the club tonight like you suggested."

Damn, I really wanted to go over to her crib and get some of that dark chocolate but I knew it wasn't going to be that easy.

"Okay. I'll see you tonight then. What time should I expect you?" I asked.

"Around seven-thirty or eight," she answered.

"Okay, well, I'll see you then."

I got my place in order; just in case we came back to my house instead of hers. I straightened up my living room, as well as the bedroom. I had to hide any sign of Jodi. Her panties she left, her clothes, makeup, pictures, shit like that. The house was perfect for my night of fun. I lay down for a few and imagined myself tasting Nakia's dark chocolate body.

The phone rang and woke me from my daze. I checked the Caller ID first to see who it was. The Caller ID read Howard University Hospital. It was Jodi. I didn't feel like talking to her so I just let the phone ring.

I decided to get dressed and head to the club. It was only six but I didn't care. I was too anxious to sit around the house and wait. Saturday nights usually filled up pretty quick so I'd have something to do until Nakia got there. I went in the bathroom to wash up. When I came out I saw the light on my answering machine was lit. She must've left me a message.

"I'll check it later," I said.

I got dressed and headed out the door.

❖ ❖ ❖ ❖

I arrived at the club and was shocked to see so many people there already. It looked like a good two-hundred-fifty people. It seemed too early to party to me. The thirty-

and-over crowd was usually there on Saturdays so it kinda made sense why there was a crowd already. It was clearly more women there than men. The fellas could scope out the women they wanted early, then put in their work to get them before the place got crowded with more niggas. It was a man's dream situation.

Most of the ladies were sitting down, enjoying their drinks and the music. The house DJ played R&B and smooth jazz until DJ Rico would take over at ten. I realized I'd been coming at the wrong times. I went to the bar to see what was up with Darin.

"What's up with you, partner? Why didn't you tell me the ladies are in here like this, this early?" I asked him, giving him some dap.

"You're the man. I thought you already knew," he said.

"It's like this every Saturday?" I asked.

"Each and every. I told you to start coming earlier. Plus, there's nothing but free game up in here 'round this time."

"I see. I'm not tripping, though. I gotta honey coming through tonight," I replied.

"You better start making those rounds before she gets here," he said.

He had a point. Why not? No need to waste a good opportunity like this one. It wasn't guaranteed that she was giving me some ass. I had one mission for that night and that was to be in some pussy. I started to try and set up some back-up pussy; just in case Nakia didn't come through. But the thought of getting in those legs erased that thought. I was determined to hit that. She could make a brother hard just thinking about it.

I felt a tap in my rib cage. I turned around and saw Nakia standing there with a smile on her face. She had on a long black dress that looked like it was painted on her. That's how tight it was. It had a slit going up her right leg, showing her plump thigh. I wanted to take her clothes off right then and there.

"Hello there, handsome. I don't remember you looking this good the first time we met," she said.

I didn't know if I should take that as a compliment or an insult. It didn't matter to me because the way she looked, she could say whatever she wanted.

"What are you doing here this early?" I asked her.

"Why? You aren't happy to see me?"

Happy wasn't the word for the sight of her. It was more like thankful.

"I'm more than happy to see you. I want to thank God for letting me see one of his angels. I just wasn't expecting you until around eight o'clock, that's all. I would've had a table ready for us if I'd known."

"Really! I tell you what. You go ahead and get things situated while I go to the ladies room," she said.

"Okay. Meet me at the bar," I told her.

She went to the bathroom. I headed toward VIP and told Janice to set-up a table for me for two. To my surprise, she'd already had it set up for me an hour ago. Talk about on your job; she was earning her paycheck.

Nakia would like the VIP section; if she hadn't been up there before. It was upstairs; separate from the club portion. There was a bar and a pool table up there. We had a glass wall where you could see the dance floor downstairs in the club. There was a $125 charge to get in VIP but it was worth it.

It was real relaxed up there. It was the perfect atmosphere for a romantic evening. Usually when musicians or athletes had birthday parties at the club, they'd spend their time up in VIP. There was a small dance floor to accommodate only the VIP room capacity. I was headed to the bar to meet Nakia when I saw April making her way through the crowd. Oh shit! I hid in the crowd so she couldn't see me when she walked by me. I made my way to the bar when the coast was clear.

"You know April's here," Darin warned me.

"I know. I just saw her."

What was I going to do? April knew her place with Jodi and how to act. But she'd fuck around and kirk out if she saw me with Nakia. She still thought Jodi and I were having problems and she was next in line. If she found out about Nakia, everything would come full circle. I became tense as hell.

Nakia came over to me and was ready to go to our table. I called over security to escort her to VIP while I ducked April. I made my way through the crowd undetected. I told Mike, who was on the door of VIP, not to let April upstairs under any circumstances. She was a regular and had privileges to go where she wanted in the club.

I went upstairs and enjoyed my dinner with Nakia. She was teasing me throughout dinner, licking her luscious lips and looking at me with her seductive eyes. The DJ started to play The Isley Brothers' new hit "Contagious."

"Would you like to dance?" I asked.

"I'd love to," she told me.

As the music played and each verse was sung, we held each other tighter and tighter. We were grinding on one another, feeling each other. I knew she could feel my soldier saluting her. I finally heard the words I was waiting to her all night.

"Do you want to get out of here and go back to my place?" she asked.

Hell yeah, I wanted to. Was she crazy? Nobody in his right mind would've turned her down.

"I'd love to but are you sure you're ready for that?" I asked.

I had to ask her that. I didn't want to get there, let things get hot and heavy, and end up having her say, *'I'm not ready for this. Things are moving too fast.'* I wanted to make sure she was ready so we wouldn't have to go through all of that.

That was how a lot of niggas caught date rape charges. They'd start fooling around with their girl and she'd want to stop but they wouldn't. Next thing you know, they're doing five to ten years. I wasn't the one to be going through that. Why put yourself in a situation that you can avoid?

"I wanted you the first time I saw you. I just couldn't do anything then. Now's a different story," she said.

That was all I needed to hear.

"Let me take care of a couple of things first; then we can leave," I said.

I had to map out an exit from the club without April seeing us. I definitely couldn't use the drama right then. I was finally about to get what I wanted; the pleasure of a night with her.

"Can we finish the dance first?" she asked.

She just wanted to keep torching me.

"Whatever makes you happy," I said.

"I'll test that tonight. We'll see."

Damn, she was talking dirty to me, too. I couldn't wait. I wanted to hurry up and get out of there. The more we danced the more my mind wandered. If she danced like that with her clothes on, I couldn't wait to see how she did with them off. My appetite for her definitely grew.

After the song ended I headed to my office to think of a plan. On my way to my office April spotted me. I wanted to run but if I had she would've just followed me. I headed towards her and met her halfway.

"I've been looking for you all night. Where have you been?" she asked.

"I just got here not too long ago. I wasn't feeling well."

"What's wrong, baby? Do you want Momma to take care of you? I'm sure I can come up with a couple of things to cure you," she said.

The girl had a one-track mind.

"Baby, I'm sorry. I'm going to have to take a rain check on that. How 'bout we hook up tomorrow afternoon or something? I could swing by your house for lunch," I said.

"I guess that's what we'll have to do, since I can't see you tonight, but I have to talk to you as well," she said sternly.

I agreed to talk to her about whatever it was tomorrow and walked off. I needed to think. I went to the bar to get a drink to calm my nerves. I could still see April looking at me when I got there. That bitch was going to sit there and watch me all damn night.

I really needed some advice on how to get out of that one. I had no idea where Jeff was and wasn't up for the lecture or his I told you so's. I couldn't call Terry because he'd probably have the same thing to say. I was stuck with this one on my own.

"D, man, you wouldn't believe how my night's going. Nakia wants to get out of here and go back to her place but April's watching me like a hawk. She's like a damn drug man; I can't shake her."

"You need to cut that bitch back. She's not worth all that drama to me. The pussy can't be that good," he said.

I looked at him like he was out of his mind.

"Damn, it's like that?" he asked.

"And them some," I replied.

We broke out laughing, but it was so true. On a scale of one to ten, I would rank her a twelve. The sex was that good. She did the three things I liked; she could fuck, suck, and then roll out. I finished my drink.

"Come up with something, D. I'm going to my office for a few," I said.

I went to my office to think and hopefully come up with a plan. I walked in and Jodi was sitting on my desk. She had on a long trench coat, like it was going to rain or something. I was in shock. I couldn't believe this was happening to me; her ass was supposed to be at work.

"What are you doing here, baby?" I asked her.

She opened her coat. "I wanted you to unwrap your surprise," she replied.

She didn't have on a single piece of clothing but that coat.

"Ahh, baby, Ahh."

I couldn't even get the words out of my mouth. I was speechless. She walked over to me and started kissing me while unbuckling my pants. I picked her up and carried her to my desk. I handled my business from there and gave her what she'd come there for.

It was a fifteen-minute fuck; nothing but raw hardcore sex.

"I thought you only wanted to make love?" I said, mocking her.

"Every now and then I just want to be fucked. Don't worry about it; you're going to make love to me when we get home. I just wanted a quickie now, to hold me over until we get home."

I was eager to get started again. I never knew she was such a freak for me. I'd always heard every woman had a little freak in them. Now I knew it was true.

"Are you ready to go?" I asked.

"Yeah, I'm ready. Excuse me, I don't have that much to put back on," she said, laughing.

"You make sure you tie that belt tight. I don't want everybody seeing my goodies. I'll meet you at the house," I said while I was walking her to the door.

I opened the door for her and realized that it wasn't even locked. Sex could really make you forget about a lot of things.

I got back to the bar and took a seat real quick.

"I thought you were gone already," Darin said.

"Maybe one day, when I have time, I'll tell you what just happened," I said.

I shook my head still in disbelief. I loved that girl; I really did.

"So did you figure out what you're going to do? I couldn't think of shit."

"Damn, I forgot all about it. I need you to do me a favor. Send a message up to table five in VIP for me," I told Darin.

I grabbed a napkin off the bar and wrote Nakia a note.

Nakia,

I'm sorry but something came up that I have to take care of. I'll call you tomorrow and maybe we can hook up then. Once again, I'm sorry.

Tyrelle

"Make sure she gets this for me," I stressed to him.

"You just make sure you tell me what happened in your office," he said with a smile on his face.

I went back to my office to get my keys. I thought about what would've happened if Jodi had caught me with Nakia, or April for that matter. None of them were worth losing her over. I couldn't believe it. Jeff and Terry were actually right. Jodi was too good of a woman to lose. She was better then any woman I'd met. She was all I needed.

Jeff
SAY YOU'LL BE MINE

"Will you marry me?" I said aloud, looking in the bedroom mirror.

I didn't like that.

"Baby, I want to spend the rest of my life with you. Will you marry me?"

That was more like it. I still needed to jazz it up and add my little touch to it. It didn't sound original to me. It sounded more like something a lot of other people had used to propose.

I'd been pumping myself up to propose all that week. Tonight was the night. Everything was planned perfectly. We were going to have dinner at Jordan's and a quiet evening at home afterwards. I finally had the ring I wanted. I still couldn't believe it had taken Jodi and me almost a month to find it. And I'd bought it from Kay Jewelers after all.

It turned out that Rhonda wasn't a salesperson. She was the district manager and that was one of her stores. She and Jodi remained friends and continued to talk after that day. She'd told Rhonda the real reason why I didn't want to buy anything from the store. Rhonda took care of everything. The ring Jodi liked was a 1-carat ring in 14kt gold. Rhonda had a 2-carat ring made just for me in platinum that had the same design as the one Jodi liked.

She had me pick it up from the same Pentagon City store. The whole scene in the store was perfect. When I came in the original saleswoman that had tried to get over on me was there. Rhonda introduced me to her formally, then refreshed her memory of the situation. She apologized to me in front of her and handed me the ring. I paid only $500 for it. The difference was deducted from the saleswoman's final paycheck. The Lord works in mysterious ways because never would I have expected that.

I kind of felt bad for the woman, too. She'd lost her job and had to pay for the cost to upgrade my ring. But they do say what goes around comes around, so I guess it came back on her. Rhonda really impressed me with the way she'd handled the situation. Customer service was definitely high on her list. She was okay by my book. She didn't have to worry about paying for anything at the club if she came; except her drinks, of course. I might've been grateful but I wasn't crazy.

Ring, Ring, Ring.

It was my phone.

"Hello."

"Hey. What's up, Jeff?" Ty said.

"Shit! Getting things ready for tonight," I let slip out.

I wish I could've taken that back.

"What's tonight?" he asked.

I didn't really want to tell him the truth. I wanted him to know after I'd done it.

"Well...tonight is the big night. I'm proposing to Chelle," I said.

I had to tell him. He wasn't just my boy. He was my blood. If anyone deserved to know, it was him.

"Look, I know I haven't been real supportive about your decision but I want you to know that I'll support you either way. Actually, I'm proud of you. It takes a lot of balls to make the step you're about to make. I have more respect for you than you'll ever know," he said.

I was shocked. I couldn't believe my ears. That was the last thing I'd expected to hear him say.

He continued, "The other night, dawg, I had this nice lil' honey at the club. We were having a good ole time when April showed up. I tried to duck her ass all night."

I interrupted him. "Stop playing. I told you that bitch was crazy."

"Well, she didn't catch me so nothing popped off. Anyway, ole girl wanted me to go back to her place with her and everything. So I went to my office to get my keys and guess who was in there butt-assed naked, sitting on my desk?"

"I told you that bitch was crazy. You need to cut her back," I said.

"It wasn't April, nigga!"

"Then who was it?" I asked.

"Jodi," he said.

"Jodi! Get the hell out of here."

"Man, I didn't know what to say. I don't know if I was more shocked that she was naked or that she was there," he said.

"Damn. Don't tell me that y'all broke up?"

"Naw! Let me finish, young. Before I could really even say anything, she walked over to me and started unbuckling my pants. So I did what any normal nigga would have."

I knew what that was, so there wasn't any need for me to even ask. "So what happened to the other girl?"

"I forgot all about her ass," he replied.

This nigga was off the hook.

"Did she cuss your ass out when she finally caught up to you?"

"Oh, naw, it wasn't like that. I went to the bar for a minute while Jodi was leaving and D reminded me about her. I wrote her a note saying something came up and then rolled. Jodi was horny as shit so I met her at my house to finish up," he said.

His ass was lucky he didn't get caught. I wanted to tell him *'I told you to slow down,'* but I didn't. I just let it ride. He needed to learn it on his own and if he hadn't learned yet, he would sooner or later. I knew he loved the challenge of getting out of it. It gave him a rush. I thought that was probably the best part about cheating; the thrill of getting out of being caught.

Cheating was like basketball in a way. If you had game, then you'd play anybody. The only problem was that you'd eventually run into a woman with more game than you and end up getting played.

"Dawg, that ain't even it." He paused. "When I went to my office to get my keys, I thought about the entire situation. None of it was even worth losing Jodi. Not dinner with Nakia."

"Who?" I interrupted.

"That was the chick's name I was there with. Being with April wasn't worth it; none of it. Later on that night I just sat around and thought about how much Jodi really does mean to me and how life would be without her. She means too much to me, young. I mean, I'm not willing to risk losing her over some ass."

I wanted to yell out, *'Isn't that what I have been telling you all this time?'* As hard as it was, I held it in. I didn't say not one word.

"It's like I'm trying to prove to myself that I've still got it by being able to get new ass. But I have the one that I want, so what do I have to prove. It just doesn't make sense, ya know?" he said.

"I hear you, but what are you saying?" I asked.

He wasn't getting out of it that easy. He was going to have to say it.

"I'm through with all these other bitches, man. I guess you were... Well, you know."

"No, I don't know. What?"

"Fine, you were right. Are you happy?" he said.

I actually was. It was rare for him to apologize. On top of that, the person who I thought would never change finally had. The reality of it was that sooner or later every man got to that point in their life when he was tired of all the women. He just wanted to be with one woman. It just took some of us longer than others. Look at Terry, he was married and it still hadn't kicked in. He still played the game, well, until recently, and he was in his thirties.

"So what's next from here?" I asked.

"Oh, I'm not at the same point as you are. I'm not ready for marriage or anything right now. I asked her to move in so we're together more. I think it will be a good test for our relationship. I mean, how can you marry someone and y'all might not even be able to live together? You need to know firsthand, I think," he said.

"Now before she moves in, you need to air your dirty laundry. Break your ties from those other chicks," I said.

"I know, I know. That's the first thing I'm going to do," he replied.

"Especially that damn April. You need to tell that bitch first."

"Okay," he said.

I wish I could've given myself the credit for his new discovery but, honestly, he'd figured everything out on his own. I'd given him advice that might've opened his eyes when it was obvious.

"Aye, I've got something to take care of. I'll talk to you later. Good luck tonight, too. I hope everything goes as planned."

Tonight, damn! I needed to get shit together.

❖ ❖ ❖ ❖

By the time I got to Jordan's, Chelle was already at our table waiting on me. Not a good way to start dinner off, being late.

"How long have you been waiting?" I asked.

"For about five, maybe ten minutes. Not long," she said.

Good. She wasn't in a bad mood over my lateness. She hadn't ordered anything to eat yet; just a glass of chardonnay. The waiter spotted me sitting at the table and made his way over to us.

"Are you ready to order, sir?" he asked, looking at me.

"I haven't really checked out the menu or anything, so I'm not quite ready yet. Can you give us another moment?"

He walked away and I began to browse the menu.

"Do you know what you want yet?" I asked.

"Yes," she replied.

After about ten minutes the waiter made his way back over to our table to take our orders. Chelle ordered a steak, medium rare, with a baked potato, string beans with almonds, and a vegetable medley. I decided to have the same thing; except I wanted my steak well done.

That was one of the things I loved most about her; we were so much alike. We liked just about the same things. I'd planned to wait until after we'd eaten to propose but I was so nervous I just wanted to get it over with.

"Are you happy with me?" I asked.

"Huh?" she said, confused.

"Do I make you happy?" I rephrased.

"Of course you do. What more can I ask for? You mean the world to me."

If I had any doubts about what I was going to ask her, after that comment, I didn't have them anymore.

"Why? Are you happy with me?" she asked.

I looked at her and smiled. "I'll show you how happy I am later on tonight."

Chelle looked at me and grinned; assuming I meant sexually. I decided not to propose right then. It would be better if I waited until after dinner. The waiter came to the table with our meals. She rushed through her meal; trying to get home quicker to start the festivities. I took my time so her sexual appetite would grow stronger. After dinner, I asked her to stop and pick up her favorite bottle of wine. I went straight home to get the house ready.

An ensemble of candles lighted the house when she walked in.

"Hello!" she yelled.

"I'm in the living room," I said.

The sweet sounds of Jill Scott awaited her as she walked in. I lay on the couch with my silk tiger-striped robe on.

"Come dance with me," I told her.

You love me; especially different every time.
You keep me on my feet.
Happily excited by your cologne, your hands, your smile, your intelligence.

She walked over to me and we danced with one another.

"Chelle, do you remember the first day we met?" I asked her while we were dancing.

"Yes. It was almost four years ago at Union Station. You walked up to me and gave me the corniest pick-up line I'd ever heard."

"I asked you if you knew what time it was," I said.

"And I said, 'Two thirty-five.' Then your crazy butt said, 'Oh my watch is broken, but I could've sworn it was time for us to get to know each other better," she said, imitating me.

We both laughed. I became a little defensive.

"But it worked because I stayed with you until it was time for you to catch your train. I think we talked for at least a good hour but it seemed like four. We just clicked from the start," I said.

"The only reason why I stayed with you that day was because I thought anybody that desperate to use a line like that was in need for some serious attention," she said.

"Well, that was the best day of my life. Every night before I go to bed I thank the Lord for bringing you into my life. Then we moved in together and I thought that was the best day of my life. I get to wake up every morning and see your beautiful face. And get to sleep next to you every night. I would just think, *What more can a man ask for?* He finally answered me and now I see what could make my life even better." I paused.

She looked at me puzzled. I stopped dancing and went down on one knee. I took the ring out of my pocket. Tears started to roll down her face.

"I want to spend the rest of my life with you. Michelle Renee Davis, you are my everything. You're the sunshine that brightens my day; the air that I breathe. You've taught me the true meaning of love. Your love gives me the strength to go on each day. My angel sent from heaven and, hopefully, my lifelong partner. Will you be my best friend, my companion, and my lover? Ms. Michelle Renee Davis, will you marry me?"

"Yes!" She paused. "Yes, I will marry you!"

I placed the ring on her finger and hugged her. I picked her up and took her upstairs to express my love for her lovingly, passionately, and without words.

Jerry

CHANGED MAN

There was just too much to do for one day. The rental car needed to be picked up by 10 a.m. I had to go to the club and sign some documents before we left. What made matters even worse; Tracy was still laying her ass in the bed. It was already 8:45 a.m. and I wanted to be on the road by 10 a.m. to beat the traffic. It took a good hour and fifteen minutes to get to Kings Dominion from home.

"Tracy, come on and get up!" I said, nudging her, trying to wake her up. "I want to be on the road by 10 a.m. Come on! Get up!" I yelled.

Talk about a hard sleeper, I wasn't even fazing her. Finally, she woke up from her deep sleep after I poured some cold water on her.

"Boy, what's wrong with you?" she asked, sounding groggy.

"Get up! We're going to be late," I said.

"I'm up. I'm up. What time is it?" she asked.

I glanced over to the clock and lied. "It's nine-thirty!"

There was no reason to tell her the truth. She'd just lie back down until nine, which would then turn into ten and, by that time, we'd be way off schedule. I'd just eliminated that process.

"Why did you let me sleep that late? You should've woken me up at eight-thirty or something. Have you taken care of your business yet at the club?" she asked.

"No. I wanted to wait until you were up. I was going to leave while you were getting ready," I said like I had an attitude.

She jumped out of bed and went straight into the bathroom. Once I heard the shower on, I knew it was safe to leave.

I walked over to the door and told her, "I'll be back in twenty minutes."

"Okay," she replied.

I went downstairs and headed out the door. I didn't have a lot of time to spend at the club. I had to sign the order slips for the chairs, tables, bar stools, and, most importantly, the liquor and beer for the new club. We still hadn't decided on a name for the club but we were narrowing it down.

Everything at the club pretty much went smoothly. I'd already pre-ordered the stuff so all I needed to do was sign the slips and the checks. I was in and out of the club in about ten minutes.

I went to my car to go back home and pick Tracy up so we could go get the rental car. Hopefully, the woman was ready.

"Terry! Hey, Terry!" I heard someone yelling from behind me.

My eyes had to be deceiving me. It was Brandi. I hadn't seen her in a while. She was looking good, too. We'd had a lil' something going on back in the day but she'd left to go to New York to pursue her modeling career. She finally made her way over to me and hugged me.

"How have you been?" she asked.

"Not too bad. I can't complain. How 'bout yourself?"

"I'm holding my own," she said.

Holding her own? Who did she think she was fooling? That had to be an understatement. Last I'd heard she'd signed a deal with Guess jeans. I'd heard it was for like two or three million dollars. That qualified her as doing a little better than holding her own in my book. She more like *had* her own.

"Yeah right! I hear Naomi Campbell doesn't have shit on you now. People are telling me there's a new sheriff in town," I said.

She began to blush.

"I wouldn't put myself on her level just yet. Hopefully one day I'll get there. Right now I'm learning the ropes. You know, getting my feet wet," she said.

I wished I was standing in the same pool she was, so my feet could get wet. Damn, I could use two million to learn the ropes. I'd settle with half a mil.

"So what are you doing in town?" I asked.

"Just chilling. I needed some time away from all the craziness of New York and the business. Plus I want to buy my mother a house," she said.

"I hear that. Gotta do right by moms. Shit, while you're at it, I need a new crib, too. You should buy me one for old time's sake," I said, laughing.

She laughed with me.

"I wish I could. I don't have it like that just yet. So how's business?" she asked.

"I can't complain. We're still in business. Actually that's what I'm doing down here. We're going to open another club over here."

"Y'all just movin' on up, huh?"

"We're trying to do a lil' something something," I said.

I couldn't help but stare at her. She was so beautiful and it was a natural beauty. She didn't have on a lot of makeup. She had on a pair of regular blue jeans and an Armani Exchange T-shirt with some black sandals. The sandals showed her nicely manicured toes. She still looked extravagant. The more I looked at her, her titties even looked a little bigger, too. I didn't remember them being that big before and I'd had several good looks at them—up close and personal.

"I see money doesn't just buy clothes these days," I said, pointing at her breasts with my eyes.

She started to blush again. "It was my agent's idea. She thinks they'll help land me some acting roles. You don't see too many little-breasted women in movies these days. You have to admit, I do wear them well," she said.

"I must agree. You certainly do," I replied.

"I came by the club looking for you last night but you weren't there. Have your days off changed? If my memory is correct you should've been there last night."

Damn, the girl had a good memory.

"I only work on Wednesdays now at Mystic and some Saturdays. I spend most of my time trying to get the new club up and running."

I checked my watch to see what time it was.

"I have to get out of here. I'm running late. I'll catch up with you later on. How long will you be in town?" I asked.

"Just for the weekend. I fly to L.A. for a photo shoot Monday morning."

She looked at me, seductively licking her lips. "So what time can I expect to see you tonight?"

I couldn't understand before why she'd gone to the club looking for me, but now I did. She wanted some weekend sex while she was in town. I wasn't sure if she thought I was one of her groupies who would jump at the chance to be with her. I'd already had her. I had who I wanted. Tracy was the only one getting any sex from me.

"I'm sorry but that can't happen. I'm with my wife and only my wife," I said.

By her laughter, she obviously thought I was making some type of joke.

"Come on, Terry. You don't have to play games with me. I'm only in town for the weekend and I really want to be with you. I miss you," she said.

"I'm sorry but I'm not joking. I don't do that anymore. I'm a married man," I said.

"You were a married man when I met you. Nothing stopped you then," she replied.

"We can go back and forth all day if you want, but I've changed. I'm not like that anymore. I'm sorry but I'd love to remain your friend. That's it; nothing sexual. If you need advice, or anything like that."

She looked at me like I'd lost my mind. I had. I was flat out head over heels in love with my wife and I wasn't going to do anything to hurt Tracy again. I'd promised her that I'd change and I had. There was no need to turn back then.

"Umm, hmm. Well, you take care," she said.

"I will and tell your mother I said hello," I said and walked off.

The whole drive home my mind was on what had taken place. I'd passed my first test, so to speak. I was proud of myself but I knew that there would be many more to come. I'd been a hoe for a long time. My skeletons were bound to come out of the closet sooner or later. I just had to stay focused on my goal. It was a lot easier to say you'd changed, but you had to prove it. After what had just happened, I believed in myself. I didn't know how I would handle the challenge of turning down pussy. I felt better knowing that it wasn't really a challenge at all. It felt good to know that I'd defied all the odds. I was living proof that the saying, '*Once a cheater always a cheater*,' wasn't true. Anyone could change; they just had to want to.

I walked in the house feeling like a new man. I felt like I was floating on cloud nine. Johnny was on the couch in the living room watching TV.

"You ready to go, Lil' J?" I asked.

"Yeah," he said.

"Go get in the car then," I said.

I went upstairs to see Tracy in the same damn place she'd been in when I'd left; the bathroom.

"You're not ready yet!" I said.

"Don't be rushing me!" she shot back at me.

I stood there and stared at her, admiring her beauty. I couldn't even get mad at her not being ready. Finally she couldn't take my staring anymore.

"What?" she asked.

"Nothing. Have I ever told you that you're so beautiful?"

Her face lit up. I walked over to her and placed my arms around her waist while I stood behind her. We looked into the mirror together.

"Look at you. You have to be the sexiest woman in the world."

Her face lit up brighter than a light bulb that time. See turned around and looked at me.

"I love you," she said.

I hugged her and gave her a soft kiss on the lips.

"I love you, too, baby, but you need to hurry your ass up before I leave you."

"I'm coming, boy. Go get in the car. I'll be down in a second," she said.

I went back downstairs to get in the car. The woman was my life. I was nothing without her. She was my everything.

We talked the entire ride down to the amusement park. It didn't matter what the subject was, we talked about it. We talked to Johnny about getting ready for school that started in a couple of weeks, the weather, issues overseas, the job market, and our relationship. You name it, we talked about it. We were so much closer as friends, which was making our love for one another grow stronger.

I pulled into the parking lot at the park and wanted to turn my ass right back around. It cost $7 just to park. They were out their minds. But where else was I going to park. I paid the $7. The prices to get in the park were even worse. It cost $36.99 each. I paid about $130.00 to just get in. I hadn't been there in almost fifteen years; now I knew why. I wasn't cheap or anything but damn. Did it cost that much to have fun.

"I'm in the wrong business," I told Tracy.

"I know. So am I," she replied.

Johnny looked around and started acting like a child in a candy store. He wanted to ride any and everything.

We had a ball the entire afternoon. We rode the Hypersonic, Shockwave, Volcano,

Flight of Fear, Anaconda, and the Grizzly. You name it, we rode it. We even got on the Hurler, Rebel Yell, Avalanche, Berserker, and White Water Canyon. I wished I'd known to bring our bathing suits so we could've gone to the water park.

❖ ❖ ❖ ❖

"I'm tired," Tracy said, getting in the car.

Who could blame her? We'd been up on our feet for six straight hours. Anybody in their right minds would've been tired.

"Well, our day isn't quite over yet, baby," I said.

"Huh! What do you mean? I'm not going anywhere else but home and in my bed to relax," she said.

I started up the ignition. "Since I'm driving, I want to see how you're going to pull this off."

"You can go wherever you want to. I'm not getting out of the car; I'll tell you that much."

"If that's what you want, fine. But I think you'll change your mind."

She sat back patiently, waiting to see where I was taking her, until I headed down a dirt road leading to the woods.

"Okay now, where are you taking us, boy?" she asked.

"It doesn't matter now, does it? Since you're not getting out of the car?"

"Yes, it does. I still want to know where we're going," she said.

I ignored her and continued driving. She kept asking me until we got to the cabin. I pulled up close to the cabin and parked the car.

"Who the hell's house is this?" she asked.

I got out of the car and didn't pay any attention to Tracy. I walked straight inside. She sat in the car and waited for me to come out, like she said she would. After twenty minutes passed and I still hadn't come back out yet, she became restless. She walked in the cabin to see what was taking me so long. I hid in the bathroom behind the door so she couldn't see me. She walked in the bedroom first to find me.

"How did my stuff get here?" I heard her say. She continued, "Terry! Where is your ass at? I know you're up to something."

I'd brought some of her clothes from the house. I'd put her negligee on the bed with her lotion and robe. She walked in the bathroom and saw a nice bubble bath awaiting her.

I didn't move a muscle. I didn't want to give away my hiding spot and ruin the surprise I had in store for her, with all the questions she'd ask if she found me. I'd had Johnny go out the back door and wait for me outside before she'd come in. She still hadn't noticed the note waiting for her on the table. She went and looked out the front door and when she turned back around, she finally saw it. She read the note and cracked a smile. She went in the bedroom to do what was asked of her. I snuck out the front door while she started taking her clothes off.

I'd made reservations at a hotel for Johnny. I knew he wouldn't want to be in a cabin by himself and he definitely wasn't staying in ours. This was our quiet time together. He didn't care. He wanted to be by himself anyway. It worked out for the both of us. He got his time to himself and I got mine. I walked him to his hotel room.

"Okay, don't be acting a fool tonight. I'm trusting you to behave yourself. I'll be here to pick you up in the morning, no later than nine. And don't be running up the phone bill!" I said.

Before I left I stopped at the front desk and left the desk clerk a number where she could reach me if he got out of hand. I put a block on the phone; just in case he tried to make a bunch of long distance calls anyway.

I walked in the cabin and there was no sign of Tracy. She had some slow jams playing. The lights were dimmed, with candles burning. I was supposed to be surprising her with the festivities and she was turning the tables on me.

"Tracy!" I yelled, heading toward the bedroom.

I saw her clothes still laying on the floor, in the same spot where she was taking them off when I left. I walked in the bathroom and she wasn't in there either. There was a note sitting up on the toilet with my name on it.

You thought you were slick, drawing me in here, then rolling. I don't know what you have up your sleeve, mister, but I'm running things now. I have a game for us to play. I have some instructions for what I want you to do.

(1). Take your clothes off and get into the tub. As you can see, your water is waiting for you.

I glanced down and saw the water. I hadn't even noticed it when I'd first come in. I continued to read.

(2). *Once you get out of the tub, in the bedroom your robe, lotion, and a pair of boxers will be awaiting you. That is all you need to put on. If you put anything extra on, the consequences will be severe.*

(3). *Last, but not least, bring your sexy ass in the living room and begin to find your prize. If anything is done out of order or not at all, the perfect night you planned will be nothing. You won't see me until tomorrow morning when it's time to go. Just in case you want to call my bluff, you shouldn't have set your keys on the table.*

Smooches

I checked my pockets for my keys, then looked out on the coffee table. They were missing. She knew me too well. I was damned sure not sleeping alone with a hard dick, so I did exactly what her letter said.

I took my sweet little time in the tub and relaxed. I'd hoped she would get restless and come out but it didn't work. She was in total control. She had to be enjoying it. I wasn't going to spoil anything she had planned.

It took me twenty minutes to relax and let my body soak. I washed off and got out of the tub. I went into the bedroom. My clothes sat on the bed, awaiting me just like she said they would be. I dried myself off and lotioned my body. I slipped into my robe and put my boxers in the pocket of the robe. I went into the living room. The fireplace was lit. There she was lying on the couch, with her robe on as well, looking at me seductively. I walked over to her.

"Wait a minute. I didn't ask you to move yet. I want to admire your sexy ass some more," she said, staring into my eyes.

"I have something for you to stare at," I said.

I took off my robe and showed off my naked body.

"You read my mind," she said, removing hers.

She didn't have anything on either. I walked over to her and started to kiss on her neck. She stopped me.

"Tonight's my night. I'm in control."

She grabbed my body and sat me down. I lay down to get comfortable. She began to kiss my neck and suck on my ears. She knew exactly where my spots were. As I started to get hot, she made her way down my body, reaching my nipples. She licked on my nipples and sucked on them. She continued her way downstairs. I began to move back and forth, as it felt so good. She stopped and got on top of me. She rode me until we both came.

After our sexual bliss, we lay on the couch in each other's arms.

"I told you to put your drawers on," she said.

"I'm sorry. I must've missed that part in the letter," I replied.

"Baby, what made you want to change?"

I knew sooner or later she'd ask me that. I had everything planned; what I was going to say. As the words to her question were coming out of her mouth, what I had planned to say left. I couldn't remember to save my life.

"Well, I was just sitting around thinking about a lot of the things I've done to you over the years. Throughout it all, you've stayed with me. I asked myself what kind of person would put someone they love through so much pain. I couldn't answer it because no one in their right mind would. I never did any of the things that I did to you intentionally to hurt you or anything, but I did them. So there was no excusing them. There was nothing I could do to change the past or take away the pain that I'd caused you. The only thing I could repair was the present so we could have a better future. In order to do that, I had to change. I had to be a better man than I was. I wanted to be the man you *thought* you were marrying, the man that you fell in love with. You mean the world to me. I can't do anything to take away any of the pain I've caused you. All I can do is promise to love you and cherish you for the rest of our lives," I said.

Tears began to roll down her face. She held me tighter. She moved back and looked me dead in my eyes.

"I love you!" she said.

We kissed. I picked her up and took her into the bedroom. We made passionate love the rest of the night.

Tyrelle

CUTTING TIES

"Hey, partner! What's up, man?" Jeff asked me as he walked in the door.

He knew he was an hour late. I couldn't believe he was strolling his ass in there like nothing was wrong.

"Your watch broke? You were supposed to be here an hour ago. I wasn't trying to spend all day moving her furniture," I said.

"My bad! My bad! I overslept," he said.

That had to be the most famous excuse ever. Thank God we didn't have a lot of stuff to move or I would've been pissed. Jodi was putting the majority of her stuff in storage, or giving it to Goodwill. All we needed to move was her armoire, TV, stereo, and clothes.

We headed to Jodi's in the U-Haul truck I'd rented. Jodi was ready, like I knew she'd be, when we got there. She had all the boxes taped up and ready to go. We decided to first take everything that was going to my house.

We packed the truck and headed to my house. Jodi took some of her clothes in her car. She met us at the house. We unloaded the truck and took her stuff into the house and went back to take the rest to storage. Jodi stayed around to straighten everything up.

I was hungry so we decided to go to Levi's Barbecue and get something to eat. I ordered a slab of ribs, macaroni and cheese, collard greens, and a side of banana pudding. Jeff got a fish dinner, string beans, and some cabbage. We sat down inside the restaurant and ate our food.

"So what made you decide to propose?" I asked him once we'd sat down.

"Well, I was sitting around thinking one day about my relationship. I realized that I was at a point in our relationship when I only wanted to be with her. But that forever shit was bothering me. I didn't think I could be with one woman forever. That word forever, it even sounded like a long ass time. So marriage was out if. I couldn't be faithful 'cause I wasn't trying to be like my uncles and shit. Anyway, I'd talked to my mother about everything. She'd told me how she'd known that she was ready to be with my dad and this story 'bout how she'd found out that he was cheating on her on their wedding day."

I interrupted, "What? He cheated on her on their wedding day! That's fucked up."

"No, you idiot. She found out on their wedding day that he'd cheated on her prior to that," he said.

"Oh, I see," I said.

"I still was confused, then she finally said something that made some sense. She asked me was there any other woman I wanted to be with and could I see myself with anyone else. She said my answer would solve all my problems and it did. I knew from that point on that I wanted to be with Chelle and only her."

"So, are you going to tell Michelle about the girls you cheated on her with, like your father did?" I asked.

"I still don't know what my father was thinking. The past is the past and if she doesn't know, there's no need to tell her now," he said.

I couldn't help but laugh at his ass. After we ate, we headed back to Jodi's apartment to move the rest of her stuff to storage. I stopped for a moment to think. It still seemed a little weird that I'd decided to settle down.

Who would have thought a year ago I would've made a decision like that? Back then I had three other girls, along with Jodi, and now it was going to be just me and her. Things really do change with time. The older you get the wiser you become. You start to see things in a different light and have a better perspective.

It seemed pointless to screw around on Jodi when she gave me more than any other women could combined. My whole philosophy had changed before my eyes. I was really excited to see what we could make out of this and how far we could go. I closed the gate to our storage room.

"You and Michelle set a date yet?" I asked.

"Not really but I was thinking about February of next year," he said.

"February? Isn't that a little soon? That's right around the corner. Do you think y'all can have everything straight in six months?" I questioned him.

"It shouldn't really be a problem. It's not like we want to have a big ass wedding where we have to fly guests in and shit. It's going to be a simple ceremony with family and friends."

"Well, whenever it is, I'm there with bells on, partna!" I said.

We hugged. We walked out of the storage place and headed back to his car. Good thing U-Haul had storage space. It cut down on the running around time. As I closed the car door, my cell phone started to ring. I checked the Caller ID to see who it was. April's number flashed across the display of my cell.

"Fuck dat! I don't feel like talking to her!" I yelled.

"Who?" Jeff asked.

"April. You would think she could take a hint by now. She hasn't stopped calling me since that night I almost got caught at the club. Every time I tell her, 'I'll call you back' or 'I'm busy,' she still just keeps calling. This bitch is blowin' the shit out of me!" I said, frustrated.

"Dawg, you just need to be up front with her. Stop bullshittin'. If you don't, the shit is going to come back on your ass; guaranteed," he said.

He was right. I was sitting there trying to be a better man but, instead of cutting my ties with April like a man, I was playing games like a lil' boy would do; hoping she'd catch on.

"You're right. I need to tell her and that's what I'm going to do. I'll tell her next time I see her but, for right now, let's get out of here," I said.

I thought it would be a while before I had to worry about April's ass but she kept calling all damn day. Finally I couldn't take it anymore.

"Hello," I said as she called my cell for the fifteenth time.

"What the fuck is your problem? I've been calling you all day," she said.

"I've been busy. Why? What's up?" I asked.

"I'm trying to see you tonight. I need some dick. It's been a while and I'm horny."

Nothing had changed with her ass. She was still straight to the point, as usual. That used to be one of the things I liked most about her. At that point, it was annoying. This was ridiculous. She knew damn well I'd been avoiding her. I guess she was just going to keep trying to push her will on me until she got what she wanted. I had to put a stop to it before it got out of hand, like Jeff had said earlier.

"April, we don't need to see each other anymore. My girl and I are starting to get serious now. I'd appreciate it if you didn't call me anymore," I said politely.

That sounded all right to me as I replayed what I'd said to her in my head. It was straightforward and to the point. Most importantly, there was no way she could get around it.

"I've heard this before, then you call me a week later trying to get some. So why don't we cut out the bullshit. I don't want a relationship with you," she said sarcastically. "I just want to fuck you. Your girl can have your heart, for all I care."

In a strange way what she'd said kind of turned me on. I turned it off though and thought with the right head.

"I hear you and I can't do anything but respect your honesty. But the fact of the matter is, things have changed. I'm not fucking around anymore. You can either take it or leave it," I said.

"Like I said, whateva, nigga. You talk a lot of shit ova the phone but once this pussy is in your face, you'll take it. You always do," she said.

She was definitely confident but my mind was made.

"Think what you want, April, but I have things to do so, bye."

I hung up the phone. Jeff wasn't lying when he said that she was crazy. She took the word nympho and turned it into something different. She was past that. She wouldn't even seduce you into asking her. She just flat out told you what she wanted and, since she was sexy as shit, any man would give it to her.

I walked in the house a little disturbed with the entire episode. Jodi detected it.

"Hey, baby, what's wrong?" she asked.

I sat down on the couch next to her and placed my hands over my face.

"Nothing, baby. I'm just tired; that's all," I said.

"You sure? We can talk about it, if you like."

I wanted to tell her so bad. I wanted to be honest and tell her everything. How could I? What was I supposed to say? *'Baby, this chick I've been fucking for a while now won't leave me alone because now I'm trying to be all about you.'* I was pretty sure she wouldn't understand that shit. There wouldn't be any good advice waiting for me. The only thing that would happen would be an argument and her walking out the front door. I wasn't going to let that happen.

"Baby, I'm okay. It's nothing a drink won't cure," I said, hoping she'd drop it.

"Well, why don't you stay home tonight so I can pamper you and take the place of that drink?"

"Tonight's my night so I need to be there. I'm okay, baby, seriously. But I will take you up on that offer after I get off. I probably can get out a lil' early tonight. How does that sound?"

"That sounds like a date to me," she replied.

❖ ❖ ❖ ❖

I planned on chilling the entire night in my office while I was at the club. I didn't feel like being bothered. I'd monitor everything from my office and if I was really needed, I'd handle it. I called the bar and had Darin send me up a drink. I should've had him send me the damn bottle. I couldn't even chill in my office without someone bothering me. Somebody was knocking on my door already.

"Come in!" I yelled.

"Mr. Lewis, you're needed at the front door," said Monica, one of the hostesses.

"Do you know what for?" I asked.

"No, I'm not sure. I think someone wants you to vouch for them," she said.

I followed behind her downstairs to the front door. There was a mob of women crowded around the front door. Moochie Norris, Sam Cassell, and Charles Oakley were standing there waiting. I nodded to security that it was okay to let them in. I should've made their asses pay though. It wasn't like they couldn't afford it with their million dollar contracts in the NBA.

The deeper we got into the club, the thicker the crowd of women got.

"Can I have your autograph?" "Do you have a girlfriend?" "Can I party with y'all?" you heard the desperate women ask.

"What y'all doing up in here?" I asked Moochie while we were walking.

"Trying to unwind, that's all," he said.

"I'll put y'all up in VIP. Everything should be straight for you up there," I said.

"That sounds good to me. Your cousin up in here tonight?" he asked.

"Naw, I doubt he'll come through."

I had Monica escort them up to VIP and made sure they were taken care of. This wasn't the first time Moochie came to the club with friends from the NBA. We didn't make them pay the door charge because they spent enough at the bar.

I didn't feel like chilling with them so I headed back to my office. I walked in and April was sitting on my desk.

"What the fuck are you doing in here? You must be out of your damn mind!" I said, pissed off.

It was one thing to be calling me all the time but popping up in my office was taking it to another level. This shit was ridiculous.

"I told you, you can't tell me no in person. Now it's time to see if I'm right," she said.

"Well, you wasted a trip up here 'cause I said no and I meant it. Now get the fuck out before I throw your ass out," I said.

She started to walk towards me.

"If you want me to leave, then I'll leave," she said. She grabbed my hands. "But I want you to throw my ass out!"

She put my hands on her ass. My dick started getting hard. I wanted her. I felt on her ass, trying to get her hot. I reached under her skirt and noticed she didn't have any panties on. She started to kiss me. I kissed on her neck and nibbled her ear. We started to passionately kiss. I stopped, coming up for air. I looked her straight in her eyes.

"Get the fuck out," I said calmly.

"You mean to tell me you don't want any of this?" she asked.

"Good-bye, April," I said.

She wouldn't give up yet. She sat down on my desk with her skirt still up. She started fingering herself, trying to turn me on. She was taking things to an all-time high.

"You know you want this. Stop trying to fight it. Why don't you come on over here and take over for my finger," she said.

I was stunned. I remained calm. I couldn't do anything with her. It was way past time for her to roll.

"Look," I said sternly. "I don't want you; none of you. I don't even want to see you again. Now you have two options; you can either walk out of here on your own or I can throw your ass out. You decide which one."

She stopped and straightened out her clothes. She walked towards the door. I kept my distance while she did because if she'd tried anything else, I might've killed her ass. She opened the door.

"There's too much dick out here to be tripping off you. It's your loss. Bye, Ty!" she said and slammed my door.

I couldn't believe that shit. She finally knew that it was over. She finally understood that I was dead serious. I felt relieved. I felt like I could finally move on with my life with Jodi.

SETTING THE DATE

Everything was getting crazy. We were about two months away from opening the Diamond Nightclub and we didn't have half the things we needed for the grand opening. Construction on the second level hadn't been completed yet. It was three weeks behind schedule. We still had to have everything inspected once construction was finally completed. Terry had been driving himself up a wall, trying to get everything done. I was more than happy to help him when he finally asked me.

We were still pushing it to make the November 18th date we'd set for the grand opening. I wasn't the only one swamped. Chelle had been putting in sixty-hour weeks on this murder case. The case would make or break her career. We still hadn't set a date yet and that was something both of us wanted to do so we could start getting things ready for the wedding. We decided to do nothing that day but come up with a date and spend a little time together.

I'd gotten up early so I could get down in the kitchen and start breakfast. I loved Chelle to death but she wasn't the best cook in the world. Eggs and bacon might be a normal task for anyone but I wasn't risking it with her. She could burn with the best of them—literally.

I got a little carried away with breakfast. I made enough to feed a family of five. I cooked pancakes, eggs, bacon, sausage, apple cinnamon muffins, fried potatoes, and oatmeal. I didn't mean to overdo it, but whenever I got started cooking I always found a way to overdo it.

I made Chelle's plate. I wanted to surprise her with breakfast in bed. I walked upstairs and opened the bedroom door. She was still fast asleep. She looked so beautiful sleeping; like an angel. I didn't want to wake her but the sight of her peaceful, pretty face was turning me on.

I ran downstairs to get some chocolate syrup from the fridge. I ran back upstairs with the syrup in my hand. She hadn't woken up yet. I poured some on her body and started licking it off.

She moved around squirming, feeling my tongue going up and down her body. She still hadn't fully wakened yet. I made my way down to her clit and poured a little there. I licked it off. That was just the trick. She woke up and began to rub my head, getting into it.

I became turned on myself. I continued eating her, going back and forth, licking all around her walls and sucking on her clit.

"Oh yeah, baby!" she moaned. "Don't stop!"

That was something she didn't have to worry about because I wasn't. The satisfaction she was getting from me pleasing her was pleasure enough for me. She tightened her grip around my head with her inner thighs. I could tell she was about to cum and picked up the pace with my tongue.

"Ohh! Don't stop, baby! I'm almost there," she said.

I sucked on her clit a little harder while I fingered her.

"Ahhh!" she continued to moan.

I felt like I was about to nut myself. She was really turning me on.

"I'm cummin'!" she said.

She finally came. That didn't make me stop. I continued to eat her. She started shaking uncontrollably. I stopped, sat back, and admired my work.

"Where did that come from?" she asked.

"What are you talking about?" I replied.

"You know exactly what I'm talking about."

"You wouldn't wake up so."

"So what?"

"So I did what I did. Why? Are you mad or something because I woke you up that way?" I asked.

"No. You can wake me up like that every day for all I care," she replied.

"I think I will. I made you breakfast, too."

"Excuse me?"

"You heard me. I made you breakfast. It's downstairs waiting for us," I said.

She got up out the bed and went into the bathroom to wash up. I went downstairs to set the table, after I'd washed my hands in the powder room. I'd just finished making her plate when she walked in the kitchen.

"This is yours," I said.

"Thanks," she replied, taking her plate.

She sat down at the table and said her grace. I finished making my plate. I sat down and said my grace. She was chewing away. She wasn't even coming up for air.

"Hungry?" I asked.

"I didn't eat last night," she replied.

"Well, slow down before you choke or something."

"Shut up! Your nasty ass didn't even rinse your mouth out or anything."

"For what? I've tasted you before! Anyway, I'm going to brush my teeth after I finish eating so I might as well do it all at the same time. No sense in rinsing my mouth out now, then brushing my teeth after I eat."

"If you say so. Just don't be kissing me until you brush those teeth," she said, laughing.

We ate our breakfast.

"I'm full," she said, putting down her fork and wiping her mouth.

I took that as a compliment that my cooking was good. She got up and went into the living room. I followed behind her and curled up on the couch with her.

"Thanks for breakfast. Why are you so good to me?" she asked.

I never wanted her to feel like I didn't love her. I wanted her to always know that, so I did whatever it took for her to feel loved. I wanted her to feel appreciated and to appreciate me. That's what escapes a lot of relationships these days; appreciation for one another. People tend to take their significant other for granted. I made it my mission to make sure I didn't. I'd do the little things like making her breakfast or giving her a back massage after she'd had a long day at work. Whatever it took, I'd do. My mother once told me that it's the little things that mean the most to a woman.

I lay on the couch and held her. I'd missed spending time with her. The relationship had a lot of firsts for me. Chelle was the first woman whose work schedule was busier than mine. When we'd first started dating she was assisting on this big case. I hardly saw her for like three months. She'd call whenever she had a chance or stop by, but I wasn't really tripping back then. I had other girls I was dealing with. Now I was with only her so I had to get used to being lonely at times.

She took pride in her work. All of her cases weren't like that, but the ones that required the extra research or more time, I had to understand. She was very devoted and that's why she was making a name for herself. It was one of the qualities I loved the most about her; her dedication.

Once we moved in together it wasn't as bad anymore. I got to sleep next to her at night and see her beautiful face before I went to sleep. I'd grown to appreciate those simple things.

"I'm only being nice because I'm trying to have some morning fun," I answered her question, laughing.

She ignored my comment and didn't say anything.

"So do you know what you want to do today?" I asked.

"It's up to you! I really don't care."

I hated it when she said that. I asked her so she would answer and, instead, she turned it around on me like I was the only one it concerned.

"I hate it when you do that. Can you give me your answer? I asked you for a reason. It's not like I'm the only one going out. You're coming," I said.

"Not yet, but hopefully you can make me cum soon," she said with a devilish grin.

I couldn't help but laugh. She didn't want to pay me any attention when I said my comment so I wasn't going to pay her any.

"Ha, ha, ha; very funny. What are you trying to do? Seduce me?" I asked.

She got up and turned to look at me. She stared at me seductively, licking her lips. She must've seen the bulge in my pajamas because her eyes were dead center on it. She smiled and came towards me. I pushed her back so I could continue to enjoy watching the show she was putting on. She stopped and looked at me as if to say, *'What are you doing?'*

She lay on her back and picked up her T-shirt. My eyes saw her body lying naked on the floor. I wanted to strip down with her and jump right into her ocean of love. I held back and continued to watch. She wasn't going to get me to give in. If she did, she was going to have to earn it. I had some control over myself;

maybe not a lot but some. I stood there looking at her, as if I was unfazed by her being naked. She was determined to break me. I could see it in her eyes. She sucked on her right index finger, then her left nipple. She'd never done that before. I was losing my mind. She was turning me on. She moved her finger slowly down her body until she reached that spot. She moved her finger in and out of her. She was so wet I could hear her finger going in and out. I couldn't hold back anymore; she'd won.

I took my clothes off and took over for her finger.

❖ ❖ ❖ ❖

I rolled over with fulfillment after our sexual encounter. Backed up wasn't the word for how we were. It had been a while since we'd had sex. Our bodies had needed it and we'd listened. That was the freakiest I'd ever seen her. I know every woman has a little freak in them, but damn. I thought I'd seen all of hers. We'd been together for almost four years.

I went to the bathroom to wash up. When I came back in the living room, Chelle was knocked out. I picked her up, took her upstairs, and laid her in the bed. I lay down beside her. The cool air felt good on my body. I just lay there and relaxed. The air was soothing me.

I glanced over at the clock. What had seemed like a five-minute catnap, to my surprise, had lasted until noon. I'd slept almost two hours. Talk about time flying. I rolled over so I could wake Chelle up.

"Baby! Get up! Baby!" I said.

"Huh," she grunted, still sleep.

"Get up, child! We're supposed to be setting a date. Remember?"

"Leave me alone! I don't want to marry you. Are you crazy?" she said, rolling over under the covers. "I just wanted your doggie-style."

"Really!" I pulled the covers back and threw them on the floor. I put her in position, like I was going to hit it from the back. "Well, I aim to please."

I tried to put it in.

"Stop! Stop! I was just playing. I'm not fooling with you right now," she said. She rolled away from me.

"It's too late now. I'm in the mood for some more luvin!" I said.

We wrestled on the bed while I tried to get some and she tried to stop me.

"Stop trying to rape me, boy. No means no," she said.

There was something about that word: rape. It was so harsh; I stopped like she'd requested.

"Come here, baby! I was just playing you, big baby. Is Big Daddy hungry again? Come here so Momma can feed him," she said.

She moved toward me and put her stuff in my face, gesturing for me to eat her.

I moved back. "Sweetie, what's gotten into you today?"

Was she that horny?

"Why? Am I bothering you?" she answered.

"It's not that. I like it, but it's just that you haven't acted like this before. I'm a lil' surprised, I guess," I said.

"Well, every woman has some freak in them. It just takes the right man to get it out of her," she said.

"Okay, that's understandable but it's taken me this long to get it out of you. This is only the what, five thousandth time we've had sex? Why now?"

I knew I was ruining the mood but it was interesting and I wanted to know.

"It's hard to explain. Our relationship has gone to another level. I mean, you asked me for my hand in marriage. You're ready to spend the rest of your life with me. I can at least give all of myself to you," she said.

I kind of understood but I didn't want to assume anything. I was still a little puzzled.

"I understand a lil' bit," I said.

"See, I want to be able to give my husband something I haven't given any other man. After I turned thirteen, my virginity was out of the question. I've loved other men in my life so that can't be it. I've never fully given my heart to anyone. I was too afraid of being hurt. That's my gift to you; my heart. I also want to be able to give my husband something sexually that I haven't given any other man. So I've never given myself fully to any man sexually either. I've only done certain things with them."

I cut her off. "I'm not sure if I want to hear this. I'm not trying to hear about you fucking some other dudes."

"Shut up! Just let me explain, please. You're the one who doesn't understand. Since we're engaged now, I just decided to not hold back with you sexually anymore. I was going to wait until our wedding night but I have something else in store for that. I'm going to let everything out then. I'm going to be as freaky as I can be," she said.

I didn't know what to say. If she could be freakier than she'd been earlier maybe we needed to get married the next day.

"Baby, we can go to Upper Marlboro to the courthouse first thing Monday morning and make it official," I said, being funny.

"I'm not getting married at a damn courthouse by a judge. Rev. Jackson will be marrying me in front of our family and friends, so tell Big Daddy he's just going to have to wait for our wedding night," she said.

Everything she'd said made sense. She'd only give everything to the man she was going to spend the rest of her life with. I wondered how many other women did, or thought the same way.

It was just like sucking dick. A woman won't suck every man's dick that she's had sex with. It takes a little more to get that privilege. Same with men; they don't eat every girl they hit. I knew a woman once who told me that she never kissed this man that she was fucking because he was only a sex partner. Sex was just another game love plays.

I walked over and hugged her.

"Your hand in marriage is the only gift that matters to me. That's it."

She started kissing my body, getting the mood right. I stopped her. It was my turn. I turned her over. She hesitated for a moment but once she saw that I wanted to be in control, she gave in. She was propped up on her knees, anticipating my next move.

I put in my *Body & Soul* CD to keep the mood right for the occasion. The CD was sixty minutes of slow jams. I hit the repeat button; just in case we went into overtime. This was our second time around so I knew it would be a lot longer than the first.

Since she was in a freaky mood, I ran downstairs to get a bedroom surprise. I came back upstairs with it hid behind my back. She was still in the same position she was in when I'd left. "I Want to be Your Man" by Roger was playing.

I started to lick her back, down to her butt cheeks. I stopped there. I might've been in a freaky mood but I wasn't ready to toss salad. I'd heard Terry mention it before but I wasn't on that level just yet.

To my delight she opened her legs slightly, enjoying the feeling of my tongue running down her spine. I turned her over on her back and started sucking on her breasts. I worked my way down and started to eat her again. I unwrapped the surprise I had for her while I continued eating her. She still hadn't noticed that I'd even brought anything into the room. I placed it inside of her while licking her clit.

"Oh, it's cold!" she said, thinking it was an ice cube.

I moved it in and out of her. She was enjoying it. I let my tongue take over for a while and tasted her. She tasted like my fruity treat.

"Ahh…. Mmmm… Baby, don't stop!" she moaned.

I switched again and started sucking on her clit, moving the surprise in and out of her again. The warmth from inside of her was turning my block of ice into juice.

"I'm 'bout to cum, baby! I'm 'bout to *cum!*" she said, excited.

I didn't want her to cum like that. I stopped and placed myself inside of her. I moved slowly with the music. Major Harris's "Love Won't Let Me Wait" was playing.

I need to have you next to me.

In more ways than one.

I sang along with the music in my head, to take my mind off how good she felt. I didn't want to cum early. I couldn't tell if she was wet, or if it was from the popsicle I'd used to get her aroused. The song was perfect. She moved faster and faster as she began to cum. I kept moving with her and singing in my mind. She couldn't hold back anymore. "I'm coming, baby! Ooo…," she screamed.

She relaxed for a moment while I kept soothing her body with soft, slow strokes. Her high from coming died down so she began to get back into it. She flipped me over so she could get on top. She wanted to be in control. She rocked back and forth slowly, then gradually picked up the pace. Singing wasn't helping anymore. I was about to cum. We hadn't even been at it twenty minutes. I tried to think of something else, anything else, that would stop me from coming. Nothing worked. She kept going faster and faster, going up and down. I could hear the sound of our bodies smacking into one another better than I heard Atlantic Starr's hit song "Forever" playing on the stereo. I couldn't hold back any longer. She felt so good. I gripped the sheets and held on for dear life as I came for the second time.

She hadn't cum again yet, but she was close. She kept going; faster and faster. I could tell she was about to cum, but I beat her to the punch. I felt like I was going to explode. She kept going faster and faster. I couldn't take it anymore.

"Ahhh!" she moaned as she finally came.

I had no energy left. I just lay still, with her lying on top of me. We held each other for a few. I felt myself starting to doze off again. I moved her off me and jumped up. I didn't want to fall asleep again. We wouldn't get anything done. I wanted to set the date and go to a movie or something. It didn't matter what, as long as we got out of the house.

"Baby, get up. Go get your calendar so we can set the date," I said.

I looked for my calendar and she did the same. We both sat back down on the bed. She browsed though her calendar, trying to find a date.

"How about April the 14th or 21st?" she asked.

That was around the time for spring break so all the college kids would be home. The club would be pretty much packed.

"No, that's not good for me," I said.

I searched for a date. "What about February?"

"February. Let me see." She paused. "That's fine with me. I'll be working on something the beginning of February so let's say the 24th."

That was perfect. I felt a big relief, now that we'd finally set a date. The wedding seemed more like a reality now.

"Have you thought about what colors you want our wedding to be?" she asked.

"Huh, colors? You can handle all that," I said.

All we were supposed to be doing was setting the date. Anything else she could handle without me.

"This is your damn wedding, too. Now what colors do you think the wedding should be? I was thinking about maybe lavender and silver," Chelle said.

I wanted to ask her what the hell we needed to pick colors out for. I didn't even know what lavender was. I was going to have on a white tux and she'd have on her white wedding dress. Those were the only two colors that mattered to me.

All that other planning is for a woman to do. Men aren't into all that. But this was going to be her day and I wasn't going to do anything to ruin it; not the preparation for it or the wedding itself.

"What's lavender, baby?" I asked.

"It's a lighter shade of purple."

"Why didn't you just say light purple and silver? I'm not sure about the lavender but I like silver."

"I want lavender. Purple's my favorite color. You should know that by now," she said.

"Well, if it's purple you want, then it's lavender you'll get. So what? Am I going to have a silver tux with lavender or something?" I asked, confused.

"No! I swear, men don't know anything! Your tux is going to be black with a silver vest. The groomsmen are going to have on the same. My bridesmaids' dresses will be lavender and, of course, I'll have on a white gown," she said.

"Don't you mean off-white? You ain't no damn virgin!" I said, laughing.

"Ha, ha, ha, very funny!" she said, not amused.

"Well, I want my tux to be white, so I guess I'll have a white tux with a silver vest. Just about everybody wears black. I want to be different. Plus, I don't want to have on the same thing as my groomsmen. I'm the one getting married; not them. I want to stick out. This is supposed to be my day."

"No, it's my day," she corrected me.

"You know what I mean," I said.

I felt like I was on a roll. I was ready to take on something else. "So what's next?" I eagerly asked.

"Well, we need to let Rev. Jackson know the date for his calendar. Do you think we need a wedding planner?" she asked.

"For what? It's not like I'm Michael Jordan or Denzel Washington or some-thing. We're not having this huge extravagant wedding. It's just going to be us and our families and friends. I'm pretty sure we can handle it by ourselves."

She thought about it. "You're probably right. Well, the only other thing I can think of we need to do is the guest list, so we can send out the invitations and pick the wedding party."

We both started on our guest lists and who we wanted in the wedding. I finished my guest list roughly quick. All I could think of was my family. I didn't have that many friends. All I knew was a bunch of girls and I wasn't inviting them.

I chose Ty to be my best man. Terry would be my best man, too, but Ty would stand beside me and handle the best man duties. Darin and my man Mike, from college, would be my other groomsmen.

Chelle was stuck between Jodi and her sister, Tiffany, as her maid of honor. You would've assumed she'd choose her sister, since she hadn't known Jodi that long, but she shocked me and picked Jodi instead. Chelle wanted Tracy and her girlfriend Kelly to be her other bridesmaids with Tiffany.

I tried to convince her to have the wedding at my church but she was stuck on being married at her family church by her family pastor. He'd married her grandmother, mother and father, aunts and uncle, and now she wanted him to marry us. How could I continue to argue or tell her no? We spent the rest of the day planning.

At the end of the night, I didn't feel like moving but we were hungry so I ordered carry-out. Chelle went out and picked up a movie and we made the rest of the night a Blockbuster night. We lay on the couch and watched *The Wood*. We fell asleep holding one another while the blue TV screen ended up watching us.

Tracy
HARD TO LET GO

I couldn't believe it was 1:30 p.m. and Crystal still wasn't here. I knew she'd be late but this was a little extreme. I wasn't even sure why I'd gotten ready, thinking she could possibly be on time. She was supposed to be there at eleven. *Damn!*

Terry was outside cutting the grass and who knew where Johnny's butt was. Since school had started, he'd been home less and less. Knowing him, it had something to do with basketball. He lifted weights after school and was at Run-N-Shoot on weekends, trying to get ready for this upcoming season. He acted like he was getting paid or something. I wished he'd put forth the same effort in school that he did for basketball. He was coming around though.

Terry had been really hard on him lately, trying to beat the importance of school-work in his head. We'd sat down one night and come up with our family eligibility rule for the season. Since the county's rule for eligibility was a 2.0 grade-point average, ours (Terry's and mine) would be a 2.5. If he had anything less, he'd be suspended for the designated amount of games.

If he came in under a 2.0, he couldn't play, so there was no reason for us to suspend him. With a 2.0, he'd miss five games. With a 2.1, he'd miss four games. At 2.2, he'd miss three games. At 2.3, he'd miss two games, and with a 2.4, he'd miss only one game. We'd put incentives in place if he got over a 3.0, to reward him. Hopefully, this would work and he'd try to excel instead of just making it.

I went into the kitchen to make Terry a grilled cheese sandwich. It was his favorite and he'd been working so hard out in the yard. I knew he had to be hungry by then. I usually had to beg him to do some work around the house but, whenever he got started, he worked.

He'd already cleaned the kitchen and living room in the morning; now he was cutting the grass. He said that he wanted to wash the cars later on, when it cooled off.

I grabbed the butter out of the icebox and put a scoop in a skillet. While the butter was heating, I placed four slices of cheese in between two slices of bread and put it in the microwave for thirty seconds. The butter started to sizzle when the timer went off on the microwave. I took the soggy sandwich out of the microwave and put it in the skillet. I cooked it until both sides were nicely toasted like he liked it. I turned the stove off and placed the skillet on the back burner to cool off. I grabbed a paper plate and put some potato chips and his sandwich on it. I poured him a tall glass of grape Kool-Aid and took his lunch to him.

"Hey, baby. Thought you might be hungry," I said.

"You read my mind, sweetie!" He took the plate from me and took a bite of his sandwich. "I thought you'd be gone by now," he said while chewing his food.

"I thought so, too, but you know how Crystal is." I followed behind him to the lawn furniture, with his drink still in my hand.

"Yeah, I do! So, what are y'all getting into today?" he asked me with a sly smirk on his face.

His birthday was coming up in a couple of days so I guess he figured I was going to get his gift.

"Crystal's thinking about getting a new living room set so we're going to Marlo Furniture to shop around," I said.

"Oh, really? Well, tell Crystal that I saw this tough ass Rolex watch she might want to get to go with it. It was up at the mall in Charles County in J.B. Robinson. Y'all might want to swing over there and check it out," he hinted.

Little did he know, I'd already gotten the watch for him three weeks earlier. I'd been hiding it in his closet, of all places. I figured it would be the last place he'd ever look for his gift. Who in their right mind would hide someone's gift in their own closet? That's why it was such a perfect hiding spot. He was such a junk fanatic, which made it easy to hide it in there. He had bags that he'd bought clothes in from two years ago. I'd just hid it in an old Gap bag and placed some bags that he had from Bare Feet on top of it.

"She's not really into watches all like that, but I'll be sure to bring up the suggestion to her," I said.

"You do that! Did you hear the door?" he asked.

I listened hard and didn't hear anything.

"I don't hear anything."

"Hello!" we heard a voice from the house say.

"I knew I wasn't lunching," he said.

"Out here!" I yelled.

I took a sip of his Kool-Aid, then stood up and walked towards the back door.

"Hey, girl! What are you doing out here?" Crystal asked.

"Nothing much. Just out here talking," I said.

"Hey there, Terry," she said.

"How are you doing, Miss Crystal? I was just telling Tracy, you need to go check out St. Charles mall. They have this tough watch there you might like," he said, being funny.

"Oh, really? We might just have to go there and take a look," she said, looking at me.

She already knew that he wanted a watch and that I'd already bought it for him as a surprise.

"I'll see you later, baby. I'm not trying to be out all day," I said.

"Yeah, I need to get back to this grass myself," he said, getting up from the table.

I walked over to him and gave him a kiss goodbye. "I'll be home around five or so."

I walked back into the house, with Crystal following behind me. I had to get my purse and keys. We got in the car and went on our way.

"So, where do you want to go first?" she asked me.

"It doesn't matter. Let's go to the mall first," I replied.

"Bitch, I know that, but which mall?"

"I don't know. Terry knows too many damn people. I want this to be a surprise."

"I know where we can go then. Let's go to Annapolis Mall. I doubt if he knows anyone all the way out there," she said.

"You would be surprised who he knows."

"I don't know why you're breaking your neck for him in the first damn place! He ain't nothing but a no-good nigga and you know it," she said.

I knew it wasn't going to be long before she started up. Crystal was my girl and all and I knew she was trying to look out for me, but she just had a deep hatred for Terry. Even she could see by then that the man had changed, unless she didn't want to. He didn't even act anything like he had before.

"Girl, I'm not going there with you today! Every time we hang out, you have something to say. If it's going to be like this, you can just drop me off at home and I'll catch up with you later on or something. I'm getting tired of this shit!" I snapped at her.

"I'm sorry. I just don't think he knows how to be a man, let alone a husband. I'm not trying to piss you off. I just don't know how to be subtle. This is your life. Only you can live it," she said.

"It's been over two months now. How long will it take for you to realize he has changed?" I asked.

"Girl, look, I just don't want you to get hurt again. I'm the one you run to when it happens. I have to see you crying. I don't like seeing you like that. I can't shoulder it anymore."

"I know you don't and I love you for being such a good friend. You've always been there for me, but listen to me when I tell you, he has changed. He does stuff now that he never did before. I've gone back to him I don't know how many times before and it was always the same old thing. He'd be this new man for a month or two and that was it. This time he's so much different. Back then he'd just spend more time with me or something like that, but now we actually talk. We talk about my day or his. We talk about any and every thing. It's not just that. When he first came to me and said he wanted to change, I could see the pain in his eyes. I could tell that he was sincere. I could see the fact that he'd hurt me so bad was painful to him. I don't know what to tell you. I just ask that you trust me on this one. Please, just trust me," I pleaded.

"Fine, child! I just hope you know what you're doing 'cause I'm not going to be there for you, if he hurts you this time. I can't deal with it anymore," she said.

"Who do you think you're fooling? You're going to be there 'cause you're my friend. You don't roll like that, but I assure you, there won't be a next time." I leaned over to give her half a hug while she was driving.

"So what are you going to do about Renard?"

"Nothing at all. After a while, he'll catch on. He probably already has. I haven't talked to him in about two weeks now," I said.

"That's wrong. You wouldn't want anybody to carry you like that. You can at least be straight up with him and tell him," she said.

"I know but I don't know what to say to him. No matter what, it's going to hurt his feelings."

"That's why you need to just tell him the truth. That's all you can do. But you can't string him along because that's only going to hurt him even more in the long run. Even though it's not like he didn't know he was dealing with a married woman when y'all started talking. If you ask me, he got what he asked for. Maybe he thought he could take you away from Terry. I don't know but the bottom line is he can't and won't. You want to be with Terry and not him, so you need to tell him and he has to just deal with it."

She was right. I couldn't just run from the problem, thinking it would go away. I'd made my bed, now I had to lie in it.

"I'll tell him when he calls," I said.

"Bullshit! Who do you think you're fooling, child? I've known your ass since we were in diapers. You're going to keep putting this shit off and he'll never know. Call his ass now and get it over with."

"No! I told you I'll do it and I will. I'm not calling him now. You just want to be nosey, that's all," I shot back at her.

"Either you call his ass now or I'm going to pull this car over until you do," she said. She didn't even wait for my answer. She pulled the car over. "Fuck it! I'll call him myself."

"Fine, I'll call him. *Damn!*" I reached into my purse and took out my cell phone. I dialed his number and waited while it rang. Hopefully he wouldn't be home.

"And don't be calling his house number either. Call him on his cell phone," she added.

"I am!"

A couple more rings and it would go to his voice mail.

"Hello!" he said.

"Hi, Renard. How are you doing?" I asked to break the ice.

"I'm fine. I figured something was wrong with you, since you don't know how to return phone calls," he said.

"I'm sorry. I've been really busy, but that's sorta kinda what I want to talk to you about. I've been doing a lot of thinking lately," I said.

He interrupted me. "About what?"

"My life, my marriage, and my relationship with you," I replied.

This was harder than I thought it would be. I really didn't want to hurt his feelings.

"So, what's up?" he asked while I paused.

I got it off my chest. "I think it's best if we don't see each other anymore."

"Why? Whatever it is, I'm sure we can work through it. Just give us a chance," he said.

"I'm sorry, Renard, but this can't be fixed. I'm still in love with my husband. I can't do anything about that. There's no way to work around it," I said.

"I can't believe you're going back to that nigga!" he said.

I didn't know if I should answer him or not. I sat there waiting to see what he'd say next.

"I can't believe this shit!" he yelled.

"I'm sorry, Renard. I wasn't trying to hurt you. Please believe me. That is the last thing I wanted to do, but I'm in love with him and I can't keep going on like this. It isn't fair to you, or to him."

"You mean to tell me, that nigga treats you like shit and you're still going back to him. Then you have the nerve to say that you're not trying to hurt me. Did you think I'd be happy about it? Was it something I did? Something I wasn't giving you? It had to be. What did I do? Give me a chance to fix it. I'll make it right, but don't just leave," he nearly pleaded.

"You haven't done anything. I'm just in love with my husband. I want to try to make my marriage work. That's all I can say. He still has and always will have my heart," I said.

He hung up in my ear. There was no way around hurting him. The truth hurt but that was exactly what he needed to hear.

"What happened?" Crystal asked as I put my phone back in my purse.

"He hung up on me," I told her.

"Give him time. He'll get over it. I know it doesn't seem like that now but it's better this way. Stringing him on like you wanted to would've hurt him more," she said.

"I hope you're right. I really do!"

I felt really bad about what I'd just done. I did care about him and had tried to spare his feelings. There was just no way to do it, and still be honest.

❖ ❖ ❖ ❖

I walked in the house, tired from a long day of shopping. I wanted to lie down and relax. The house was still clean, like I knew it would be. I didn't think Terry was home. I walked over to the window to make sure I hadn't missed Terry's car. It wasn't out there, like I'd thought. I went into the kitchen to make a quick sandwich so I could get in the tub. My body felt drained physically. There was a note waiting for me on the refrigerator.

Hey, baby. I figured you'd be hungry when you got home, after you called and said you'd be late. I made some lamb chops for dinner. I made your plate for you and put it in the fridge. All you have to do is put it in the microwave and heat it up when you're ready.

I should be home around midnight or so. If not, I'll call and leave a message to let you know I'm running late because I know you'll be sleep. I love you!

Terry

He'd read my mind just as I'd done his earlier. I was starving. I took my plate out of the fridge and put it in the microwave. I went upstairs while my food was heating and ran some bath water. The house was too quiet for Johnny to be home. I didn't see a note from him, letting me know where he was. I hope he'd told his father something, or maybe he'd left it in his room.

I went in his room to check and see if he had. There he was, lying in the bed sleep. I couldn't believe my eyes. This was a first for him. It was only 7:45 p.m. Usually he'd be out ripping and running the streets.

He'd been working hard lately, trying to get ready for the season. He reminded me so much of his father. In high school Terry had been the same way. I closed his door and went to the bathroom to turn my water off.

I went downstairs to get my food. I brought it back upstairs with me and got in the tub. The water was nice and hot, just like I liked it. I ate my food and enjoyed my bath. My muscles received the attention they needed. The steamy hot water soothed every inch of my body. I finished eating my meal and relaxed.

I thought about my husband. I couldn't believe he'd cooked for me before he'd left. That was so thoughtful of him. Those were the things he did then that he hadn't done before that I was trying to get Crystal to see. I couldn't give up on my marriage. I loved the man to death and if we could make it work, that's what I was going to do.

I wished he was there with me. I grabbed a towel and got out the tub quickly. I called my husband on his cell phone.

"Hello," he answered.

"Hello to you," I said.

"Hey, baby! Are you just getting in?" he asked.

"No, I've been home a while now," I said.

"Oh, so, what's up?" he asked.

"Nothing. I was just lying in the tub, thinking about how much better it would be if you were here with me now. All the things I could do to you. Thinking maybe we can make these thoughts a reality," I insinuated.

"Well, I'll be home in a lil' bit, so just hold those thoughts until then," he said.

"I would but, by then, they'll probably be gone and I'll be sleep."

"I don't see why. I'm sure you can hold off until I get home."

"I'm sure I can, too, but I want you now so I want to resolve them now."

"Do you have something specific in mind you want resolved?" he asked.

"I'm pretty sure if you're real hard, I mean if you *think* real hard, we can come up with something. What do you think?" I asked.

"I think I'll be home in fifteen minutes," he said.

"You do that and I'll be waiting."

I hung up the phone and went back into the bathroom. I turned on the shower and unstopped the tub. I looked around the bathroom.

"What do I want to feed him tonight?" I asked myself.

I grabbed my strawberry kiwi body wash and got in the shower. I figured me smelling like strawberries, instead of Ivory, would make the mood a little better. I rushed out of the shower, thinking I needed to straighten up the room a little bit. I'd totally forgotten that Terry had already cleaned the house.

I hated making love in a dirty room. I'd be on top, looking at a pile of dirty clothes. That shit was a turnoff. I put on some lotion so I wouldn't be ashy. I heard a knock at the door. Damn, that was fast!

I put on my robe and went downstairs to let him in. I opened the door and Renard was standing there.

"What the hell are you doing here?" I asked.

I was ready to cuss his ass out for showing up on my doorstep. The nigga had to be out of his mind.

"I need to talk to you and I knew you wouldn't answer the phone if I called," he said.

"Call me tomorrow. I'll answer. We can talk then. I promise!" I said.

"I'm here now, so I might as well get it out of the way," he said.

"Now's not a good time. My husband will be home in a minute," I told him.

"It won't take me but a minute," he pleaded.

I could tell he wasn't going to leave until he said what he had to say. I nodded okay to him.

"Look, I'm not sure why you're doing what you're doing. I don't even really care anymore. The only thing I care about is you. The only thing I'm sure of is that I'm in love with you. I don't want to lose you. I can't! He doesn't appreciate you. He doesn't know how to treat you. I do. I can give you the world and so much more, if you let me," he said.

"Renard, I'm sorry but I can't. I'm trying not to hurt your feelings, but I'll never love you. My heart belongs to Terry. He's the man of my dreams. He's all that I'm looking for and all I want. Can't you understand that?"

"If that's the case, why were you with me?" he asked.

"I don't know. To get back at him, I guess. I wanted to show him that I could find someone else. I didn't need him. I was hurt. I thought by being with you, it would relieve some of the pain and show him at the same time. I was wrong. I'll be the first to admit that. I can't take back being with you but if I could, I would. It was a mistake."

"A mistake? You don't mean that. You're just confused right now."

His determination was blocking reality. My mind was made. There was no way I was going to be with him. No matter what he said I was going to be with my husband. My time and patience was wearing out. Terry would be home soon and that was the last thing I wanted him to see.

"Look, I know what I want. You just need to face the fact that it's not you," I said.

He became angry.

"Fuck you then, bitch! You think you're going to have your cake and eat it, too? I'll just stick around until Terry gets home and we can tell him the truth! How 'bout that?"

My mind went blank. I didn't know what to do. He looked every bit serious when he said it.

"If you don't leave, I'll call the police to make your ass leave! I don't know who the fuck you think you're dealing with! I'm not one of those little bitches from the club that's trippin' off you! You're not going to make demands at my fucking house! I suggest you be on your merry way!" I yelled at him.

"I don't give a shit who you call!" he replied.

"And you say you love me. That's a bunch of bullshit. You only love your damn self. If you loved me, you'd respect my feelings. You'd respect the fact that I'm in love with someone else. If you truly love a person, you want them to be happy; regardless of whether they're with you or not. That's true love," I said.

"Well, if you loved me, then you wouldn't be leaving me to go back to him."

"Renard, I never told you I loved you. I never said it because I don't. I love Terry. I'm in love with him. I can never love you. Terry's the only man I've ever loved and always will!"

He became silent. It had finally sank in that I didn't love him and never had. A tear started to come down his face. I really hated myself for putting that pain in his eyes. He realized that our relationship was nothing but sex to me.

"I'm sorry. I guess that my love for you blinded me. I love you so much I just wanted you to love me. I'll leave you alone. I'm sorry. Bye, Tracy!" he said.

He turned around and walked to his car. I closed the door. I went in the living room and sat down on the couch. I couldn't believe what had just happened. My legs were shaking uncontrollably. I had to tell Terry about my affair. I'd always wanted him to be a man and tell me when he'd cheated, so I needed to as well. I needed to be a woman and confess my faults.

I picked up the phone to call Crystal, hoping she could help calm my nerves. The phone just rang.

"Damn it!" I yelled.

I went into the kitchen to get a glass of wine. I downed my glass and poured me another one. I took my second glass upstairs with me. I lay on my bed and just thought of the web I'd woven. I sipped on my wine and plotted how I'd tell him.

The front door opened. I still had no clue what to say or how to say it. I put my glass down and went into the bathroom. I splashed cold water on my face, trying to relax myself. I came back out to see Terry sitting on the bed waiting for me.

He could detect something was wrong with me. "What's wrong, baby?" he asked.

I walked over to the bed and took another sip of my wine. I wished I were drunk. It would've been much easier.

I blurted it out. "Terry, I had an affair!"

His face dropped. I downed the rest of my drink. My heart pounded while I waited for his response.

"I know, baby. I figured you did," he said.

"What? How?" I asked, puzzled.

"That night I told you I wanted to be the man for you. I just sat around and thought. It seemed like almost every weekend you were going somewhere with Crystal or your girls. Most of the time, you wouldn't even come home until Sunday. I knew something was up. It was like you wanted me to catch you. I thought you were using it as a way to get my attention and I thought, *she shouldn't have to do all this.* Plus, the way I cheated on you, it was bound to come back on me. In the back of my mind, I always knew you were cheating. I just didn't know if it was with a man or a woman," he said.

I couldn't believe it. He'd known all that time and had never said anything.

"Why didn't you ever say anything?"

"I didn't really notice until that day. I was so wrapped up in trying to get something while you were gone, I didn't care where you were. I looked at it as: she's not home; that's more pussy I can try to get. Then, when I realized it and reflected on my life, it was just like it's in the past now. I've made a lot of mistakes over the years and now you've made one, but that's all in the past now. If we're going to make this thing work, that's where they need to stay; in the past. I was more concerned about whether you'd forgive me and want to start over fresh," he said.

I sat there speechless. He walked over and gave me exactly what I needed; a hug.

"Baby, I'm not mad at what you did. If anything, I'm pissed at myself for the way I've treated you over the years. If I'd treated you like I was supposed to, we would have never gone through any of this bullshit. I'm actually shocked you didn't do more. A lot of women would've just packed up their bags and left me after they'd cheated, because of the way they were treated. You stayed. You want to give our marriage another chance and, by you telling me, that just shows me how much you love me."

I finally felt the completeness in our relationship that had been missing for so many years. The trust that I'd lost in him over the years was being rebuilt but, most importantly, my respect for him was back. I loved that man and nothing in the world could change that.

Tyrelle
AN UNFORGIVABLE MISTAKE

The monogamy thing hadn't been that bad. I found myself looking at a couple of chicks here and there but overall I couldn't complain. I was a little nervous when Jodi had first moved in. I thought things might change for the worst but they'd actually gotten better. I loved sitting around, talking to her. We'd talk for hours. I enjoyed her company and companionship.

We'd grown so much closer over the past month or so. Her schedule was going to take some getting used to. She was working nights and I hated it. The 11 p.m. to 7 a.m. shift was killing me. The only good part about it was that she got a week off every two weeks. Lately she'd been coming home on her lunch break since the emergency room hadn't been that busy. If it got busy while she was gone, someone paged her. Overall we were making the relationship work so I couldn't complain.

I was running late. I was supposed to be over Jeff's almost an hour ago. He was throwing a Halloween party and I was helping him set up for it. I wanted to come dressed as a pimp but I settled for myself. I wasn't in the mood to be role-playing that night. I actually didn't even feel like going.

I arrived at Jeff's and it was packed outside. I didn't have a place to park. I knew he was pissed. I walked in and tried to blend in with the crowd, which wasn't easy. Everybody had on a costume and I had on jeans and a T-shirt. Jeff spotted me in no time.

"First, your ass was supposed to be here two hours ago, then you don't even wear a costume," he said.

"Nigga, I wasn't supposed to be here no damn two hours ago. You're always exaggerating about everything," I replied.

"I asked you to come ova an hour before the party started, right?" he asked.

"Yeah!"

"All right then. It's 8:30 p.m. now. The party started at 7:30 p.m.," he said.

Oh shit, I was two hours late. I hadn't even realized it.

"Who actually comes to a party on time? I thought I had a lil' time left; my bad," I said in my defense.

"Whateva, nigga! I'm not even trippin' anymore. The shit got done regardless," he said.

"Jodi here yet?" I asked.

"No, not yet. Well, I haven't seen her, if she is. Why didn't she come with you?"

"She had to work, so she was coming straight here once she got off," I said.

"What happened to the costume, though?" he asked.

"I really didn't feel like coming. I feel drained. It's like I have no energy. By the time I convinced myself to come, I wasn't wearing any costume. I was just ready to go," I explained.

"Well, Terry's in the back room playing pool. You know where the bar is, so go find something to do. I'm 'bout to entertain my guests. I'll catch up with you later," he said.

"All right. I'm just going to go back here and holla at Terry. If you see Jodi, tell her where I am."

I walked to the bar and made me a rum and Coke. A drink was probably exactly what my body needed. I went to the back room to catch up with Terry. He didn't have on a costume either. He was on the stick, just like I thought he'd be, kicking everybody's ass. I don't think there was a sport he couldn't play. Some people are just gifted like that.

There were four people in front of me for the table. I drank my drink and watched him clean the table on the first two people in front of me. I went to go make me another drink while they were racking up the next game. I came back into the room and Terry was actually down two balls. I was kind of shocked. That didn't last for long. Terry didn't miss another shot.

"Good game," he told the guy he was playing.

"That shit ain't going to fly with me," I said, racking the balls.

That was the last word I got to say. He cleaned the table. I didn't even get a shot.

"It was nice playing you," he said with a smile on his face.

"Whateva, nigga! I got you next time," I said.

"Maybe later. I'm 'bout to chill and start up a spades game," he said.

"Jeff get on you 'bout the costume thing, too?"

"You know he did. I'm a lil' too old for the costume thing," he said.

I finished up what was left of the drink I'd made. "I'm 'bout to make me another drink."

"All right. I'll be on the patio trying to get things started."

I stepped off to the bar to make my drink. I felt my cell phone vibrating on my hip.

"Hello," I said, not even looking at the Caller ID.

"Where have you been? I really need to talk to you," April said.

She was getting on my last nerve. I wasn't about to let her blow my high. The drinks had me feeling nice. I was tired of playing games with her.

"Look, Shortie, I don't want to fuck you anymore, see you anymore, and definitely not talk to you anymore. I tried to be nice about it at first but you keep thinking I'm playing. I have a girl. I'm going to be with my girl; end of story. You'd think your dumb ass would know that by now," I said.

The alcohol was doing most of the talking but she needed to know either way.

"Is that what you think this is about? Don't nobody want your stupid ass. She can have you for all I care. You were just dick to me, boo! I have to talk to you about some real shit," she said.

"Well, if that's the case, please stop fucking calling me. The dick don't want you no more, dumb bitch!" I yelled.

"Nigga, I just wanted to tell you..."

I hung up on her before she could even finish her sentence. I didn't want to hear anymore. I downed my drink and made me another one. I went to catch back up with Terry. He was on the patio talking to Tracy, Michelle, and Jodi. Aw shit, my baby was here!

"Hey there, handsome," she said as I approached them.

"Hey there to you, sexy. When did you get here?" I asked.

"I just walked in not too long ago," she said.

"So are y'all going to get the cards or continue to talk this bullshit?" Terry said.

"Nigga, I'll show you how much I'm bullshittin!" Michelle replied.

She walked back into the house to get the cards. Michelle came back with three decks in her hand. There were enough tables set up on the deck for more than three games. I ran in the house to get Jeff. He was my partner. Jodi and Michelle partnered up and Terry played with his wife. Jeff had been my partner since we were little. We'd never switched up since then.

"Baby, hope you don't think we're going to take it easy on you!" Jeff said to Michelle.

"Whateva, nigga. I'm not tripping off you or your drunk-ass cousin," she said.

"Well then, listen to this ass whipping we're about to give you. And for your information, I'm not drunk. I'm nice. There is a difference," I said.

"Jodi, please don't pay any attention to them. All they're going to do is talk shit the entire game, trying to frustrate you," Michelle said.

"Yeah, don't listen to us. We're just going to sit here and talk shit while we're taxing that ass," Jeff said, laughing.

Terry and Tracy sat down to play two dudes from the party. Jeff shuffled the cards.

"We're playing joker, joker, deuce," he said.

Michelle interrupted. "No, I hate playing that way. Let's play straight-up. The deuce is a regular card."

"Okay then, fine. Dealer calls the rules," he said.

Jeff spread the cards on the table.

"High card deals," he said.

Michelle picked the four of diamonds. Jodi pulled her card. It was a jack of spades. I couldn't beat that. I only had a nine of spades. Jeff pulled last. He picked a king of hearts.

"Like I said, we're playing joker, joker, deuce with no kitty," he said, laughing.

"Fine," Michelle agreed.

She had no choice. He took the two of diamonds and two of hearts out of the deck. He started to shuffle the cards again.

"Jodi, watch these two. They'll cheat like shit and swear they didn't do anything," Michelle said.

"Aw, there she goes. How do we cheat? We're just good. Why can't you just accept it?" I said.

"Good, my ass; y'all niggas cheat. Droppin' cards on the floor or misdealing when y'all hands are shitty. I know. I've watched y'all play so don't try to act all innocent and shit," she said.

Terry's game was already started.

"Terry, what are y'all playing to? Three fifty or three hundred?" Jeff asked.

"Three fifty or two bumps," he replied.

"There you go. Game is to three fifty or two bumps," Jeff said.

He started to deal the cards. I could tell what Jodi had in her hand just by her expression when she picked up each card. Jeff knew how to set the deck while he was dealing. Another trick the two of us had learned from Terry. He used to do it all the time when we were younger and we would never catch on. One day he finally showed us and we'd done it ever since.

I picked up my hand and sorted my cards. I looked up at him and he had a smile on his face. I knew he had something to work with in his hand. He dealt me a bomb hand. I had both jokers, the ace of spades, the jack of spades, the five and three of spades, plus the ace of hearts and the kings of diamonds and clubs.

"What are y'all going?" Jeff asked.

"Y'all can bid first," Michelle said, trying not to back down.

"I dealt. Come on now. You know the rules," he replied.

"How many do you have, Jodi?" Michelle asked.

Jodi shook her head. "I can get you one, maybe," she said.

I bursted out laughing.

"That's all you have is one?" Michelle asked.

"That's it," Jodi replied.

"Damn! We're going board," she said.

"You sure? I know y'all can squeeze out five or six books. Come on," Jeff said, laughing.

"I said we're going board," Michelle repeated again.

Jeff wrote down their four on the paper.

"What do you have over there, partna?" Jeff asked me.

"I can pull you five, maybe seven, over here, so I'm going to say six," I said.

He wrote down ten for us to lock the game up. There are only thirteen books in a game, so one of us would bump.

"Let's get them off the table early tonight. Remember, two bumps and you're up. Don't try to get all forgetful and shit later on," Jeff said.

"You don't try to be getting forgetful. You're the damn cheater!" Michelle said.

Michelle threw out the five of hearts first. I threw out my ace of heart. No one could beat it. Jeff picked up the book. I only had two clubs and two diamonds, which I wanted to get rid of fast so I could cut.

I threw out my eight of clubs, hoping my partner could do something with it. Jodi played the two of clubs, putting the pressure on Michelle to win the book. Jeff threw out the ace of club. I started to grin while he raked up the book.

Jeff led out with the king of hearts. Michelle threw out the three, I threw out the seven, and Jodi played the eight of hearts. I knew the game was in the bag then.

Michelle switched two cards in her hand over. That was a rookie mistake. I knew that she didn't have any more hearts and probably had only two clubs left. She mismatched her suits by color so it was red, black, red, then black.

Jeff threw out the ace of diamonds next. We might actually be able to run a Boston if we play this right. Diamonds hadn't been played yet so I knew they at least had one. No one could beat Jeff's ace.

He came right back with another diamond. He played the three. Michelle threw out the five, I played my king, and Jodi played the ten of diamonds. Jeff started to count how many books we had after he raked that last one. We had five books.

"Ty, I kind of feel like going to Boston. How 'bout you?" Jeff asked.

"I was just thinking about that myself," I replied.

"Shut up! Y'all ain't getting no damn Boston," Michelle said.

I led out with the king of clubs. Jodi played the six, then started to rearrange her hand. She was done with clubs now. It didn't matter because so was I. Jeff threw out the four and Michelle played the five of clubs. I only had one heart left and the rest spades. I didn't want to throw my heart because Michelle was cutting hearts and she played last that round.

"Bring them out!" I said as I smacked the big joker on the table.

Jeff started smiling his ass off. That was the highest card so I knew they couldn't beat it. I smacked the little joker on the table as Jeff raked up our last book.

"Come on, bring them out!" I said.

Jodi shook her head, knowing there was nothing she could do. She played the ten and Jeff threw out the eight of spades.

"God damn it!" Michelle said.

She threw out the two of spades. I knew we'd run a Boston then. Michelle was out of spades and Jodi had just thrown out a ten. She had to be almost out, if not on her last spade.

I smacked the ace of spades on the table. Jodi played the queen and Jeff played the nine of spades. Michelle wasn't a factor anymore.

I wanted to see what my partner was working with so I came out low this time with the three of spades. Jodi couldn't beat it because she was out of spades. She played the ten of hearts. I knew she'd be out, sooner or later. Jeff won the book. He played the king of spades. Michelle threw out the eight of diamonds.

Jeff came out this time with the ten of clubs.

"Shit!" Jeff said.

Michelle threw out the jack of clubs before Jeff could pick his card back up. She started to get happy because they'd finally won a book. I played the six of spades and watched her face crumble. She knew there was no way to stop us from running a Boston. We rarely made mistakes, so when she'd see one she'd try to capitalize. Unfortunately for her, she'd forgotten about me. Jodi played the jack of diamonds.

I led back out with the jack of spades since everyone was out of spades.

While Jeff raked up the last book we'd won, I said, "Watch this lil' muthafucka walk!"

I played the four of hearts. Michelle sat there pissed. She couldn't do anything with it since she was out of hearts and couldn't cut with a spade. She started to move her chair back from the table, since they'd lost.

"Chelle, I don't know about you but I hate Boston," Jodi said.

She threw out the queen of hearts. Jeff had the jack of hearts left but that wasn't high enough. There was nothing we could do. Michelle became excited again, knowing that the game wasn't over yet. They started high-five'n each other like they were winning or something. We paid no attention to their newfound excitement.

After the next hand, their smiles were quickly erased. They bid six but only got five books. GAME OVER! We sat and waited to see who would win at the other table to play them. It didn't take long for Terry and Tracy to get them off the table.

"We'll see you later, ladies. Nice doing business with you," Jeff said as we switched tables.

We didn't do so well against Terry and Tracy. It was a good game but in the end we lost three fifty to three ten. It probably would've been more than that but we didn't play over books. We kept going back and forth with Terry and Tracy all night. Those were the only two we lost to for the rest of the night. Michelle and Jodi never beat us nor did Mike and Tony (the other team). I don't think Mike and Tony won a game all night. That was the only team Michelle and Jodi could beat.

As the night wound down everyone started to leave one by one. I was ready to go myself. I went over to Jodi.

"You ready to go?"

"Yeah, I'm getting tired," she said.

We started to say our goodbyes to everyone.

"You riding home with Jodi?" Terry asked me.

"Naw, I drove," I said.

"I know you drove, but you don't need to be driving tonight," he said.

"I'm straight. I can make it home."

I knew how to drive drunk and besides, I wasn't that drunk. I was a lil' tipsy but most of the drinks had already worn off.

"Don't pay him any mind. He's riding home with me," Jodi said.

"I'm fine," I repeated.

"I'm not trippin' off what you think you are. All I know is you're getting in the car with Jodi before I have to put you in it," Jeff said.

I couldn't fight all of them.

"Fine," I said.

"Wait right here. I have to go to the bathroom," Jodi said.

I needed to sit down. I was tired.

"Tell Jodi I'm in the car and to hurry up. I'll catch up with y'all tomorrow or something," I said.

I went outside to get in the car. I sat in Jodi's car, waiting for her to come on. I saw Terry and Tracy come out the house and head to their car.

"Where's Jodi?" I asked.

"She's coming. She's in there talking to Michelle about the wedding. Good night," Tracy replied.

"Good night."

I swear, that girl could run her mouth. I was tired and ready to get in the bed. I already had to get up early in the morning and come back and get my car. I cut out the middleman. I got out of her car and into mine. It didn't make any sense to have to drive all the way over there in the morning when I was fine then. I started up the ignition and drove myself home.

There was a note waiting for me outside my front door when I pulled up. I took it off and opened the door. The envelope was addressed to me. I walked up the steps to get in the bed. I sat on the edge of the bed and read the letter.

First, let me let you know that I don't want shit from you. I just wanted you to know because you have a right to. I'm pregnant with your baby. You don't have to be a part of the baby's life if you don't want to. Just let me know and I'll get an abortion but you will be paying for it. I really don't want to get one and as I'm thinking, I take that back. I won't get one. It's not the baby's fault that it's being brought into this world, so why should I punish it. If you don't want to be a part of the baby's life, that's fine. I'll take care of my child with or without you. I'm hoping that we can set aside our differences and do right by our child. I'm ten weeks now. My due date is March 31st if you wanted to know. It's up to you what part you're going to play? Just let me know. You know the number.

April

I began counting back the weeks. Ten weeks was a while ago; it couldn't be mine. I looked for my calendar. I counted back the weeks on it. If she was ten weeks, that meant I would've had to gotten her pregnant in June. I thought about when Jodi was gone for the conference. I could've sworn that was the end of May. If it was then it couldn't be mine because that was the last time we'd had sex. I looked for Jodi's calendar.

"Shit!" I yelled.

I didn't need that right then. I put the letter down on the bed and sat there. I needed to think of my next move. There was no way I could know if she was telling the truth or not without going to the doctor's and verifying everything. Even then, I still wouldn't know. She could've been with someone else then, too. I mean, how did she know I was the father? I needed to relax and think of something. I needed a plan.

I took my clothes off and sat them on the bed. I got in the shower to relax myself. I could picture Jodi walking out the door if I told her. I couldn't let that happen. I needed to tell her though. I wanted our relationship to be built on trust. I just didn't know how to tell her because I couldn't trust April's word. I wanted to make sure the baby was mine first, before I said anything.

Jodi walked in the bathroom and opened the shower curtain.

"What the fuck is this?" she asked.

She had the letter in her hand. I was speechless. Lying wouldn't help the situation because if the baby was mine I could never tell her. I was obviously fucked. Jodi knew I had to have fucked April because why else would she think the baby was mine. I didn't know what to say. Tears started coming down her face while I was thinking of what to say.

"Let me explain. It was on the door when I got home," I said.

It was all I could think of. She walked out of the bathroom. I jumped out the shower and grabbed a towel. I went after her but it was too late. By the time I got to the front door she was driving off. She needed to be alone. She needed time to think. I'd only make matters worse. I was scared. The thought of losing her scared the shit out of me.

That wasn't the first time she'd caught me cheating. The last time she'd come back but said if I ever did it again, she'd leave for good. Things were different then. We lived together and I was actually committed to her. I stared at the street for twenty minutes, hoping she'd pull back into the driveway so I could explain. She never did. I closed the door and went upstairs.

I lay on the bed and started to cry. I was the one who'd cheated but I was crying. The fact that I'd lost her trust hurt. I'd hurt her; something I'd never wanted to do. I had to get her back. I would get her back. I was determined. We'd come too far to end. I'd come too far. I only wanted to be with her. I cried myself to sleep that night. I tossed and turned all night long. It wasn't the same without her next to me.

❖ ❖ ❖ ❖

I wondered where she was. Where she'd slept. I hadn't heard from her since she'd left. I was worried out of my mind. I sat at the kitchen table, trying to force myself to eat something. I couldn't. I didn't have an appetite. My baby had left me and I didn't know where she was or if she was all right. I didn't know anything.

I heard the front door open. I went to see who it was, hoping it was her. It was.

"Baby, I'm so, so sorry. I really don't know what to say. I know I fucked up but I swear to you I wasn't the same man I am now when all of this happened," I said.

"So you did have sex with her? It's possible that this is actually your baby?" she asked.

"Yes. I cheated on you, if that is what you want to know. I'm not sure if the baby's mine. But, going by how many weeks she is, we did have sex around the time she would've gotten pregnant," I answered.

Tears began to trickle down her face.

"I'm glad that you at least told me the truth," she said.

"Baby, please. I swear to you, I'm not like that anymore," I said.

"Just like the last time, huh?" she asked.

It didn't look good for me.

"I didn't change the last time. I just wanted you back. I was willing to say anything to get you back. But I've changed this time. I changed before I asked you to move in with me. I knew then that the cheating was useless. You give me everything that I want. I'm sorry I cheated. I wish I'd seen things then like I do now. Then we wouldn't be going through this. I wish I could change the past. I really do," I said.

"So do I, Tyrelle, but I can't. Neither can you. Right now, this has nothing to even do with her. This has to do with us. I can't trust you anymore. You broke our trust the first time you cheated on me but it was rebuilt. This time you've destroyed it. I could never trust you again. Without trust we can never have a relationship. I can't be with someone I don't trust," she said.

"Baby, I'm sorry. Please, don't do this! Give me the chance to rebuild your trust. Let me earn it back. Just give me that chance. I'm telling you, I've changed. I'm nothing like that anymore," I pleaded.

"I did give you a chance and this is what you've done with it," she said as the tears kept rolling down her face.

No matter what I said it didn't faze her. She had her mind made to leave. She took the keys to the house off her keychain.

"I'll have my brother stop by and get my things," she said.

I couldn't hold back my tears anymore. She tried to hand me the keys. I wouldn't accept them.

"Baby, please! I love you! Please, let's work this out," I pleaded again.

She looked me in my eyes. "Unfortunately, I love you, too. I always will. Bye!"

She put the keys on the table and walked out the door. I fell to the floor and started crying. It was like a scene right out of a movie; except this time I didn't get the girl. She wasn't coming back. There was no happy ending and it was all my fault.

Jerry

A FIGHTING SECRET

Everything was finally on schedule for Diamond to open the following month. I could relax and stop stressing over getting things ready. Jeff, Ty, and I sat down and decided to go back to our old schedule until Diamond opened. I was going to run Diamond, Ty would run Mystic, and Jeff would float back and forth between the two until we open another club the next year. In ten years, we should have a club in every major city on the East Coast.

Tracy didn't like the fact that I was gone more at night again, but she said she'd have to deal with it. Things would get a little better when Diamond opened because I'd mostly work during the day. We'd hired a manager for the club that would handle all the nighttime activities. We'd done it mostly because of Ty's situation. He was going through a tough time, dealing with the breakup between him and Jodi. I didn't feel like being at the club every night and I knew Jeff didn't either so we hired Donovan.

I'd forgotten how rowdy the women would get on Wednesdays. The line was around the corner, as usual, when I got there and it was only 6:30 p.m.

"Some things will never change," I said.

Jeff was probably already there. I doubted Ty would be there. I went straight to the back to see who was there. I didn't see anyone. I stopped at the bar to get a quick drink and relax.

"What's up, D?" I said.

"Nothing much! It's strange seeing you up in here," Darin said.

"I know it is. I feel strange," I told him.

"You seen Jeff yet?" I asked.

"Yeah, he and Ty are upstairs in VIP," he replied.

I grabbed my drink.

"I'll catch up with you later on. I'm a go and see what's up with them."

I went upstairs to catch up with the fellas. I was shocked to hear Ty was there; especially this early.

"What's up with y'all?" I said.

"Nothing much; just talking. How 'bout yourself?" Jeff asked.

"Can't complain. It feels different up in here. Shit, I don't even have an office anymore! How you feelin', Ty?" I asked.

"I'm chilling. You know me. There isn't anything a drink can't handle," he said.

"He's chillin'. He just needs to get his mind off Jodi, that's all," Jeff added.

"Man, fuck Jodi! I'm not worrying about her ass anymore. She's made it very clear that she doesn't want anything to do with me. Right now I'm worried about April. I'm 'bout to have a baby by this chick. What kind of shit is that?" Ty said.

I didn't know what to tell him. I could see exactly what he meant. She wouldn't have been my first choice to have a child by either.

"Are you sure it's yours?" I asked.

"Hell no, but I won't know for certain until the baby is born," he said.

"You think about giving her the money for an abortion?" Jeff asked.

"Fuck that shit! We don't believe in abortion," I said.

"Honestly, y'all, I thought real hard about getting one. But I can't. I don't believe in that shit. It's like I'm punishing my child for something I did and that's not right. Even if I did believe in that shit, April made it very clear in the note she left that she wasn't getting one, no matter what," Ty said.

He continued, "What's really fucking me up is that she hasn't filed for child support yet. You know you can file while you're pregnant now. I would've thought she would've run to the courthouse."

"For real, I didn't know that shit," I said.

"Yeah. I called her the other night to, you know, see how she was doing. She acted all civil and shit. We were on the phone for like two hours almost."

"Talking 'bout what?" Jeff asked.

"Baby names, her doctor's appointment, shit like that. It was jive shocking to say but, then again, we always got along. I just didn't like it when she'd call me all the time. Come to find out she was trying to tell me she was pregnant. I think she thinks we're going to get together or something though," he said.

"That bitch is lunchin'," Jeff said.

"Who you telling!" I added.

Ty didn't say anything.

"Don't tell me you're actually thinking 'bout being with her?" I asked.

"Naw, he wouldn't do any shit like that. Would you, Ty?" Jeff asked.

"I don't know. I mean, why not? Maybe we can be together and make it work. If not for ourselves, at least for the baby. I'm not trying to be one of those weekend fathers, you know. I want to be able to see my child all the time, tuck him in at night, shit like that," Ty said.

"I understand what you're saying but a child's not a reason to stay together or, in your case, get together. You can't even stand her. How can you honestly believe you can be with her?" I asked.

"Terry has a point, Ty. Nobody really likes her ass. I know I don't. I hate that bitch," Jeff added.

"Go 'head, young. You don't have to keep calling her a bitch like that. I might like her. I wouldn't say I can't stand her. The situation's really complicated. If I was in her shoes, I would've called my ass all the time, too. I honestly don't know shit about her. I really never took the time to get to know her. She was just some easy pussy to me. I had Jodi then. I wasn't trying to get to know her like that," Ty said.

"Speaking of Jodi, how can you try to have anything with April when you're still not over Jodi? There's still a chance she'll come back," Jeff said.

Ty became excited. "What do you mean? Did she say something to Michelle 'bout coming back or something?"

"See, look at you getting all excited and shit. No, I'm saying though, it's possible," Jeff replied.

Ty came back down to reality after getting his hopes up.

"'Bout as much a possibility as me winning the lotto. She's not coming back. I saw her face that night; you didn't. It's over between us and there's nothing I can do about it but move on. I think it's time I do that," he said.

He actually had a point. He probably did need to move on but I wasn't sure if it was with April and definitely wasn't sure if the time was right then. But I wasn't the one to decide or judge who he was with or what he did. I knew that if he got that excited about hearing Jodi might come back, he wasn't over her yet. And if he wasn't over her there was no way that he could love April, or any other woman for that matter. I was looking at the entire breakup through my past experiences. I'd fucked up way more than him and Tracy had found a way to forgive me. A part of me thought Jodi could and would do the same.

"You just need to give it time, dawg. Jodi's hurt right now. It's going to take some time for her to get over it. Once she does, then she can think about what she wants to do. Right now she's just acting off pure emotion. This shit with April is the same for you. Take this time and think about what you want to do before you actually do it," I said.

"Yeah, I guess you're right."

"Excuse me, Terry, can I talk to you for a minute," someone behind me said.

I turned around and it was Midnight.

"What's up, Midnight?" Jeff said.

He didn't say anything back. He just looked at him, then back at me again.

"What do you need to talk to me about? If you're having a problem, Donovan handles that now. Take that shit up with him," I said.

I didn't like the way he was coming at me.

"All I have to say is you better treat Tracy right," he said.

I jumped up from the table. "What!"

Ty and Jeff got up from the table.

"I don't want to hear shit about you doggin' her or..."

"Or what?" I asked, cutting him off.

"Like I said, you better treat Tracy right. I don't want to hear shit," he said.

I couldn't believe this nigga had the balls to come at me like I was soft or something.

"Me and *my wife's* concerns are none of your muthafuckin' business. You just worry about not getting butt-fucked by one of your lil' backstage buddies before the show," I said, looking at the two niggas with him.

"Tracy is my business, since I'm the one fucking her! Yeah, bet your ass didn't know that shit, huh, bitch ass nigga."

My mind began to wander. I didn't know what to do or say. I stood there, frozen in the same spot.

He continued, "All those weekend trips, she spent them with me, dumb ass. I was the one digging up in your wife. Just remember that shit! When you're kissing your wife, you're tasting my dick!"

POP!

I knocked his ass on the floor with the first punch. His man hit me on the top of my head before I could duck the punch. Ty followed up behind him. The next thing I knew it was an all-out brawl. Midnight tried to get up when I hit him again.

"Talk shit now, you bitch-made nigga! You're fuckin' my wife, huh!?"

I didn't see or feel anything. I tried to kill his ass. I kept swinging and swinging. Security made their way upstairs to break up the fight. It took almost every security guard in there to stop it. I finally calmed down when I realized I couldn't get to him anymore. There were four dudes alone holding me back.

"Get this bitch up out of my damn club! Let me see your ass on the street!" I yelled.

Jeff came over to try and calm me down. Midnight still hadn't gotten off the floor. He just lay there bleeding. I'd beaten the shit out of his ass. I was still fired up. I looked around for one of his boys. I didn't care which one.

"Where are his lil' bitch-ass friends?" I said.

BOP!

Someone hit me in the back of the head. Darin swung back to get him up off me. Everyone rushed us again to break it up.

Once everything had died down, I went in Ty's office to calm down. Someone had called the police earlier so they were still getting statements from everybody that had seen the fight. Midnight and one of his boys had to go to the hospital. I really got a hold of his ass.

Jeff walked in. "What the hell is going on?"

"He wasn't going to disrespect me like that," I said.

"I wouldn't have even tripped. Tracy wouldn't do anything like that. Not with his ass," he said.

"She already told me that she cheated a while ago. It had to be with him. He knew too much shit," I said.

"I can't even see her doing some shit like that; especially with his ass!" he replied.

"Maybe you're right. I don't know but I'm damn sure enough going to find out," I said.

I drove home doing a good eighty miles per hour. All kind of thoughts raced through my head. I'd fucked around but I'd never done anything with someone she knew, or worked with even. That was dirty and beneath even me. How could she? Why would she?

I stormed through the front door. Tracy was sitting on the couch reading her book.

"What's wrong?" she asked.

"Midnight!" I said. Her face said it all. It was true. "How could you? Somebody I worked with. Why Tracy? Why?"

"I'm sorry. I tried to tell you but when you said you already knew, I figured there was no point. If you knew what I did, I didn't think it mattered with whom," she said.

"Midnight!" I repeated.

I couldn't believe it. I couldn't get past the fact that it was with Midnight. He'd touched my wife in ways that only I should have. He'd tasted my wife, caressed her. I thought about what he'd said, '*When you kiss your wife, you're tasting my dick!*' I became even angrier at the thought of it.

"Midnight! How could you? I'd never do any shit like that to you! Never!" I yelled.

"You've already done it to me, and a lot more. You've cheated with way more damn girls than I have on you. I did it once and you accepted it. You've done it since we were fucking kids and I've stuck by your ass still like a fool. I'm sorry for what I did but don't try to sit here and judge me because you've done far worse," she said.

"I never did shit with any of your fucking friends. I showed you that much respect. I wouldn't hurt you like that," I said.

"What the fuck is wrong with you? It all hurts. There's no way to show respect when you're cheating. And furthermore, he's not your friend. You hardly even know him," she replied.

"He fucking works for me. I must know him somehow. What kind of shit is that? I'd never do some shit like that!"

"So, is that what this is about? The fact that I fucked Renard? Let me ask you this. Would it have been better if I'd fucked Joe instead?" she asked.

"Who the hell is that?" I asked.

"I just made a name up. Would it have been better if I'd cheated with someone you didn't know?"

"Yeah! I'd never do some shit like that to you! How would you feel if I fucked Crystal?" I asked.

"She wouldn't do that to me," she replied.

"Neither would I, but you would. Shit, you did. I'm just saying, how would you feel?" I asked.

"That's different. She's my best friend. You hardly even know Renard. You didn't even know his real name. This shit is starting to piss me off. You've cheated on me since I was fourteen. Fucking *fourteen*!" she said, getting excited.

"Why do you keep bringing that shit up? I know what I did. You know what I did. You chose to stay with me. It was your decision. You could've left a long time ago but you didn't, so stop bringing that shit up," I said.

"That's right, I didn't. I stayed hoping you'd change. I stayed because I loved you. I could've taken this house, gotten child support, and a whole bunch of other shit. I stayed though. I made a vow to you before God, through good times and bad, and I meant that shit. I can just about count the good times on one fucking hand so don't turn this shit around on me. I'm wrong for cheating, I know that. You're the one who chose to stay with me, too. You're the one who said let's keep it in the past; that's where it belongs. Don't try to act all different now. The *one* person I cheated with doesn't come close to comparison with the hundreds of girls you've cheated with," she said.

"I didn't fuck no damn hundreds of girls and I didn't know who you cheated with before I said that," I said.

"Cheating is cheating, I don't care who you cheat with. It doesn't make it any better or any worse. It's wrong regardless. I'm not going to keep going through this with you. I can't change the past and neither can you. You cheated with who you did and I did with Renard. Either you can accept it like you said you did or you can't. That's a decision you have to make on your own," she said.

I walked upstairs to the bedroom. I grabbed a few of my clothes and packed up one of my old gym bags. Tracy walked in the room a couple of minutes after me.

"So that's it? You're just going to leave just like that? What about all the things you told me? Like you love me and only want to be with me. If that were true you wouldn't let this come between us. We've *both* made mistakes; not just me," she said.

"Tracy, I'd never do what you did to me. At least I showed you that much respect," I said.

"Don't keep trying to talk to me about respect! You fucked anything that moved and you call that respect because I didn't know them. You never respected me. If you did, you wouldn't have ever cheated on me. You say I didn't respect you when I cheated. You're right, I didn't. But don't you sit here in my fucking face and tell me that you respected me," she said.

I finished packing my bag.

"Well, since you don't respect me and I don't respect you, we don't need to be together then. If you need me I'll be at Ty's house. I'll stay there until I find an apartment," I said.

"You're actually going to leave over this? I can stay and try to work things out for your ass because I love you and the first time I do something, you run. Go then! You don't love me," she said.

She started to cry. A part of me wanted to wipe her tears away and hug her but my pride wouldn't let me. My mind was made and I needed to stick to my decision.

"Bye, Tracy." I walked out the door and went downstairs to leave.

"Leave then! Run like you always do! You haven't changed! It's still all about you! All you've ever cared about is you! I fucking hate you!"

My heart dropped when she said that. "I never did that shit to you."

I walked out of the front door and our marriage.

A CONSCIOUS CALLING

Things were getting out of hand between everybody. First, it was Jodi and Ty, then Tracy and Terry. I hoped I wasn't next. It seemed like everything was happening back to back. I wasn't losing Chelle over some bullshit. Ty had it the worst, in my opinion. He'd actually changed this time. I couldn't say he didn't bring it on himself though.

I wasn't tripping about Tracy and Terry. That was temporary. He knew he was dead wrong for leaving that girl. As much of his shit that she'd put up with, I would've been thankful to even have her. She could've fucked the Pope for all I cared. I think the entire scene at the club was what bothered him the most. People hearing his business about what Tracy had done and the way Midnight said it didn't help matters at all.

It was scaring me, how everyone's past was coming back to haunt them. I was no saint. I'd done my fair share of dirt over the years. I could've easily been in the same predicament as everyone else. The story my mother had told me about my father stuck out the most. Had he not come out and told her what he'd done when he did, he would've lost her. I wouldn't even be alive.

Chelle walked in the living room while I was thinking.

"Hey, you want something to eat? I'm about to fix a sandwich or something. I don't know yet," she said.

I sat there, still deep in thought. "Naw, I'm okay."

She could detect something was on my mind. "What's wrong?"

"Nothing really! I was just sitting here thinking about everything that's going on with my friends," I said.

"It's a mess, ain't it? But both of them brought it on themselves. What's done in the dark always finds its way to the light," she said.

"Yeah, but we all have pasts and that's all it is, the past. Not to say that what Ty did wasn't fucked up but he actually did change," I said.

"Is that supposed to change the fact that he cheated on her and got another woman pregnant?"

"No! I just feel bad because he finally did change and wanted to settle down with Jodi. It was too late though. For some reason it takes us longer to settle down than women," I said.

"That's fine and dandy but if that's the case, why not be honest about it from jump. Why even play those games? He should've just told her that he wasn't ready to settle down when they first hooked up," she said.

"We all play games, in a way," I said.

"Maybe you did, but I didn't. I never had time for games," she said.

"Yes, you did. The first time we met would you have given me some booty if I tried?" I asked.

"No."

"Why not?" I asked.

"Because I didn't know you like that. I have more respect for myself than to just sleep with anybody," she said.

"I can take that. So, how long does it take for you to get to know someone?"

"I'd say about two or three months. By then I should have a pretty good feel for you," she answered.

"Then why did it take us four, almost five months, before we had sex? You knew me; definitely by the third month. Shit, we talked every damn day. You probably knew me after the second month," I said.

"Yeah, but I still couldn't give it up that early. I really liked you and I didn't want you to think I was that easy or I let just anyone get this. I wanted you to know that you had to work to get it," she said.

"Exactly! What you did was nothing but playing a game. We all do, whether it's not trying to give it up too soon or putting on the big front in the beginning of the relationship to get it. It's all a game," I said.

"But that's different than what we're talking about. He wasn't honest, so that means he was breaking the trust they were trying to establish. You can't have a relationship without trust," she said.

"I see what you're saying but put yourself in his situation," I said.

"I can't. I wouldn't do something like that," she replied.

"Imagine if you did. What if you never really had a boyfriend before you met me, just friends? Then, when we first started talking, you still remained friends with them until you realized you wanted to be with me. Once you realized it, you cut all your old friends back," I said.

"Okay."

"Now we become serious and you're with me now and only me. I find out that when we first started messing with each other you were cheating on me and I break up with you," I said.

"I understand what you're trying to say but that's different. We were only talking. Had we been a couple from jump, then it would be the same."

"We're not kids anymore. Talking, chilling with each other, and being a couple is all the same damn thing and you know it. If it wasn't, then when did we become a couple? When I asked you to marry me?"

"No. We became a couple on July 15th. That's our anniversary date," she said.

"No, that's the day we met, which is my point exactly," I said.

She thought back. She was stuck.

"I see what you're saying. I really don't know when we had the actual title boyfriend/girlfriend. We just did after a while," she said.

"Right! Once you realized you wanted to be with me then we had the title in your eyes. So, what if I realized it before you? I'm going around thinking we're a couple and you don't. You're still fucking with other dudes. Still think he's wrong?" I asked.

"I see what you're trying to get at but it didn't take him no damn three years to realize he wanted to be with her so, hell yeah, he was wrong," she said.

"What I'm trying to say is in his situation it took him that long to realize that Jodi was the one he wanted to be with. He needed to be committed to her. If I tell you something, it stays between you and me?" I asked.

"Who am I going to tell?" she replied.

"Jodi! Y'all have become real tight over the last month or so," I said.

"Fine, I promise," she replied.

"Okay, like round the end of July, I think maybe sooner, he took this girl out to dinner. Something was going on with him and Jodi. Anyhow, April, the girl he got pregnant, showed up at the club that night so he had to duck her. He went back to his office for something and Jodi was in there waiting for him. She wanted to surprise him. I think they had sex that night in his office—yeah, while April was in the club and the other girl upstairs.

"Anyway Jodi wanted to go back to his place to finish up so he rolled with her. But he didn't want to get caught and have one of them see him leave with Jodi so he made up something he had to do before he left and told her he would meet her at his house. While he waited for her to leave the club, he sat there and thought. He realized that those other women weren't worth losing Jodi over. She gives him what all of them did and more. It's like he learned what love actually is and that he was in love with Jodi. After that, he cut all the other chicks back and asked Jodi to move in with him," I said.

"I told you I understand that but what I'm trying to get you to see is that while he was discovering himself or whatever he was doing, he should've told her from jump what his process or agenda was so that way she would've known where she stood and wouldn't have expected more out of him," she said.

"Okay, y'all say that now, after the fact, but if he did do that before things had gotten serious she wouldn't have stayed with him. She would've left the minute he told her that shit," I said.

"You're probably right but she would've had the choice. She couldn't have done anything but respect him for his honesty."

"So, what if it was me and you? What if we were in the same situation but I was honest with you from the start. What would you have done?" I asked.

"I wouldn't have been with you. I was looking for something serious," she said.

"So, me being honest wouldn't benefit me? And to think, we're getting married now," I said.

She thought about it. "Well, once I think about it, I'd rather not know. I don't know. I still think I'd rather be able to make that decision first."

"If you did, you already said you wouldn't have been with me so we wouldn't be getting married now," I said.

"I know. Honestly, I don't know, now that I know you. I can probably overlook it because of how much I've grown to love you. But I understand where Jodi's coming from. She can't overlook it. But, then again, neither could I before I understood the entire situation. I'm pretty sure once Jodi really thinks about it and gets the whole scenario, she'll see things the way I do now. She really wasn't even mad at the fact that he cheated or that the girl was pregnant. Well, naw, the pregnancy really hurt her also, but what did it was the way she found out. I think if he'd come clean about everything when he asked her to move in, it wouldn't have hurt as much because she would've already known," she said.

"Really? Do you think she would've stayed?" I asked.

"I don't know; probably. She told me that when she caught him the first time, she'd given it another go around because he'd promised that it would be the last time. If he did it again, it was over. So I'm really not sure what she would've done. I hope that he learns from all of this, whether they get back together or not," she said.

"Has she been talking about going back to him?" I asked out of curiosity.

"Not in those words but she keeps bringing him up, which means she's thinking about him. She just needs some time to herself to think about what she really wants."

I thought about telling Ty what Chelle had just told me so he could get any thoughts about hooking up with April out of his head, but I didn't want to be wrong and have to hear his mouth.

"I'm sorry, baby, but I'm hungry. I need something to eat. You sure you don't want a sandwich?" she asked.

"I'm sure," I replied.

She got up from the couch and went into the kitchen. I thought a lot about what she'd said. What stuck out the most though was when she'd said if he would've told her once he'd asked her to move in with him, she might've tried to work things out. I could've easily been in the same position as Ty. What if I'd gotten some girl pregnant when I'd cheated on Chelle and she'd come and told me in like two years or something? The same shit could happen to me.

I had living proof of the honesty approach working. It had worked for my father; why couldn't it work for me. My mother was going to leave him until he'd told her everything. Chelle had even said that you had to respect the honesty in it. I wondered whether to tell Chelle about my past or not.

I decided to call my father and ask him what he thought. He'd already done it. He'd been in this situation before. I could see what made him do it. I went into the bedroom, in case Chelle walked in the living room. I didn't want her to over-hear anything. I closed the bedroom door and turned the TV on, just in case she tried to listen at the door. I was paranoid. I wasn't about to say anything just yet to her and I didn't want her to find out like that.

"Hello," he said as he answered the phone.

"Hey, Pops! You gotta minute?" I asked.

"Yeah, why? What's up? It must be something serious. You're cutting out the small talk," he said.

"Is Mom around?" I asked.

"No, she went to the grocery store. What's on your mind, son?" he asked.

"Okay, well, lately things have been going crazy with my friends. Ty and his girl broke up. I'm not sure about the exact specifics because Ty was drunk and really doesn't remember what happened. But this girl Ty was messing around with a while ago got pregnant. So she leaves him a note on his door telling him, because they were beefing, and he wouldn't answer her calls. Somehow, after he read it, his girl got a hold of it and she rolled out. Now, I can't help but to think that could've been me, Pop," I said.

"But it wasn't, so what's the problem? A lot of things could've been you, but they weren't," my father said.

"But see, Chelle and I were talking about everything earlier and I explained Ty's side of it. Well, she said that Jodi might've stayed if Ty had come clean when he asked her to move in with him. That made me think about you," I said.

"What about me?" he asked.

"Mommy told me the story about your wedding day, when you told her about the woman you'd cheated on her with. She told me that she was ready to call the wedding off until you told her. She said that you didn't have to tell her but you risked losing her by being honest with her," I said.

"So I take it you're asking me if you should tell her about the times you were unfaithful in the relationship?"

"Yeah."

"That's a tough one, son. What your mother doesn't know was I saw her in the window. I had to tell or I would've lost her. I probably wouldn't have said a word had I not seen her or had she not overheard. Everything worked out for me, but that was me. It might not be the same for you, if you say something. Michelle might not be as understanding.

"I know she's telling you that she can't do anything but respect you but she's speaking from the outside. It's a totally different story when you're on the inside. You don't see things the same because it's you. It's like I told you about your cousin. Just because he was caught in his wrongdoings doesn't mean you will be. The same goes with me telling your mother. Just because it worked out for me doesn't mean it will for you," he said.

"So, you wouldn't tell her if you were in my situation?" I asked.

"I'm not in your situation, nor have I been. My circumstances were a lot different than yours, son. You want me to tell you what to do and I'm not going to do that. You have to decide for yourself, son. You're a grown man. I'm going to give you what you should've called here for in the first place: advice.

"You have to do what your heart and your conscience tell you. That's all you can do, son. If you feel you should tell her, tell her. If not, then don't, but either way, you have to live with the consequences of your actions. If you tell her and she decides to leave you, you have to live with it; just as if you don't and she ends up finding out and leaves you.

"I'll tell you this; I admire you for wanting to tell her. A lot of men wouldn't even think about saying a word, but not you. I applaud your thoughts, son. Put it in God's hands and He'll take care of everything. He'll give you the answers that you're searching for."

He always told me what I needed to hear instead of what I wanted to hear. I got off the phone with my father, still not knowing what to do. I didn't want to lose her, regardless of what decision I made, but the reality of it was that I could lose her either way.

Tyrelle

LIFE GOES ON

I picked up the phone and started dialing her number. I hung up when it started ringing. I was nervous. I didn't know how to approach her. I wanted to talk to her though so I called her again.

"Washington Hospital Center. Mrs. Clark speaking," a woman said, answering the phone.

"May I speak to Dr. Freeman, please?" I asked.

She placed me on hold while she paged her. "Dr. Freeman," Jodi said.

It felt so good to hear her voice.

"Hello, this is Dr. Freeman... Hello!"

I just sat there listening to her voice. She hung up the phone. I pulled myself together and called again.

"Washington Hospital Center. Dr. Freeman speaking," she said.

"How are you?" I asked.

She hesitated, then replied, "I'm fine."

"I just called to see how you were. I haven't talked to you in a while."

"Well, I'm fine."

"Okay," I said.

"It was nice talking to you but I have to get back to work. Take care of yourself, okay?" she said.

"I will and you do the same." Before she hung up, I said, "Wait a minute! Jodi, I miss you. I really do. I wish I could go back in time and do things differently. I'm sorry, Jodi. Every day I pray that you'll come back and say we can work things out, and every day I'm disappointed because you never do. I fucked up but I swear I've changed. I'd cut all ties with everybody before we moved in together. I should've done it when we first hooked up. I didn't know any better then, but now I do. I've never felt this way about any other woman. I can't sleep at night without you beside me. I can't eat. I can't do anything because I don't have you in my life. Please, Jodi, just give us another chance," I said.

"I'm sorry, Tyrelle, but I can't ever be with you again. It would be best if you just moved on with your life. There'll never be an *us* again. I can't trust you and I can't be with anyone I don't trust," she said.

"I love you and I know you still love me. That has to count for something. As long as we have love for one another, there's always a chance to start over fresh. I'm sorry, baby. I made a mistake. I've made several but I can't go on without you. I love you! Do you hear me? I love you!"

"Listen to me, it's over between us. I'm not nor will I *ever* come back to you. We're over. I'd appreciate it if you didn't call me anymore. Thank you. Bye, Tyrelle," she said as she hung up the phone.

My heart was crushed. It couldn't be over with. I called her right back. I wasn't finished saying what I had to say.

"Hello, Washington Hospital Center. Mrs. Clark speaking," the woman said.

"Dr. Freeman, please," I replied.

"I'm sorry, sir, but she's with a patient right now. Can I take a message?" she asked.

"I just got off the phone with her. I know she isn't with a damn patient that fast," I said.

I hung up the phone. It was obvious she didn't want to talk to me. I called all throughout the day, hoping to get her back. Every time I called I got the same reply: "She's with a patient." It was bullshit. I thought about going down there and talking to her in person but I didn't. I might've messed around and gotten arrested.

I didn't feel like doing shit. I couldn't move. My body was numb all day long. I called Jeff and told him I wasn't coming in; I needed him to cover for me. He tried to talk to me about what was on my mind but I wasn't in the mood. I needed to be by myself. I was tired of everyone else's opinion; people telling me to move on. I wanted Jodi. She just didn't want me.

I went to the liquor store and bought a half-gallon of Bacardi. I played the first CD I spotted and sat on the couch and drank drink after drink. I drank until I passed out, still holding the bottle in my hand. I woke up the next morning and the pain still was there. It wouldn't go away as long as Jodi was gone. I picked up my cup and made another drink. Terry came downstairs and saw me.

"Okay, this shit is getting ridiculous. You need to snap out of it," he said.

"How the fuck do you snap out of love? Huh, Terry, tell me that! Where's the switch to just turn the shit off?"

I downed my drink and poured another one.

"I can't tell you how to snap out of love but I can tell you this isn't the way. What are you going to do? Just sit around the house and drink all damn day for the rest of your life?"

"That's what y'all don't understand. Without Jodi, I don't have a life. *She* is my life." The tears began to come down.

"Do you think you're the only one hurting? I'm going through some shit my damn self. I'm fucking staying with your ass, but I'm still living my life. How can Jodi even think about coming back to you when you're not even you anymore? And even if she doesn't come back, there are too many damn women out here. Move the fuck on!"

"I don't want to move on. I want Jodi," I said.

I took another sip of my drink.

"I'm going to say this because you need to hear it. She doesn't want you and you can't make her. You need to just move on with your life and find someone else. But before you do that, find yourself first. Life's too damn short to let it pass you by. Learn from this so you don't make the same mistake the next time. That's what part of life is about; learning from your mistakes. Right now I know it hurts and it's going to for a while. But you've got to move on," he said.

I finished my drink. He was right. I needed to move on with my life, and find someone else who wanted to be with me.

"Thanks, man! I needed to hear that," I said.

"No problem. That's what I'm here for. Just do me a favor and take your ass upstairs and wash. You smell like you slept in the alley," he said.

I didn't notice it before but I did smell like shit. I went upstairs and took a shower. I got out the shower feeling fresh and brand-new. My head still felt like shit. The effects from my all-night drinking binge were starting to set in. I lay back down and slept the day away. My body needed time to recuperate.

❖ ❖ ❖ ❖

That night was the grand opening of Diamond. We'd been hyping up opening night for several weeks. We'd booked Chuck Brown and the Soul Searchers and Suttle Thoughts to perform. We'd even gotten SOULO to open up for them. We wanted to have a club opening to compete with Club U and 2K9, as far as the bands. What better way to start the club off than with the Godfather of Go-Go himself? People that didn't even like Go-Go music liked Chuck Brown. We couldn't go wrong. We'd already signed SOULO to play every Friday and Suttle to play every Saturday so this was their coming out.

We decided to close Club Mystic for the night so the employees could have the night off to come and share the moment with us. We threw the party in VIP for invitees only; mostly our family and friends. I didn't have a date and I was content to go alone but I changed my mind. I needed to start dating again, so why not start now? I thought of the perfect date. I just hoped she didn't have plans.

I walked in Diamond with a beautiful woman on my arm and everyone was shocked.

"Hey, now, what's up, y'all? Darin, Jeff, and Terry, y'all know April," I said.

"Hi, how are you doing?" April said.

I pointed at Michelle.

"April, this is Jeff's financée, Michelle."

"Hello," Michelle said.

I glanced back at Darin. "I'm sorry, I don't know your date's name."

She reached her hand out. "Hi, I'm Tammy."

"It's nice to meet you," I said.

I pulled April's chair out so she could sit down.

"Ty, can I talk to you for a second?" Jeff asked me.

"Sure. April, you want anything to drink? Soda, juice, anything?"

"No, I'm fine," she replied.

We got up from the table and went to the bar. Terry followed behind us.

"What are you doing? Why the hell did you bring her here?" Jeff asked.

"Huh? Excuse me? Since when did you become my fucking father? You're not in the position to judge anyone I'm with. I asked her if she wanted to come, she accepted, and here we are," I said.

"All right, both of you calm down. I think what he's saying is we thought you said that you weren't going to mess with her? We're just a lil' shocked to see her, that's all," Terry said.

"I'm a grown ass man. I can date whoever I choose. I have the right to change my mind about someone I want to date or whatever. You were the one who gave me the big speech yesterday about moving on. I'm doing exactly that; moving on with my life. Y'all acting like I asked the girl to marry me or something. I just asked her out for tonight," I said.

"You're right, Ty. You're a grown man and you can make your own decisions," Terry said.

Jeff looked at Terry like he was out of his mind.

"I'm not going to sit here and sugarcoat the shit. I can't even see how you'd even think about looking at the bitch, let alone trying to be with her. You're dumb as shit if you fuck with her ass," Jeff said.

"Then let me be a dumb bitch because I'm going to mess with her," I said.

"You sure, Ty?" Terry asked.

"Yeah, I'm sure. If I'm wrong about her, then I'm wrong, but I'm going to see where we can go," I said.

Jeff started shaking his head.

"Ay, I already told you, Ty, it's your life so it's your call," Terry said.

"You know what? I don't have anything to say to you. Fuck you and that bitch. I hope y'all are happy together," Jeff said.

"Call her a bitch again, hear? I'm tired of you thinking you can just disrespect her in my face. Call her a bitch one more damn time," I said.

"What are you going to do, swing? You're going to swing on me over her. You're right; this shit is for the birds. Have a good night, Terry," he said. He turned and looked at me. "Fuck you!"

"Come on now! Come back here, Jeff," Terry said as Jeff walked away.

"Man, fuck that nigga! Let his ass leave! How the hell is he going to criticize somebody and he ain't going through shit," I said.

"Look, there's too much tension built up right now. Come on, let's party. We're supposed to be celebrating," Terry said.

We went back to the table.

"Is everything okay?" April asked.

Jeff and Michelle were gone; so were Darin and his girl.

"Yeah, I'm straight," I replied.

"Oh, because your friend and his wife just left. He looked pissed," she said.

"Fuck him! I'm not trippin' off his ass. Where did the other dude and his girl go?" I asked, referring to Darin.

"They went out on the dance floor," she said.

"That sounds like a good idea. Would you like to dance?" I asked her.

"Sure," she replied.

We went to the dance floor. The DJ was tearing it up. He played old school, new school, hip-hop, and R&B. He did his thing. We stopped and sat down for a minute while Suttle Thoughts was setting up. Terry didn't get up at all. He just sat there and drank. I knew he missed Tracy. He didn't even bring her up anymore. It was like he was trying to make himself forget about her or have us forget about the situation.

I could see the pain in his eyes though and he hadn't danced with anyone. Usually he was the first one out on the dance floor. All he did was drink. I saw a couple of women swing past the table and he'd just turn them down. I excused myself from the table and went into the office. If he wasn't going to call her and ask her to come, I damn sure was.

"Hello."

"Hey, Tracy, this is Ty," I said.

"Hey," she replied.

"Look, I know you and Terry are going through some things right now but I think you should be here sharing this moment with him."

"I'm sorry, Ty, but he's made it very clear that he doesn't want anything to do with me."

"As long as I can remember, you've always been there for him. Don't start not being there now. This is a night he should never forget but he's sitting here moping around because he can't spend it with you. He's stubborn. You know that. If you don't come, the both of you will regret it for the rest of your lives," I said.

"Ty, I don't want you to think that I don't want to be there. I love Terry and I always will but he doesn't want me there, so I'm not coming. I'm not going to impose on his night," she said.

"How can you impose? He's your damn husband."

"I'm sorry, Ty. I just can't. I hope y'all have a good time though. Bye," she said.

There was nothing I could do. I'd gotten my point across and, ultimately, the decision was hers. I went back to our table. Suttle started playing and rocked.

Diamond in the back
Sunroof top
Diggin' the scene with the gangsta lean
OOO ooo OOO

I moved back and forth, rocking with the band. I went to the table to get Terry.

"Come on. Let's go downstairs and party with the band," I said.

"Naw, I'm straight," he said.

"Come on, young. This is supposed to be our night," I said.

"I don't feel like it, for real. I'll party when SOULO and Chuck get up there," he said.

I left it alone. April didn't feel like being downstairs so she stayed upstairs with Terry while I went downstairs and partied. Darin was already down there so it was just me and him. We partied the entire time. I couldn't sit down. I'd hoped Terry would come down but he never did.

I went back upstairs to check on him and April during intermission. Nothing had changed. She was dancing on the floor upstairs and he was sitting at the table drinking. He'd promised to come downstairs while SOULO played. He tried to weasel his way out of it but I wouldn't let him. He finally got up and started to enjoy himself. The way Suttle had played earlier, SOULO had to bring it and they did.

Now did they go down low
All the way to the floor
Ladies don't stop
When ya pop pop pop
You make your booty go
Up
Down
To the left
To the right
Move it in
Move it out

The crowd went crazy. SOULO had the floor and everybody knew it. The women in there were working it. They didn't disappoint at all. In the D.C. area, you have only a couple of premiere bands. SOULO was definitely one of them. They rocked non-stop. Even when they slowed things down, they were still thumping.

Terry and Darin stayed downstairs during intermission this time. I couldn't forget all about April. I went upstairs and spent some time alone with her.

"Where are you going when we leave?" I asked.

"Hopefully to your house," she said.

"That's no problem, as long as you're staying the whole night. I want breakfast in the morning and everything," I said.

"Breakfast? I'm pregnant with your child. You should be cooking breakfast for me," she said.

"How 'bout we make it together?" I asked.

"That sounds like a plan to me."

"You're not upset at the fact that I'm downstairs while the bands play and you're up here by yourself, are you? If you want me to stay up here, I will."

"Not at all. I'd be down there with you but I'm not trying to be in that crowd. I'm holding my own up here, thank you," she said.

"Okay, I'm 'bout to go back downstairs. Do you want anything?" I asked.

"I'm just fine. What I want you can't give me now," she said.

"Tonight, baby, tonight."

I got down the steps and started making my way to the bar. I knew they'd be somewhere close by. Chuck Brown got up on stage and it seemed like there were nothing but ladies around. The ratio had to be at least six to one. I caught back up with Terry and Darin as Chuck took the mic.

"I want to thank y'all for coming out and celebrating this night with us. First and foremost, I want to thank the three special brothers for inviting me to spend tonight with them. Jeff, Ty, and Terry, come on up here real quick."

I didn't even know Jeff was still here. We made it up to the stage and Jeff was already up there.

"Fellas, I've seen y'all grow from boys to men. I always knew that y'all would make something of yourself. The sky's the limit for the three of you. I wish y'all continued success and if it's all right with you, we're going to party until five in the morning."

The crowd started cheering. Chuck wasn't going to let another band outdo him. None of us had any objections. We knew how Chuck partied and we were in for a treat. I noticed Tracy standing in the back with a long black dress on, looking ever so sexy. I pointed her out to Terry. His face lit up like a lamp. I knew he missed her. I was glad I'd put that bug in her ear to come. Terry fought his way through the crowd to be with her. The band started to play.

Give me the beat now
Give me the beat now

The band started to play.

I feel like bustin' loose
Bustin' loose
Give me the beat now

Chuck put the lasting touches on a memorable night.

❖ ❖ ❖ ❖

I walked in the house worn out. I went straight to the couch and fell out. It had been a long time since I'd partied like that. April went upstairs to change her clothes, then came back downstairs. She sat down on the couch beside me and we cuddled.

"Did you have a nice time?" I asked her.

"The best! I'm glad you asked me to come," she said.

Terry walked through the front door. I didn't think he'd be there that night, or anymore at that. It looked like he and Tracy were back together, the way they'd been all over each other.

"April, I'll be right back," I said.

"Go 'head; your boy needs you. Family comes first. I'll just call you tomorrow," she said.

I felt bad that our night had to end that way but my cousin needed me. I walked her out, then went to check on Terry.

"All right, Terry, what's going on? I didn't expect you home tonight," I said.

"I don't know. I couldn't do it. I couldn't be around her alone so I left."

"What? What do you mean, you couldn't be around her?"

"All I kept picturing was her and Midnight together and it kept fucking with me. I just can't get over that shit. Fucked up, ain't it? Here I am telling you that you need to move on and I'm not. I can't be with her anymore. I just can't," he said.

"Look, man, I'm 'bout sick of this shit."

He cut me off. "Don't try and change my mind or lecture me because I'm not trying to hear it. I know I've done some nasty shit but I've never done anything like that. I've never fucked someone she knew."

I wanted to tell him off right then and there, but it wouldn't have done any good. I decided to let him calm down and talk to him later, when both of us were coherent. I'd been drinking and so had he. The shit would've gotten out of hand. We would've been arguing instead of talking.

"You gave me some advice, now let me return the favor. Right now you're still hurt and you're talking off emotions. You need to use this time away from her and put things in a better perspective," I said.

"I don't need to do anything. My mind is made," he said.

"You've been drinking and so have I. We don't need to have this conversation tonight. We'll have it another time but you really do need to take time and put your life in perspective," I said.

He walked away from me and went upstairs. Sometimes people just don't realize how lucky they are.

Terry
WRONG IS WRONG

I couldn't believe I was running late. It seemed like every time I tried to wrap things up so I could leave, something else came up. Johnny's game started at 7:15 p.m., as long as the Junior Varsity game didn't run late. I hoped it did. This was his first game of the season and I didn't want to miss a thing.

I flew through traffic and made it there at 7:15 p.m. exactly. I ran inside and paid the $4 door charge to get in. Both teams were still warming up on the floor. I looked up at the clock and there were still three minutes and some change remaining until tip-off. I blew out a sigh of relief.

Johnny was in the lay-up line, warming with the rest of his team. I looked around to see if Ty was there already. I spotted him behind the Crossland bench, on the top bleacher. I went up and sat next to him.

"What's up?" I said.

"Shit! Your ass is going to be late for your own funeral," he said.

"They wouldn't let me get out of there," I replied.

The one-minute horn sounded to inform both teams there was one minute until game time. Both teams went to their benches for last-minute instructions.

"Have you heard anything about Westlake?" I asked Ty.

"No. All I know is they're from Charles County," he replied.

They had pretty good size for a high school team. Their center looked a good 6'7". Tracy walked in as both teams' starting lineups took the floor. She sat down a couple of rows in front of us. She looked good. I wanted to say hello or something, but I didn't.

The referee threw the ball in the air for the jump ball. Crossland won the opening tap. Crossland's point guard brought the ball over half court. He fired a pass to Johnny, standing wide open in the corner. He shot it. SWISH! It hit nothing but net.

"That's the way you start the game, baby!" I yelled.

Crossland set up in their full-court press. It was a 2-2-1. Westlake threw the ball inbounds and two Crossland players trapped him in the corner. He threw it to a man he thought was open. Johnny stepped in front of the pass and stole it. He pulled up at the top of the key behind the three-point line. SWISH! He was on fire early.

"That's what I'm talking about right there," I said.

"They need to find that lil nigga. He's hot. Y'all gotta hot man!" Ty yelled.

Crossland set back up in their full-court press. Everyone was matched up with a man, denying hard. Crossland was working, trying to get a five-second count. Westlake got the ball inbounds barely. The Westlake player who caught the ball was standing almost in the same spot he was before. The second Crossland defender was rotating to trap him. He tried to get rid of the ball quickly but threw it out of bounds. Crossland forced another turnover.

Crossland took the ball out on the side. The point guard caught the ball in the backcourt and set up the play. He threw it to the shooting guard standing on the left side of the floor. The power forward came up to set a pick for him. As the shooting guard ran off the pick, the power forward went toward the basket. The shooting guard lobbed a pass toward the rim. All of a sudden the center came out of nowhere and caught the alley-oop and dunked it with two hands. The crowd started to go wild.

The opposing team's coach called timeout to stop Crossland's momentum.

"These boys came ready to play tonight," I said.

"You ain't lying," Ty replied.

Tracy stood up and applauded Crossland's 8-0 lead to start the game. I couldn't help but stare at her. She looked so good. She had on a pair of blue jeans, a black turtleneck sweater, her leather coat, and her black boots. Her hair and nails were done, like always. She was radiant. Nothing she had on was extravagant but she looked enticing.

"Why don't you go and talk to her?" Ty commented.

He noticed me staring at her.

"Huh? What are you talking about? For what?" I asked.

"Nigga, everybody in the gym sees your ass staring at her. Go talk to her and stop being so damn stubborn," he said.

The horn sounded for both teams to take the floor.

"I'm not being stubborn. I have nothing to say to her. I was just looking at what she had on. That's not a crime, you know."

"No, but not working out your marriage because of your damn ego should be," he said.

"I don't know why you keep thinking I want to work things out with her. If I did I would, pride or not," I said.

"I don't know who you think you're fooling because you're damn sure not fooling me. The only reason your ass hasn't tried to work things out is because of your damn pride. This shit is stupid anyway. How are you going to get mad at her when it's nothing but your shit coming back on you?" he asked.

"Who are you to talk about someone's shit coming back on them?" I said sarcastically.

"Mine came back on me so that puts me in a pretty good position to talk," he replied.

"That's right, yours did and hers did, so I'm going to ask you again, what position are you in to give me any advice? I could see if you were Jodi telling me this, but you're not. You can't say shit to me," I said.

"You know what? I should've said this a long time ago. Your ass was wrong. The world does not revolve around you. If your ass didn't dog the shit out of Tracy none of this shit would've happened. You're to blame for this shit; not her. I don't care if she cheated. I don't fucking blame her. You're lucky she didn't fuck your father, videotape it, and show it to you, after all the shit your ass put her through. All this shit about you never fucked anyone she knew is a bunch of bullshit. I don't care if you knew 'em or not. Wrong is wrong and your ass is fucking wrong. Here you have a woman that loves you and will do anything for you but you're willing to fuck it up. That's fine but don't point the finger at her. If you're looking for someone to point the finger at, point it at your damn self," he said.

I was stuck. Other parents and fans in the stands were trying to listen in on the side. I was embarrassed.

"Fuck you. You don't know what you're talking about," I said.

"Yeah? That's all you can say, huh? That's because you know I'm right. It doesn't matter. The truth hurts but it's still the truth. You can run from the truth all you want but remember this. No matter how far you run from it or hide from it, it's still the truth. Nothing you do can change the fact that it is, so either you can face it, move on, or continue to run and hide. I had to deal with the truth that I was the reason Jodi left and the reason she isn't coming back. It's time you do the same and put this shit behind you and get your wife back," he said.

I sat there the whole game thinking about what he'd said. I was speechless and had no comment. For some reason I couldn't put one and two together. I was so confused.

Crossland ended up blowing Westlake out, 101-47. Johnny led six Crossland players with twenty-five points. He hit six three-pointers. All of his hard work from the summer had paid off. Mine with my marriage hadn't. I really worked to change and be the man that Tracy deserved but there we were; not together. I needed to get out of the gym. I walked up to Johnny before he went into the locker room.

"Lil' J!" I said to get his attention. He turned around and gave me some dap. "Hey. Good game but I gotta get out of here. I'll call you tomorrow."

"Okay," he replied.

I gave him a hug and left. I needed to be by myself. I needed time to think about everything that was going on and everything Ty had said. I drove around the city, thinking about whether I was to blame for everything. I knew I was to blame for my own cheating but how could I be for hers.

I drove until I had no more gas. I stopped at a gas station and refilled my tank and then drove some more. I couldn't get what Ty had said out of my head.

"You're the reason. YOU are! If you want to point the finger at someone point it at your damn self!"

I replayed his words in my head over and over. I stopped at a liquor store on Florida Avenue. I needed a drink in the worst way. I drove all night until I found myself back at the same place where all of it had started: Crossland.

I walked over to the football field and sat in the bleachers. I hadn't owned up to my responsibilities. My lil' cousin was right. I'd brought this on myself. I needed to feel like I wasn't the only one who did anything wrong. But the fact was that had I never cheated on her she wouldn't have cheated on me.

I wanted my wife back. I missed her. I missed talking to her, holding her, being with her, and making love to her. It was time to put my ego aside and correct the mistake I'd made because of my pride. Even if she didn't want to take me back, I needed to apologize to her for walking out.

I got in the car and went home. I pulled up in front of our house and sat there thinking of what to say. I thought of holding her, caressing her, and making love to her. I thought that could only be just a dream then. I laid my chair back and finished off my fifth of vodka.

❖ ❖ ❖ ❖

The sunlight woke me from my drunken sleep. I'd passed out in the car in front of the house. It was time for me to make my move. The longer I waited, the harder it would be. I got out of the car and knocked on the door. It dawned on me that it was still my house. It had been so long that I forgot for a moment.

I took out my key and opened the door. Tracy was coming down the steps to answer the door. She ran over to me and hugged me. This was easier than I'd thought. I hadn't even said a word yet and she was already in my arms.

"Where have you been?" she asked. She continued before I could answer. "Do you know how worried I've been? I didn't know what happened to you."

She let go of me and walked in the living room. She picked up the phone and started dialing.

"I needed time to myself last night to think."

She cut me off. "Hey, Ty, it's Tracy. He just walked in the door. Okay, I'll tell him. Thanks, Ty. Bye," she said. She hung the phone up and turned and looked at me. "You had all of us worried sick. Don't do that anymore. Okay?"

I ignored the question. "I'm sorry, Tracy."

"Just don't do it again."

"No, I mean, I'm sorry about everything. I'm sorry I walked out on you. I'm sorry I cheated on you. I'm sorry I was such an asshole. I'm sorry for everything. I love you so much. I can't even explain it. I'm not the same without you. You and Lil' J mean the world to me. I don't know what I'd do without either one of you.

"I don't know why I tripped off the fact that it was with Midnight. I knew you cheated. I accepted it and was ready to move on. It shouldn't have mattered who it was with. It was just that night at the club when he approached me, I was embarrassed. Everybody heard that he was with you. My mind just got away from me. I knew I was wrong for leaving but I just kept letting my pride and ego get in the way of my heart. You're all I want. I want to come back home. Do you forgive me?"

"Only on one condition! You bring your fine ass over here and give me a kiss, then take me upstairs and make love to me," she said.

"I think I can handle that," I replied as I walked over to her, ready for what I was missing.

"I love you, Terry. I always will," she purred.

Tyrelle
AS THE WALLS START COMING DOWN

I was finally starting to get used to the idea of being a father. The first time I'd gone with April to the doctor's and heard the baby's heart beat, I'd felt a chill. I was excited. I could hear my child's heartbeat. It was a feeling that was unexplainable. I hadn't missed a doctor's appointment since. I enjoyed them.

The whole process of having a baby was growing on me. I was looking forward to our doctor appointments. That was why I was extra happy that day. I knew as soon as we got in the exam room he was going to listen to the baby's heartbeat. I couldn't wait. Plus, that day he was doing a sonogram to measure the baby. I'd missed the first sonogram so this was going to be special.

Hopefully, he'd be able to tell if it was a boy or a girl. I wasn't tripping because I knew I was having a lil' man. My mother swore up and down it was going to be a girl because of all the hell I'd put women through. God's way of giving me my own medicine, I guess.

I called April to see how she was doing.

"Hey," I said once she answered the phone.

"Hey."

"Have you been drinking your water, like the doctor said?" I asked.

"Yes, Ty, for the thirteenth time," she replied.

"I'm just checking. I want to make sure nothing goes wrong. You've already gotten to see the baby. I haven't," I said.

"I know. That's why I'm being patient with you. Other than that I would've told your ass off by now," she said.

"You trying to go to a movie after the appointment?" I asked.

"That's fine but I have something I've been meaning to talk to you about." She paused. "I just want to know. What's going on with us?"

"What do you mean?" I asked to get a better idea. I didn't want to jump to any conclusions.

"Where are we going? At times I think we're moving towards starting a relationship and other times I don't. I'm unsure now. I don't know where we stand or where you want things to go," she said.

"To be honest with you, I've never really thought about it. I've just enjoyed spending time together and being with you."

"Well, I'd like for us to have a relationship. I want to be with you, but I understand your situation with Jodi and all. I know you're still kinda trying to get over her and so forth, so I'm not trying to rush you. I don't wanna be some substitute for her. If we're going to be together, I want it to be because you want to be with me. If that's not possible, I'm content with us being friends," she said.

It felt like I was losing her and I didn't even know why.

"April, I'm not going to bullshit you. At first, I did miss Jodi. I couldn't help that. We were together for four years. But it's really not like that now. I want to see how far things between us can go and no, not just for the baby either. I want us to take our time though. I'm tired of rushing. If we do things right, we'll have the rest of our lives," I said.

"I can respect that. I just had to see what direction we were going. Whether you were going to be my man or just my baby's daddy," she said.

"I'm still your baby's daddy," I said.

We both started to laugh.

"What time do you want me to pick you up?" I asked her, changing the subject.

"My appointment's at ten forty-five so you might as well come now," she said.

I glanced over at the clock to see what time it was. It was 9:30 a.m. already. "Okay, I'll be there in about twenty minutes. Be ready please. I'm not trying to wait for you all day," I said.

"Excuse me? I *know* you didn't just say that."

We both said our goodbyes and got ready. I grabbed my sweatpants and threw on a T-shirt. There wasn't any need to get dressed up for the appointment. I wasn't trying to meet anybody. I grabbed my keys and headed out the door.

The doctor's office was off Branch Avenue by Iverson Mall. We made it there at 10:15 a.m. Not bad for someone who was always late. April went upstairs and checked in while I parked the car.

"I can't believe I'm so nervous," I said.

"Why?"

"I'm about to see my baby. My baby. It's something that I can't explain," I said.

"I understand. That's how I felt right before my first sonogram," she replied.

I looked over to another woman in the lobby waiting as well. She looked like she was about to burst.

"Excuse me, miss! How many months are you?" I asked.

I wanted to know when April would look like that.

"I'm thirty-seven weeks," she replied.

"Not that much longer," I said.

"Nope! I wish he'd hurry up and come on but he'll probably come late," she said.

"Oh, so you already know what you're having?" I asked.

"Yeah. It's a little boy," she said.

I rubbed April's stomach. "This better be a lil' man, too."

"You're so silly," April said.

"What? It's got to be a lil' boy," I said.

"Ms. Thompson," the nurse opened the door and said.

The woman I was just talking to got up and went to the back for her appointment.

"I can't wait until you're that big," I said.

"Why? Are you going to leave me or something?" April questioned.

"Oh no, baby, it's going to take a lot more than that for me to leave you," I said.

She started to blush.

I continued, "Now, if you don't lose the weight after you have the baby, that's another story."

She hit me on my arm.

"Whateva! You better not even think about leaving me. I don't care how big I am," she said.

"I'm not going anywhere, baby. Let Daddy rub on that beer belly," I said.

"Shut up, boy! You have some serious problems!" She paused. "Who would've thought I'd be pregnant. I couldn't even see myself settling down a year ago. Now here I am, about to be a mother," she said.

I understood exactly what she meant. My life had gone in another direction than I'd thought it would have. The whole thing was mind-boggling. There I was about to be someone's father. I could see myself, taking my son to the park or going to one of his football games or, if the Lord blessed us with a baby girl, sitting in the front row at one of her dance recitals or watching her playing with her dolls and jumping rope. I couldn't wait.

"Ms. Harris, have you used the bathroom yet?" the medical assistant asked.

"No," April replied.

She got up and went to the back to use the bathroom. She opened the door and told me to come on once she was finished. I followed her to the exam room.

"Take your clothes off and put on the gown," the medical technician said.

April started to undress. I turned away.

"What's wrong with you? You don't have to turn away. You've seen me naked before."

"I know. I was checking out these baby charts," I replied.

I didn't know why I lied. I didn't know why I felt uncomfortable looking at her undress. That was the main reason why we hadn't had sex yet. I didn't feel ready and it felt weird. She hadn't been pushing the issue so I hadn't had the pressure to rush.

April put on the gown and I helped her get on the table. The doctor had perfect timing. He walked in as I was going back to my seat.

"How are we doing today, Ms. Harris?" he asked.

"I'm fine," she replied.

He pulled the sonogram machine close to the exam table. I scooted up so I could get a better look. April lay flat on her back.

"Now this is going to be cold," he said.

He squirted some gel around her stomach. I looked at the black screen. There were these white flashes on it. I had no idea of what I was looking at. All I knew was that somewhere on the screen was my baby and I couldn't believe it. I sat in silence while he took pictures and measured the baby.

"There's the baby's heartbeat," he said.

I could see it. Its little heart rapidly pumping. A tear started to form up in my eye.

"Let's see if we can tell what you're having," he said.

He searched and searched for an angle that would indicate what we were having. The baby didn't want to be cooperative. A part of me was disappointed. I really wanted to know what we were having. He checked one more time and, sure enough, the baby was spread eagle.

"Do you see that right there?" he asked, pointing at the screen.

I couldn't tell what that was.

He continued, "Congratulations. The two of you will be having a baby boy."

"Are you sure?" I asked to double-check.

He printed out the picture for us.

"See this right here. This is his penis. If it was a girl, there wouldn't be anything right here," he said.

I wanted to jump up and down. I was having a boy. I knew it. The doctor wiped the gel off April's stomach.

"You can get dressed and come in the office," he said.

He grabbed April's medical chart, the pictures, and walked out.

"Did you hear that? It's a boy," I said.

"I heard him," she said.

She got up and put her clothes on. We walked out of the exam room and went into the doctor's office.

"Come on in and sit down."

He paused. "It seems as if we made a mistake with your due date. You're further along than what we first projected. The baby's too developed to be twenty-four weeks. You're actually twenty-nine weeks, which puts your due date at February 17th instead of March 31st," he said.

"What?" I blurted out.

As he continued to explain the mix-up, I kept thinking that this wasn't my baby. I wasn't a doctor or anything but that would put us having sex in late May, early June. I wanted to break down in tears. I went from finding out that I was having a baby boy to finding out the baby wasn't mine at all. I fought it off. I didn't want the doctor in our business.

I cut the doctor off. "Are you sure she's that far along? I mean, isn't it possible that the baby's just big?"

I didn't know what I was talking about but I wanted the baby to be mine so badly, I was desperate.

"Yes, it's possible that he's big but not that developed. The date that I've given her now is correct. There's no doubt in my mind medically about that," he said.

I didn't know what to do or say. I couldn't believe I'd just lost my child that fast. What was I going to lose next? I needed some air.

"I'll be downstairs. I need some air. This caught me by surprise," I said.

"Well, I'm pretty much done. I just need you to come every two weeks now instead of once a month," he said.

We walked out of his office and back to the lobby. April stopped at the counter to make her next appointment. I didn't stop. I needed to get out of that office and fast. I went straight to the elevator and outside.

I couldn't believe my ears. I'd lost my girl because I'd gotten April pregnant. I'd accepted responsibility for getting her pregnant and was ready to take on the task of being a father. Then I lost my son the day I found out that I was having a boy. Why was the Lord punishing me?

I got in the car and laid my head on the steering wheel. April got in, I started the car up, and put it in reverse. April stopped me.

"I'm sorry, Ty. I know how you must be feeling right now. I didn't know. When I first found out I was pregnant I asked him around what day the baby was conceived and that was around the same time we were together. That's why I thought the baby was yours. Had I had the correct date from jump... I'm sorry, Ty."

"Well, we've already established that," I snapped at her.

"Why are you mad at me? I didn't know."

"My life was fine until you came along with this *I'm pregnant* shit! Now Jodi doesn't want anything to do with me because she knows I cheated and I don't even have a son."

"I knew you still wanted to be with her. I knew it! You can try to blame me all you want but any woman would've done what I did. I didn't know! I thought the baby was yours. How was I supposed to know the doctor had the wrong date?"

"I don't even care anymore! Move your hand so I can take your ass home," I said.

"I thought we were going to a movie. So, what? Now that you're not the father, you don't want to be with me?" she asked. I just looked at her. "You think you're the one hurting? I don't know who his father is now. You're the closest thing that he'll ever have to a father," she said.

"Yeah, well, I'm not, so go find someone else to play *daddy* for you!" I shot back at her.

Tears started coming down her face. "Fuck you, Ty. I don't know what hurts more. The fact that you were only with me because I'm pregnant or that I'm some replacement for Jodi. But guess what, I won't be either one," she said.

She opened the door and got out. I got out the car to catch up with her.

"Come on, April! Get in the car! I'm sorry. I didn't mean to snap at you. Come on, please!" I pleaded.

She kept walking. I realized I'd left my keys in the car. I ran to the car to get them. She was halfway up the street. For a pregnant woman she was moving fast. I jumped in the car to catch up with her. She was standing at the bus stop waiting. I pulled up across the street and parked as the bus pulled up. She got on and the bus pulled off while I was running towards it.

"Damn it!" I yelled.

I'd really handled that well. I shouldn't have lashed out at her. I drove to her house and waited. I lay back and listened to the radio, waiting for her to come home. I saw her walking up the street towards her house. I got out the car and walked towards her.

"April, I'm sorry. I didn't mean to yell at you," I said.

She kept walking, ignoring me.

"April, please stop," I said, grabbing her arm.

"Get the fuck off me! You've said enough!"

She jerked her arm away.

"April, please," I pleaded.

"Fine, just don't touch me. You have five minutes," she said.

I took a deep breath. Getting her to stop was a task all by itself.

"April, I didn't mean to take it out on you. I'm sorry for that."

She cut me off. "I'm not really even trippin' off that right now. I'm pissed at the fact that you lied to me. I asked you earlier if I was a replacement for Jodi and you said no. You could've told me the truth. We're all adults here," she said.

"I didn't lie to you. You're not a replacement for Jodi. I'm with you because I want to be with you. Not because of the baby and not because of Jodi. You can't ever replace Jodi; just like she can't ever replace you. I was upset and needed to vent. When the doctor said the baby wasn't mine, I felt like I kept losing everything that I loved. I lost Jodi; now my son. What was I going to lose next?"

I fought back the tears.

"You haven't lost me or your son. I told you, you're the closest thing he'll ever have to a father. As far as I'm concerned, you are his father. It's up to you to decide whether you want to be or not," she said.

I looked around and thought about what she'd said. Did she really feel that way and for how long? Would she throw it in my face that I wasn't his father whenever we got into an argument?

"Can we go into the house and talk about this?" I asked.

We walked towards the house while I continued to think. I loved that little boy. I knew that much. I couldn't just turn it off like a light switch. I turned and looked at April.

"I'm not going anywhere. I want to be with you and nothing has changed that. As far as my son..."

She cut me off again. "Your son?"

"Yes, my son. He started out that way and he's going to stay that way. That is my son. I don't want you throwing that shit in my face though. I don't want us to get in an argument or something and you start saying that bullshit. *'That's not your son'* or *'You're not his father.'*"

"I won't. That's a promise. So, what are you going to tell your family?" she asked.

"I'm not telling them anything. Nothing's changed; that's my son."

"That's fine by me but I don't want you to run out on him if we break up or something. You say he's your son, then he should stay that way; regardless of whether we're together or not," she said.

"I told you, I'm not going anywhere. I'm always going to be there for him and you; whether we're together or not," I said.

I meant it, too. I'd made my decision and I was going to stand by it.

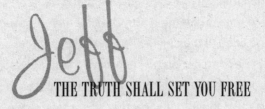

Jeff
THE TRUTH SHALL SET YOU FREE

"You and Ty need to cut this shit out," Chelle said.

"I have no words for him," I said.

"That's your cousin. Y'all have been tight since birth. He's a grown man and if he wants to be with April, then you should respect that and stand behind him. This has gone on long enough. I should've put a stop to it a long time ago. It's been almost three months now. He and Jodi aren't going to get back together. He's going to be with April. There's nothing that you or I can do to change that," she said.

"I just don't see what he sees in her. She's nothing like Jodi," I said.

"Of course she's not; they're two different people. This is childish. It really is. I didn't have any right judging her without even knowing her and neither did you. We both need to apologize to Ty and move past this," she said.

"I'm not apologizing to him. For what, speaking my mind? Since when did that become a crime? I don't like her ass. I think she's scandalous. Plus, the only reason he's with her is because she's pregnant."

"That might be true but he is with her. As far as her being scandalous, how would you know? You don't even know her. Let's at least get to know her before we judge her."

"I don't wanna know her ass. She knew what she was doing when she fucked him. She knew exactly what she was doing!"

"Now you're not making any sense. How the hell could she know that she was going to get pregnant, unless they didn't use any protection and, if that was the case, how can you blame her? Ty's the one who should've been like, *'Naw, boo, let me get a rubber,'* or something. And let's not forget the fact that he did have a girl. None of this would've even happened if he was faithful like he should've been. You can't put the blame all on her. He needs to shoulder some of it, too," she said.

I changed the subject before we ended up arguing.

"So what time are you meeting with the caterer?" I asked.

"Don't try and change the subject. You need to call your cousin. But to answer your question, I need to get out of here now. I'm supposed to be there by ten," she said. "Don't forget we have to meet with Rev. Jackson at two today."

I was hoping she'd forget but knew that was a fat chance. I really wasn't trying to play 20/20 with some preacher. I was sure I wanted to get married and that should've been that.

"Why do we have to see him again?" I asked.

"You already know why, so don't even try to act dumb. Please don't be late, Jeff."

"I don't see why we can't just go to Upper Marlboro before a judge and get married. We can still have the reception, if you want to," I said.

"Yeah, you and some other bitch can do that because I won't be marrying you like that," she said sternly.

"Fine! I'll be there but I'm telling you now, I'm not going to be going through a rack of questions," I said.

"You're going to go through whatever he puts you through. Now I'm serious, have your ass there before two o'clock, Jeff," she said again.

"I heard you the first two times, woman. You just make sure you heard me. I'm not going through a rack of questions," I said.

"I'm not thinking about you," she said. She gave me a kiss goodbye. "I'll talk to you later."

She walked out the bedroom. I still had a good five hours until I had to be at the church so I decided to go back to bed. My body could use the extra rest.

I woke up from my nap and went to use the bathroom. I got back in the bed. I was still tired. I rolled over to set my alarm clock to wake me up at 1:00 p.m. so I'd have enough time to get ready. It was too late. It was already 1:17 p.m.

"Shit!" I shouted.

I jumped up and went to wash up. I didn't have time to take a shower. The church was a good fifteen minutes from my house. I washed up and rushed and got dressed. I made it out of the house at 1:40 p.m.

I flew there. I made it there before 2 p.m. luckily. I was glad we didn't live that far away. I walked in the church and Chelle was sitting in the lobby waiting for me.

"You're late!" she said.

I looked at my watch. It was only 2:01 p.m.

"You've got to be kidding me. I'm a minute late. Come on, give a nigga a break," I said.

"Watch your mouth. I was just playing. Our appointment isn't until two-fifteen anyway," she said.

"I hope, for your sake, you're just playing," I said.

"No, I'm serious. You're either right on time or late. How could I go wrong by telling you two? Either you'd be here at two or around two-ten. Either way you'd be early," she said.

I wanted to smack her ass. Having me rushing to get there thinking I'd be late and all that time I was early. I had to give it to her. She had my number. I couldn't help but laugh. I wished I'd gotten there early so she would've been wrong.

"Sister Davis, you can come on back now," the reverend came out and said.

He had on a pair of blue jeans and a Redskins sweatshirt. His attire caught me off guard. I thought he would at least have on a suit or something. He reached his hand out to shake mine.

"How are you doing there, Brother Jeff? It's finally nice to meet you. We haven't been able to see you in service on Sundays yet but we just ask the Lord to bless us with your presence one of these days," he said.

I became defensive.

"I know. I'm sorry, reverend, but I work late on weekends and I sleep in the mornings."

He sat down in his chair and got comfortable. "So what line of work are you in?"

"I'm a part owner of LIPHE Entertainment. Currently, we have two nightclubs open and we're looking to open another one in either Baltimore or Philly. We also have been thinking about starting a record label and a clothing line but that's still in the developmental stages right now," I said.

"It sounds like you're doing quite well for yourself. That's always good to know. Your mind must be thinking all kinds of thoughts right now. First, let me tell you that I'm not here to ask you a bunch of questions or question your love for Michelle. I use this time to get to know the two of you better and make sure you have a plan for your life together," he said.

I felt a little at ease, now that I knew his intentions, but I was still a little skeptical.

"Let's see here. What's your full name, Jeff?" he asked.

"Jeffery Long," I replied.

"No middle name?" he questioned.

"No," I answered.

He jotted it down on his notepad.

"Okay, Michelle, I just need your middle name," he said.

"It's Renee," she replied.

"All righty now, who's going to be the best man and maid of honor?" he asked.

"Jodi Freeman and Terry Shaw," Chelle said.

"I'm sorry, reverend, but there's a change on the best man. It was going to be both Tyrelle Lewis and Terry Shaw but Tyrelle will handle all the best man duties," I said.

Chelle looked at me and smiled. I read her lips as she said, "Thank you," without speaking. She was right. I had to put aside my pride. Ty and I had been through a lot worse things than this. He was the man I wanted standing next to me on the most important day of my life. It wouldn't be a real wedding without him; at least not one for me.

"Okay, now, I just want to talk to the two of you about this marriage and the union the two of you will be making. I do this because of the high divorce rate we have nowadays. Marriage is supposed to be a lifelong union between a man and a woman; not as long as the two of us can be together, then get a divorce. The Bible doesn't recognize divorce so I talk to my couples now to make sure they understand how to prevent a divorce.

"I know there's no way you can tell me now that when problems arise you'll do whatever it takes to work things out until death do you part. A lot of times you find that the couple gets married and one of them didn't want to in the first place, so they use the first sign of trouble as an early exit. They did it because they were pregnant or got someone pregnant or, if they've been together for a long time, they were pressured by the other person in the relationship to get married or by family or peers. Whatever the case may be, you have too many couples out here married and they shouldn't be because they weren't ready in the beginning for that type of commitment and figured they'd get through it somehow and it wouldn't be that bad. I'm not saying that's the case between the two of you but, if it is, let's talk about it first so we can make sure it's the right decision for the both of you," he said.

"No, that's not the case with us. I want to marry her. I'm ready to spend the rest of my life with her," I said.

"And there's nothing more in this world that I want than to be his bride," Chelle added. She paused. "I understand what you mean though, Rev. Jackson. There was a point in time last year or so when I wanted him to propose to me so badly. I felt like our relationship was at a standstill. I wanted more. I needed a stronger commitment. But then, as time went by, I had to rethink my train of thought. I didn't want to pressure him into proposing to me. He would've only been doing so to please me and not because he wanted to."

I was shocked, mainly because I'd never known that. I didn't even remember her bringing up marriage back then. Maybe she'd said something about it in general, but nothing pushing me to propose to her or her wanting to get married.

"That's interesting, Michelle. Do you still feel like you need to get married because of the timetable or because you're getting *older* and you're looking at your own clock?" Reverend Jackson asked.

"Oh, no! I didn't want to pressure him into marriage. I wanted him to propose to me whenever he was ready. There's no question in my mind who I want to spend the rest of my life with. I want to grow old with him. He just had to know who he wanted to be with. Once he proposed to me, I felt like I was the happiest woman in the world," she said.

"Well, it sounds like to me that the two of you are going to be all right. I just want you to remember one thing though. Times are going to get rough. There are going to be times when you're not going to know whether you're going up or down. But trust in one another to work through it and ask the Lord to show you the way," he said. He paused. "I also counsel a lot of couples and I find that the biggest reason a lot of them are having problems is because of lies. Please do not lie to one another. No matter how big the situation is or how small, be honest with one another. Usually when we do lie, the lie always seems to come back and haunt us. So, if there's anything that you take from this conversation today, please let it be this. Secrets ruin marriages. An open and honest marriage usually will turn into a long lasting one," he said.

"Thank you, Reverend. I must say it's been a pleasure talking with you today," I said.

"I just hope I've been of some help today in any way. If there's nothing else you'd like to discuss, I wish the two of you well and I'll see you next month. Make sure you call my secretary to schedule the rehearsal some time next week. It needs to be at least a week before the wedding," he said.

Chelle wrote that down in the to-do list section of her planner.

"I'll make sure I do, Rev. Jackson."

He stood up to shake my hand.

"It was finally nice meeting you, Jeffery. We'd love it if you could bless us with your presence one Sunday morning," he said.

"I will, Reverend. I'll make sure of it."

I shook his hand and headed to my car.

❖ ❖ ❖ ❖

I thought about what he'd said during the car ride home. *"Always be honest." "Secrets ruin marriages."* Was God speaking to me through him? I wasn't the most spiritual person but I didn't think that was a coincidence. I'd been debating over whether I should tell Chelle about my past for months. I needed to tell her. I had to.

Chelle walked in the house ten minutes after me. I didn't want to waste any time. I needed to tell her then. If I didn't, I'd keep on procrastinating.

"Chelle, come in here for a minute!" I yelled before she could go upstairs.

She walked in the living room. "Yes," she said.

"Come, sit down. We need to talk. I've been thinking about what Rev. Jackson said ever since we left."

She cut me off. "Don't tell me you're not ready to get married? I knew his talk was some sort of sign from God."

"No, no, it's not that. I just hope you still want to marry me after I say what I have to say," I said.

Her full attention was mine and she sat down, but not too close, turning her body to face me at an angle.

"What is it?" she questioned.

"Chelle, I've cheated on you in the past. When we first met I was messing with someone else and it continued on throughout our relationship," I came out and said.

She looked stunned. "I always knew it but never really knew. There was no way your boys could be the dogs they were and you be a saint," she said. "I just really hoped differently." She paused. "How many girls or, should I say, times are we talking about here?"

"You don't want to know," I said.

I didn't know why I'd said that. That just intensified it. Now she had to know.

"I wouldn't have asked if I didn't want to know," she said and then stood up. "So how many girls have you been with while you were with me?"

"Honestly, I don't know. I stopped counting after five."

She put her hands over her face and froze. I started to think it wasn't such a good idea. I could picture Terry and Ty telling me how dumb I was for saying something.

"When was the last time?" she asked, moving her hands and slowly sitting down again.

"A little over a year ago. It was when I took that business trip to Atlanta," I said.

"So you're telling me that you going down there for business was all a lie?" she asked.

"No. We actually had business in Atlanta. We were looking for possible sites to open a club. That is the truth," I answered.

"Is this what our marriage is going to be like if we get married, me wondering if you're cheating on me when you're not around or with your boys?"

"No, baby, it's not. Before I even proposed, I thought about all this. I was scared to tell you then, but now I feel like I must. A long time ago, I sat back and thought that there was no need to cheat. You do everything and more than any other woman could do. You're all I want. You're all I'm interested in. You're the woman I want and if we do get married, you won't ever have to worry about me cheating," I said.

She sat there thinking. "I'm only going to say this once. I'm not going to go through this again. I'm not going to have this talk again five years from now. I'm not going to go through any of that shit that Tracy did with Terry. I'm glad you told me now but, at the same time, I'm pissed that you cheated. You know how I feel about that whole thing. If you feel unsure about whether you're going to do it again, then we need to call it quits now and save ourselves the heartache later. Because regardless of what Rev. Jackson said about divorce, if you cheat on me ever again—I don't care if you just smell her panties—I'm gone. I'm not going to deal with that. I won't deal with it."

"There's nothing to think about. I sat down and thought about all this the day before I proposed. I don't want to be like my uncles; running around cheating on my wife. I want to be bigger than that. I want to set an example for my child, if we ever have one. I only want to be with you and only you," I said.

She sighed and leaned back and looked at me.

"So does that mean you forgive me?" I asked.

"Yes, I forgive you. But don't confuse forgive for forget. I mean it, Jeff. I'm gone if you do it again," she reminded me.

There was no need for her to remind me because I was going to stick to my word like I had been. I felt like I didn't have the world on my back anymore. A lot of the men in my family had cheated on their wives. It was time that someone broke the mold. Why not me?

Tyrelle
THE BIRTH OF MY HAPPINESS

"April's starting to lunch because we haven't had sex yet. She hasn't accused me of cheating or anything just yet but I know she is thinking it," I told Terry.

"Well ...are you?" he asked.

"No!" I replied.

"Come on now, you must admit, it's not like you to go so long without any pussy. And y'all practically live together, too. I can see why she thinks you're cheating. I can't even see how you're doing it. When was the last time you got some, with Jodi? My dick would've fallen off by now. I can't go longer than two weeks and I'm running, looking for Tracy," he said.

"On the real, I don't get in the mood like that. I don't know why. It's like something's wrong with me or something. I don't know what it is," I said.

"I don't know what to tell you. I don't have those types of problems. I always want some. I wish she'd hurry up and hit menopause so she'll stop coming on her period. That shit be blowing me," he said, laughing.

I started to crack up, laughing at his ass.

"How's the baby?" he asked.

"Oh, everything's straight. I've been buying clothes for lil' man like shit. It's still unbelievable. I'm having a lil youngin," I said.

"She's due in March, right? You've only got a good month or so, so your ass better get ready," he said.

"Young, if I tell you something, you've gotta keep the shit between us. I mean, don't tell nobody," I said sternly.

"Okay, what?" he replied.

"She's due on Feb. 17th; not March 31st," I told him.

"Okay so... What does that mean?" he asked.

I'd forgotten how slow he could be sometimes.

"It means that the baby isn't mine," I said.

"What? Are you serious?" he asked.

"I'm dead serious. When we went to the doctor's the last time he did a sonogram and measured the baby. That's when he realized they'd made a mistake on her date. She's further along," I said.

"Damn, so what you going to do?" he asked.

"I'm not going to do anything. I'm still carrying on like nothing's changed. I'm too attached to that lil' boy now. I can't just turn that shit off," I said.

"I know what you mean. I remember way back when Ebony called me and told me she was pregnant. I just assumed the baby was mine. We both did. When I found out she wasn't mine, I was all fucked up. I still swing past there every now and then to check up on the little girl and all. I guess a part of me still looks at her as my lil' girl," he said.

I had forgotten all about that.

He continued, "So how are y'all going to do this? I mean, is she not going to tell the real father about the baby or is the baby just going to have two?"

"She doesn't even know who the father is so we're going to leave things like they are. Nobody knows that I'm not the baby's biological father and we're going to keep it that way. That means what I told you stays with you. Don't tell anybody, including Jeff or Tracy," I said.

"I said fine. I don't know why you want to keep things a secret, but fine. You at least need to tell Jeff," he said.

"I am but just not right now. I don't want to add any more fuel to his hatred towards her."

"So what are you going to do about April?" he asked.

"Huh! What do you mean?" I asked.

"You said that she thought you were cheating because y'all ain't fuckin'. What are you going to do?" he said.

I'd forgotten I'd even brought that up.

"Oh, I don't know. That's why I called you for some help with this one," I said.

"I don't know what to tell you. Why haven't you tried to get any? Is it because you think you're going to hurt the baby?" he questioned.

"No, it's not that. I know my dick isn't that big," I replied.

"Her stomach. That's it, huh?" he asked.

"No. I told you, I don't know what it is," I said, aggravated.

"Well, I don't know what to tell you. I can't help you if I don't know what the problem is," he said.

"Shit, if I knew the problem, then I probably wouldn't need help," I replied.

"Well, let me know what you think of it. I gotta get ready to get out of here so I'll talk to you later," he said.

I lay back on my bed thinking about the situation at hand. I'd never had a problem wanting sex before but it was like I didn't have the appetite I'd once had. I didn't have the desire anymore.

"I'll take care of it tonight," I said.

❖ ❖ ❖ ❖

The sound of my doorbell woke me up from my nap. I went downstairs to see who it was. It was April. I needed to get her ass a key.

"Hey! You're not ready yet," she commented.

"Ready for what?" I asked.

"We were supposed to go out to dinner, then the movies tonight," she said.

"Oh shit! I'm sorry, baby. It totally slipped my mind. Give me a minute to get ready. I'll go take a quick shower and then we can be on our way," I said.

She agreed. I ran upstairs and jumped in the shower. As I washed my body, the bathroom light shut off. I opened the shower curtain and saw April taking her clothes off. I hurried and rinsed the soap off my body. She got in the shower with me.

"Now you just told me to hurry up and you want to start stuff," I said.

"I'm not starting anything, yet. I just decided to have my dinner now," she said.

She began massaging my back. She worked her hands down to my dick and caressed it while kissing my chest. Everything felt good. I had the desire then. Her tongue gently made its way down my chest to replace her hand. I leaned back as the combination of the water and her tongue on my body started to overwhelm me.

What the hell was I thinking, holding back on her? I wanted her. I was tired of the foreplay. I positioned her leg up on the tub so I could place myself inside of her. She felt so good. I became excited prematurely. We'd only been at it five minutes and I felt like I was on the verge of coming. I tried to think of something that would take my mind off the excitement. I couldn't. The feeling was uncontrollable. There was no stopping me.

"I'M CUMMIN'!"

"Wait a minute, baby. I'm almost there," she said.

I couldn't hold back anymore. It was too late. She began to move faster and faster after I'd come. She was determined to get the orgasm that was due to her.

"Okay baby, I'm 'bout to cum. Oh... I'm cummin'! Yes! I'm cummin', baby!" she said.

I felt like I was about to explode as her body moved. She stopped. My body began to shake as I felt a tingle. I put my head up against the wall to regain my composure. She started to wash up. I felt relieved. I turned around and she was rinsing off. I grabbed her and held her while the water ran over both of us. The silence spoke volumes. She was as happy with me as I was with her.

"I have something I want to tell you. Now I don't know if I should but I feel like I must. Promise me that no matter what I say, things won't change between us. Okay?" she said.

"All right," I replied.

I braced myself for what she was about to say.

"Ty, I love you. I always have. Now, I know you might not feel the same way and that's fine. I don't really expect you to but I needed to tell you how I felt. Hopefully, with time, you can grow to feel the same way about me," she said.

I gazed at her, speechless. I wasn't expecting that. I thought she was going to tell me that she knew who the baby's father was or something along those lines. This was a complete shock.

She continued, "Now please don't tell me that you love me because you feel like you have to; since I said it. You won't hurt my feelings if you don't. What will hurt is if you tell me you do and you actually don't. I only want to hear those words come out of your mouth when and if you really do love me."

I leaned over and kissed her, firmly gripping her ass. I wanted to please her. I stopped and turned the shower off. I wasn't trying to struggle by picking her up and ruining the mood with her thinking about the weight she'd gained. I grabbed her hand and guided her into the bedroom.

We started to kiss again passionately. I nibbled on her lip gently while we kissed. We finally made our way to the bed. She lay back on the bed and I kissed on her breasts. I moved my tongue up and down her wet body, bathing her like I was a cat and she my kitten.

Her hands became active, rubbing my back and gripping my ass. I made my way down her body and gently caressed and kissed her stomach on the way. As I put my fingers inside of her, I could feel that she was warm and was getting warmer and wetter. I kissed from her hips to her inner thighs and then moved my tongue in her pussy slowly at first, then deeper to make sure she knew I loved the way she tasted. She started to squeal and moan, moving her hands through my hair. I became hard again. I was ready to get down and dirty. I stopped eating her and placed myself inside her. We moved together like synchronized swimmers.

She finally came after twenty-five minutes and I followed behind her shortly afterwards. We lay on the bed and relaxed. I felt drained and couldn't move.

"Are you nervous?" she asked me.

"About what?" I replied.

"This baby. I'm almost thirty-eight weeks now. I can have this baby any day now."

"How do you figure? You still have a little over two weeks until your due date," I said.

"They say your first born is usually either two weeks early or two weeks late," she said.

"I've never heard that before."

"Ask any woman. They'll tell you," she said.

"We don't even have a name picked out yet. It seems like everything's moving so fast," I said.

"I know but you still haven't answered my question."

"Hell yeah, I'm nervous. I'm probably more scared though. I'm going to be some one's father. All I can picture is the stuff my father used to do and say to me. Now that's going to be me with my son. It's a trip. What if I fuck up? I think about shit like that all the time," I said.

"I know what you're talking about but I think you'll be just fine. The two of you will probably get along just fine. Me, on the other hand, I don't have half as much as you to offer. My mother didn't set a good example for me to follow and I don't want to be like that. I'm scared shitless," she said.

"Don't even worry about that. Your mother set all the example you need. She showed you exactly how you don't want to treat our son and how you do. Your motherly instincts will do the rest for you. All y'all women got that shit. You see it every day. A woman can be out here and can't even take care of herself, then she has a baby and finds a way to succeed for herself and her child. You'll be fine. I keep having this dream that one day his father comes back and he finds out I'm not his real father and starts to hate me," I said.

"That'll never happen because you're his father. You're the one raising him. You're the one who'll be in his life. That's one dream that won't come true; believe me. Plus, I don't even know who his father is so how could he find out and come back. I was out there back then, trying to find love in all the wrong places," she said.

"Do you think I should still tell him when he gets older? So he'll know the truth. I don't want to lie to him. I want my son to always be honest with me and how can I expect him to be if I'm not with him," I said.

"Why are you asking me? It sounds like you already have your mind made up," she said.

"I wanted to see if you objected to me telling him when he's old enough to handle it."

"The only thing I object to is you continuously saying you're not his real father. You're his real father. A *real* father is a man that takes care of his child; financially and emotionally," she said.

A part of me needed to hear that. I felt better about the situation.

She continued, "Now I want you to promise me that I won't hear you say that anymore."

"I promise, baby, but you know what I meant by it," I said.

She shot back at me, "I might know what you meant, but that doesn't change the fact that I don't like hearing it. No, your sperm didn't create our baby but *our* love will nurture and raise it."

"So what are we going to do about a name? Don't you think we need to start thinking of one?" I asked.

"Well, what do you want to name him?" she replied.

"I don't know. That's why I asked you. What about Derek or James?"

"Naw, I don't like those. They're too plain. How about Harold or Malik?"

"Harold's okay but it sounds like a white boy's name. I don't like Malik. Every time I hear that name I think about the movie *Higher Learning* when the white boy says, '*Fuckin' Malick.*' That shit just makes me laugh," I said.

"You're a fool! I like Harold; it sounds professional. There are a lot of black men named Harold," she said in her defense.

"Well, I don't like it for my son. How about Shawn or D'Shawn, RaShawn, you know, something like that?" I asked.

"RaShawn is cute but that sounds more like a girl's name to me. *Come here, Ray-Ray!*" she said funny, shaking her head. She continued, "Let's just make his name like yours but instead of Tyrelle, Terrell. Yeah, I like that," she said.

"I don't. I want him to have his own identity."

"I see what you're saying but, in this case, he will. His name's going to be Terrell," she replied.

"I still don't like it. People will be able to put one and two together."

"Fine, you think of another name then," she said.

"I'm hungry. Are you?" I asked.

"Kinda," she replied.

"How 'bout this? How 'bout we finish this over dinner?" I asked.

"How 'bout we finish something else first?" she said with that determined look in her eye.

I grinned and moved in to kiss her.

❖ ❖ ❖ ❖

I felt April nudging me on my side. She was sitting up, breathing heavily. I glanced at the clock. It was four in the morning.

"What's wrong?" I asked, rubbing my eyes.

"My back's killing me and my stomach keeps cramping. Call the doctor," she said.

I didn't hesitate. I'd programmed my phone with the doctor's office number and his emergency number; just in case something like this happened.

"Dr. Thompson's office. What's the emergency?"

"My girl's having cramping in her stomach and back," I said.

"What's her name? How many weeks is she and how far apart are the contractions?" she asked.

"Her name is April and she isn't contracting; just cramping," I replied.

"The cramps she's feeling most likely are contractions. How frequent are they coming?" she asked.

"Oh, I'm sorry!" I turned and looked at April.

"How far apart is the pain?" I asked.

"Every ten minutes," she replied.

"They're every ten minutes," I told the woman on the phone.

"Hold on for a minute while I contact the doctor. What's your name, sir?"

"Tyrelle Harris," I replied.

I sat there and held April's hand, timing the contractions to be certain of the time.

"Hello, Mr. Harris, how are you doing? What seems to be the problem?" Dr. Thompson asked.

"Well, April's having contractions," I replied.

"How far apart are they?" he asked.

"She said every ten minutes but I'm timing them now to make sure," I said.

"Has she had any spotting or bleeding?" he asked.

April said she didn't.

"No," I replied.

"Has her water broken?"

"Your water hasn't broken, has it?"

She shook her head no.

"No."

"Okay, well, you need to take her to the hospital so she can get monitored," he said.

"Okay."

I hung up the phone.

"Come on, we have to go to the hospital," I said.

"Why? What did the doctor say?" she asked.

"He said that I need to take you to the hospital so you can get monitored. Now let's get you dressed so we can go," I said.

I picked up a pair of my sweatpants from off the floor.

"Here, put these on." I helped her get dressed and then threw a sweatsuit on myself.

I helped her down the stairs and into the car. Her contractions were coming harder and faster. She was contracting every five minutes. I was scared shitless. I wanted to comfort her but nothing I did would take the pain away. I held her hand, hoping it would comfort her in some way.

I pulled up to the emergency entrance to Columbia Hospital for Women off L Street in Northwest D.C. It had taken us a good twenty minutes to get there. I ran inside and up to the first nurse I spotted.

"My girl's in labor," I said to her.

I didn't know what else to say. She grabbed a wheelchair and followed me to the car. She rolled her into a delivery room and I followed behind them.

"How far apart are the contractions?" the dark-skinned African nurse asked me with her thick accent.

"They're coming every five minutes now," I said.

I sat down next to April as they took her vitals.

"If you could, take off your clothes for me and put on this gown. We need to examine you and see if you've dilated any," she said to April.

The nurse stepped out so April could change. She was in serious pain as another contraction came. We waited until the pain subsided, then finished taking off the rest of her clothes. The contractions lasted about a good forty-five seconds.

Once April got the gown on, I went to get the nurse so she could see exactly what was wrong with April. I didn't have a clue what was going on. This was nothing like on television when they had babies so I knew it wasn't time for her to deliver yet.

The nurse came back in the delivery room a few seconds behind me. She washed her hands, then put on some latex gloves. She lubricated two fingers and stuck them inside of April. April squeezed my hand tight as she was being examined.

"She's already dilated to four centimeters. Who's your doctor?" she asked.

"Dr. Thompson," I replied.

She hooked up a monitor to April's stomach to monitor the baby's heartbeat and her contractions.

"I'll be back in a couple of minutes with some paperwork for you to fill out. Have you already completed your pre-admission forms?"

April nodded her head yes. She gripped my hand tighter as another contraction started to come.

"I need something for the pain! Give me some damn drugs!" April yelled.

"I'm going to call the doctor now," she said.

"The doctor? Why? What's wrong?" I questioned.

"Nothing's wrong. Your wife's about to deliver. Just breathe with her and keep her calm," she said.

About to deliver? Fuck keeping her calm. Who the hell was going to keep me calm? I wasn't ready for this shit. We both weren't. We didn't even have a name for him yet. This shit was happening all too fast.

I called April's mother, then my own to let them know the news.

"Ty, I can't take it any more. I need some drugs. I need something for the pain," she said, tears streaming down her face.

The pain was becoming unbearable to her.

"Okay, I'll get the nurse," I replied.

"No, no, don't leave me. Please, don't leave! I need you with me," she pleaded.

"I'm just going to get the nurse for you so you can get something to help for the pain."

"Please just stay with me," she said.

I stayed, hoping my presence would ease her mind off the pain she was experiencing. Another contraction started. She clamped down and started to breathe.

"I told you I need some damn drugs! Now go get somebody!" she snapped at me.

She was losing it but I couldn't blame her. I tried to walk away but she had too tight a grip on my hand. I waited until the contraction subsided.

"I'll be back, baby. I'm going to get the nurse so she can give you something," I said.

"No, baby, I need you here with me. Please don't leave me," she said.

I didn't know what to do. She was confusing the hell out of me. Luckily for me, Dr. Thompson walked in.

"How's she doing?" he asked.

"She needs some drugs! Well, she wants something for the pain. That's what she has been complaining about for the last ten minutes," I said.

"I think we can take care of that for her. Let's see how far along she is now first, though," he said.

He examined her the same way the nurse had earlier when we'd first gotten there.

He looked at the nurse. "She's at five. I'm going to go ahead and break her water. That will speed things up," he said.

I stood over April and held her hand like I'd been doing.

"What the hell was I thinking, having this baby?" April screamed.

Tears started a continuous stream down her face.

"I can't take it anymore, Ty! I can't do it! It hurts," she said, crying.

"I know, baby. I know. It'll all be over with soon. Just hold on, baby. He's getting you something for the pain now. Just hold on, baby," I said, rubbing her head trying to comfort her.

All the pain April had been experiencing had worn her out. She took naps in between contractions. She said the pain was coming harder. Dr. Thompson walked in the room.

"Okay, the anesthesiologist will be down in a couple of minutes to give you an epidural," he said.

It was about time. She had been asking for something for the pain for nearly two hours.

"Thank God! She said the contractions are coming in harder now," I said.

"Really... Let's check her and see how far she's progressed," Dr. Thompson said.

He examined her again to see how much she'd dilated. I stood in my same position, by April's side, while he examined her. He looked at the nurse.

"We need to prep for delivery. She's at eight now."

"What does that mean?" I asked, concerned.

"The baby's ready for delivery. We need to start pushing him out," he said.

"Will she have enough time to still get the epidural?" I asked.

"I'm sorry but she's too far along for that now. By the time he gets down here, the baby will be already out," he said.

The nurse assisting him prepared everything for delivery. Dr. Thompson scrubbed off and prepared himself as well. I couldn't believe how fast things were moving.

"Y'all have to stop. I have to use the bathroom. Move! I have to shit!" April said.

"That's just the baby getting into position. It's applying pressure that makes you feel like you have to use the bathroom. You're okay," Dr. Thompson said.

The nurse propped April's legs up.

Dr. Thompson continued, "Now, Mrs. Harris, when I count to three, I want you to sit upright and start pushing until I tell you to stop. All right?"

"Okay," she replied.

I got myself ready. I kept telling myself, '*I have to be strong for her. I have to be strong for her!*' I was all the support she had.

"Here we go now. One! Two! Three! And push!"

"Ahhhhhhhhh!!!" she screamed, pushing.

"Now breathe. One! Two! Three!"

"I need to go to the fucking bathroom! I'm going to shit on myself!" April yelled.

I was jive embarrassed for her.

"It's the baby, boo. You're not going to shit on yourself," I whispered to her.

"I should shit on your ass for getting me pregnant!" she snapped at me.

"You're doing just fine, Mrs. Harris. Okay now, One! Two! Three!" Dr. Thompson said.

"AHHHHHHHHH!!!" she screamed.

I could see the top of the baby's head. My son had hair on his head. I could see the hair on my son's head. My excitement began to grow. Dr. Thompson positioned his hands around the baby's head to guide him out.

"Now breathe. One! Two! Three!" April let out a big sigh.

"Baby, we're almost there. I can see his head, baby," I said.

"That's right, Mrs. Harris. One more good push," Dr. Thompson added.

"I don't think I can do it. I'm too tired. I don't think I can do it," she said.

"Baby, we're almost home. You're too strong to stop now. Come on, baby, I'm right here with you," I said, holding her hand.

"Here we go now! One! Two! Three! And push!" Dr. Thompson said.

"AHHHHHHHHHHHH!!!!" she screamed.

The baby's head came all the way. Dr. Thompson guided his shoulders out, trying not to tear April's vaginal wall. I could see my child. I became overwhelmed with happiness. Dr. Thompson cleaned his mouth out and placed some type of ointment in his eyes. The baby started crying as soon as Dr. Thompson finished suctioning his mouth out. Dr. Thompson looked at me.

"Would you like to cut the cord?" he asked.

"I would be honored," I replied.

I cut my son's umbilical cord. April was exhausted. Dr. Thompson handed our son to the nurse assisting him and she took him to the other side of the room. He was so pale he looked white. She weighed and measured him.

"He's six pounds four ounces," the nurse said.

She took out the measuring tape to measure his head and how long he was.

She continued, "He's nineteen inches long."

She wrapped him up and placed him under this bright light. It looked like one of those lights they had in restaurants to keep your French fries warm.

I walked over to April and kissed her on her forehead.

"You did it, baby! You did it," I said.

"No, *we* did it. Can I see my baby?" she asked Dr. Thompson.

He was still stitching her up.

"Of course you can," he said, still working.

The nurse brought April our baby. April started crying as she held him.

"So what are you going to name him?" the nurse asked.

"Khalil Terrell Lewis," April said.

"Lewis? I thought your last name was Harris?" the nurse asked.

"It is. His *father's* last name is Lewis," she replied.

I wanted to burst out in tears. I kissed her and looked her in the eyes.

"I love you," I said.

She became teary-eyed again. "I told you, you don't have to say it."

"I know. You said you wanted me to say it when I meant it. So, April Harris, I love you," I said.

"I love you, too," she replied.

I leaned over and kissed her again.

The night wound down. April laid in her bed sleeping from exhaustion. I couldn't sleep. This was undoubtedly the happiest day of my life. I sat in my chair, staring at my son while he slept in my arms. My body tingled with joy, just knowing I had a son.

"I promise to give you the world and more. I'll always be there for you and your mother. No matter what!"

Terry
SURPRISE! SURPRISE!

"Congratulations, nigga. I'm sorry I haven't been able to get up there yet. How's April doing?" I said.

"She's straight. I'm supposed to go up there later to pick her up," Ty said.

"Already! Damn! When Tracy had Johnny she was there for a good two weeks, I think. Something like that. I know it was for a good lil' minute though," I said.

"Oh, well, it's not like that anymore. Two days, then you're going home on the third. They wouldn't even let me sleep in her room overnight since she had a roommate last night. Nothing was keeping me out of there when Khalil was born though," I said.

"Times are either changing or I'm getting old."

"I think it's both," I said.

"Ha, ha, ha, very funny. So that's lil' man's name, huh? Khalil?"

"Yeah, Khalil Terrell Lewis."

"What? Excuse me? Lewis?" I asked.

"I know, right, but April wanted him to have my last name," he said.

"Damn, dawg. I guess things between y'all are getting pretty serious," I said.

"Pretty much! I really do love her. It's not like when Jodi and I were together either. It's like April and me are more compatible."

"I can dig it. Maybe April was actually the one; you never know. You always hear people saying the Lord works in mysterious ways," I said.

"Yeah, maybe!"

"I'll have to stop past there and see lil' man later on today. Better yet, I'll stop past tomorrow to see my godson. That way April can enjoy her first day out of the hospital without people being all over there in her face," I said.

Ty caught on to the hint I'd given him.

"Correct me if I'm wrong but, uh, I don't remember telling you that you were his godfather?"

"You didn't have to. I already know that I am. I fucking better be! You and Jeff are Lil' J's godfathers," I said, raising my voice.

"Don't get your panties all up in a bunch, nigga. You know you and Jeff are his godfathers," he said.

"That's what I thought. You were about to make a nigga get physical for a second," I said.

"Whatever, you weren't going to do shit!"

"You talk to Jeff lately? How's he taking things?" I asked.

"How's he supposed to be taking it?" he fired back at me.

"You know what I mean. Y'all haven't been on the best of terms lately. I just didn't know how he took it," I said.

"Well, yeah, we've talked. He called a while ago and apologized for the part he played in everything. He said that he was just trying to look out for me and all. I told him that I could understand that and we left it at that so we're jive chill now. But he called up to the hospital to see how the baby was doing and to say "congrats" yesterday. He asked what we needed for him, stuff like that. Other than that, nothing major."

"So I guess you didn't tell him about your newfound love, huh?" I asked.

"Didn't see a need. He's trying, you know, to be understanding of the situation, but I don't want to put too much on him too soon. It's better with time, I think," he said.

"I feel you. What, having a baby make your ass smarter and shit?" I asked, laughing.

Ty seemed more patient and had a better perspective about things. He was definitely handling things differently.

"*Anyways*, so what's going on over on your end? How's the household holding up? Things back to normal yet?"

"It seems like things are normal but something's fishy with Tracy though. I can just tell, young. She isn't acting the same."

"You sure you're not overreacting?"

"I thought about that, but I don't think so. It just seems like she's hiding something," I said.

"What's there left to hide? She's just about told you everything. I think you might be paranoid with this one."

"You might be right on this one, but I'm not sure. I know one thing. I'm not going to accuse her of anything without any proof though."

"I wouldn't worry too much about Tracy. I'd concentrate more on keeping Lil' J's head on his shoulders. With them being the number one team in the area, all this recognition might start to get to him," he said.

"Might start? It already has and him being only fifteen doesn't really help the situation either. When I was in school I didn't really start to dominate on a constant basis until I was in the eleventh grade. He's only in the tenth and he's already the man.

"Coach Franklin's doing all right with him though. He doesn't allow the media attention to get to him since he only allows seniors to talk with the press. So really all he has to worry about is the basketball side of it. You know there were even some pro scouts at one of his games last week. This shit is getting ridiculous. I don't think he knew, but still. My main concern right now is these little fast ass girls."

"I can only imagine," he said.

"They're calling the house left and right. I went and bought him a twelve-pack of condoms and left them on his dresser. I know he's getting some, so I don't want him bringing nothing home."

"Yeah, but you still need to talk to him. Maybe we all do because we've been there. You know, like his first boys' night out, to make it nice and really talk to him about how to handle himself and those fools that are just trying to be part of the spotlight."

"Probably. That sounds cool but, aye, let me get off this phone and clean up a lil' bit. I'll call you tomorrow and let you know what time Tracy and I are coming over," I said.

"Okay, holla."

I hung up the phone and started cleaning. I washed the dishes and cleaned the kitchen. I thought about what I'd told Ty about Tracy hiding something. I searched around the house, looking for any type of clue or evidence. To my luck, I found nothing. Hopefully there was nothing to find.

❖ ❖ ❖ ❖

I sat in the living room wondering if April was up yet that morning. I'd promised Ty we'd swing around there some time later on in the day. I'd forgotten to tell Tracy that. I went upstairs to see what she was doing.

"Baby!" I yelled, trying to find out where she was exactly.

No answer. I went in the bedroom to check; nothing. I went back downstairs to check out back. Sometimes she'd sit outside to think when something was bothering her. Sure enough, there she was. Now I knew something was wrong.

"Hey, baby! What are you doing out here?" I asked.

"Nothing, just thinking," she replied.

"About what? What's wrong?" I asked.

"Nothing. I just haven't been feeling well lately, that's all. I think I'm coming down with the flu or something," she said.

There was no need to invite her to come along with me if she was sick, so I'd keep going over Ty's to see the baby for myself.

"Oh, so what's on your mind?" I asked.

"Nothing specific. I was just thinking in general about life and so forth."

"Oh, well, have you called the doctor?" I asked.

"For what? Why do you say that?" she asked.

"Because you said you think you're coming down with the flu," I said.

"Oh, no, it's not that serious. I took some Advil for my headache and I'm going to go in and lie down for a few. I just need some rest, that's all," she said.

She got up to go in the house. "Thanks for caring though." She kissed me on the forehead and went into the house.

Now I knew something was up. For one, she never kissed me on the forehead like that and two, she was too jumpy. Usually when she was sick she'd call the doctor and make an appointment. Now, all of a sudden, she didn't want to go. She was definitely keeping something from me. I'd have to find out what.

I went in the house and up to our room. She was in there, lying on the bed.

"Baby, you're not keeping anything from me, are you?" I asked.

I was going to find a way to get it out of her and what better way than to ask.

"No. Why?"

"Because you're not acting like yourself, that's all. You know you can tell me anything, no matter what it is," I said.

"Yeah, I know," she said as she grabbed her stomach.

"What's wrong, baby? Is it your stomach?"

"I'm 'bout to throw up," she said, getting up.

She rushed into the bathroom. I felt bad for questioning her. She actually was sick. I closed the door and went downstairs to the kitchen. I grabbed the Thera Flu from out of the cabinet. I made her a cup and took it back upstairs to her. She was still in the bathroom, bent over the toilet.

I put her cup down on the nightstand and walked in the bathroom. I rubbed her back to comfort her. She sat there, bent over the toilet while nothing came out.

"Come on, baby," I said.

I helped her up. She washed her mouth out and then I helped her into bed.

"I made you some Thera Flu. Drink it and you should feel better. If you need anything, just let me know and I'll bring it to you. I'll be right downstairs, okay?"

She nodded her head yes. I left out and closed the door behind me. I sat down on the couch and turned on the TV. The phone rang.

"Hello," I said.

"Hey, Terry, how are you doing?" Crystal asked.

"I'm living so I can't complain," I said.

"That's good. Let me talk to your wife for a minute. She called me earlier."

"She is in the bed lying down. She's not feeling well. I think she's coming down with the flu."

"I've got it, baby! I need to talk to Crystal," Tracy said.

"Oh, I'm sorry," I said.

I hung up the phone. A minute ago she was throwing up everywhere and now she was fine to talk on the damn phone.

"Whatever!" I said.

I wasn't going to allow the situation to stress me out. I needed to get ready to go and see my godson. I got my cell phone and called to make sure Ty was home.

"Hello," April said, answering the phone.

"Hey there, Miss Lady. How are you feeling?" I asked.

"I'm fine. A little sore but your boy's taking pretty good care of me," she said.

"I know he is; he better be. Well, I was just calling to make sure someone was home. I told Ty yesterday I'd come around there and see my new godson," I said.

"Yeah, he told me. Well, we're here. We aren't going anywhere."

"Who is that?" I heard Ty yell from the background.

"It's Terry," she replied. "Hold on. Let me put your boy on the phone."

"Naw, that's okay. I'll be over there soon," I said and hung up the phone.

I didn't want to talk to Ty right then because he'd want to know about Tracy and I really didn't have any answers. I went upstairs to get dressed. Tracy was still on the phone with Crystal. She started to whisper once I walked in the room so I couldn't hear what they were talking about.

"I'll be back in a couple of hours. I'm 'bout to go over Ty's house and see the baby," I said.

"Wait a minute. I want to come. Crystal, I'll call you back later on, girl," she said.

She got off the phone and washed up quickly. Things weren't making sense to me. She was sick earlier but she was fine to talk to Crystal and now she wanted to go with me to Ty's.

I yelled into the bathroom. "You sure you want to go? I thought you weren't feeling well. You need to lie down."

"I'm fine now. That Thera Flu really worked," she said.

"Okay, I'll be downstairs waiting for you," I replied.

I grabbed the dishes in our room and took them downstairs with me. I put them in the sink and sat down at the kitchen table while Tracy got dressed.

❖ ❖ ❖ ❖

Ty opened the door and I rushed past him.

"Where's that baby?" I asked.

"Can I get a hello, a what's up, or something? I didn't sleep with your ass last night! When you walk into someone's house, you're supposed to speak. I know Aunt Bunny taught you that much," Ty said.

"Nigga, move! I didn't come here to see your ass. I came to see my godson. Now where is he?" I asked again.

I didn't see the baby so I figured he was upstairs with April. I walked upstairs to the bedroom. The bedroom door was closed. I didn't want to burst in and find her sitting there breastfeeding or something. I knocked on the door.

"Are you decent?" I asked.

"Yeah, come on in, child," she replied.

I walked in the room and there was this tiny white little baby lying on the bed next to April.

"Come here, lil' man," I said. I picked him up. "Aw, look at him. Hey there, lil' man! How you doing, Khalil?"

"Well, hello to you, too," April said.

"He doesn't know how to speak to anybody today," Ty said, walking into the room. "The nigga is just rude!"

"I didn't come to see either of you. I came to see Khalil. Ain't that right, man?" I said.

He lay in my arms sleep.

"Let me hold him," Tracy said.

I handed him to her.

"He's so precious. Are you going to open your eyes for me? Huh, Khalil? Come on, precious, open those eyes for me, man," Tracy said in a soft voice.

"Now, I'll talk to the two of you. So how are you doing April?" I asked.

"Oh, no, it's too late now," she said, putting her hand up to signal me to just stop.

"Fine then, I tried!"

"Boy, hush! How you feeling, April?" Tracy asked.

"I'm fine," she replied.

"Ty hasn't been acting trifling, has he?" Tracy asked.

"Come on now, Tracy! I'm handling mine over here. I'm taking care of her," Ty said in his defense.

"I can't even lie. He's been such a sweetheart. Sometimes I want to strangle his ass though. He won't even let me move. The only time I can get up is to go to the bathroom. Even then, he's escorting me," April added in Ty's defense.

"Let me find out, Ty!" Tracy said.

Ty started blushing.

"So when you moving in?" I asked April.

I didn't mean to put Ty on the spot like that, but I wanted him to catch my hint.

"We talked about it and I think it'll be best if we keep our own houses for now. We're just going to alternate for a while," she said.

"What's the difference? It sounds like y'all are already living together; just in two places," I said.

"Boy, get out of their business," Tracy said.

"It's okay. This way we can still have a place separate from one another. There are going to be times when he isn't going to want to be bothered by me and I don't want to be bothered by him. This way we still have our separate space. I don't want us to rush things because of the baby," she said.

"Sounds more like y'all are breaking up than staying together," I said.

"Don't get me wrong. I want to be around him all the time but I think this would be best," she said.

"I tried to talk her into moving in but she won't listen to me," Ty said.

I couldn't help but laugh at everything. April hit me with a line Ty would have back in the day and Ty played the role the woman would have. I left things alone because I could kinda see where April was coming from. There wasn't any reason to rush things.

"I feel ya," I said.

"Girl, he is so precious. Doesn't he make you want to have another one?" Tracy said, looking at me.

"Yeah, it's about time y'all do. Lil' J is what, fifteen now? He needs a little brother or sister," Ty added.

"I've thought about it but we really haven't had the time. I don't know; maybe one of these days," I said.

I'd only planned on staying over Ty's twenty minutes, no longer than a half an hour. Time flew by as we all sat around talking and it was going on three hours.

"Baby, look at the time," I said.

"I know Johnny's sitting around wondering where we are," she said.

"You ready?" I asked.

"Yeah," she replied.

"All right, partna! I'll holla at you later. We'll take the baby one weekend and give the two of you a break," I said.

"You mean *I'll* have the baby one weekend," Tracy said.

April and Ty started laughing.

"We don't care who watches him. We're going to hold you to that," Ty said.

"Me, too," April added.

Tracy and I got in the car and headed home. Spending all that time with the baby had me actually thinking about having another one. I wasn't sure if Tracy had been serious though.

"Were you serious about wanting another baby?" I asked.

"Why, you don't want to?" she replied.

"I don't know. I was just thinking about it. Why? You don't want to?" I threw back at her.

"I really haven't thought about it. I wouldn't mind it if you wanted to," she replied.

"We always did say we'd try and have a girl," I said.

"So you want to? Try, that is?" she asked.

"It's up to you. You're the one who'll be carrying it for nine months; not me," I said.

"So we can start trying to have another baby?" she asked.

"Yeah!"

She started smiling.

"You don't know how happy I am to hear you say that. Terry, I'm pregnant," she said.

"Ha, ha, ha, very funny. I'm pregnant, too," I replied.

"Terry, I'm serious. That's why I've been throwing up lately. It's morning sickness. I haven't had my period in two months now," she said.

I pulled the car over.

"You're serious?" I asked.

"Yes! We're going to have a baby. I was scared to tell you because I didn't know how you'd react. I was trying to find a way," she said.

"How long have you known?" I asked.

"For about two weeks. I wasn't positive until I took a test the other day though."

I thought back and I couldn't remember if she'd come on or not. I'd thought she did but, in actuality, I wasn't honestly sure.

"What's wrong? You were just excited at the thought of having another baby. Now that I tell you I'm pregnant, you're not," she said.

"That was when we were discussing it. Now, I find out you're actually pregnant and you've been keeping it from me," I said.

"I wasn't trying to keep anything from you. I just didn't know how to tell you. I didn't know if you were ready or even wanted another baby," she said.

"So what if I said I wasn't ready to have another child, then what?" I questioned.

"Then nothing! I would've still told you; maybe not today. But I would've still told you!"

"What good is it to make promises to one another if we're just going to break them?" I asked.

"I wasn't trying to break my promise to you. I was going to tell you. I just didn't know how. I was trying to find a way to tell you and wait for the right time. I wouldn't keep anything like this from you!" she said.

I calmed myself down before things got a lot worse. This was something both of us wanted and it was a blessing.

"I'm sorry if I seem upset, boo, but I don't want you to feel that you can't come to me about anything. No matter what it is, good or bad, you can always tell me. I don't want us to keep any secrets from each other," I said.

"I'm sorry, too, for not telling you right away. I should have; regardless of your reaction. I'm sorry, baby," she said.

I leaned over and kissed her.

"It's over with now! Let's just concentrate now on my little girl," I said, rubbing her stomach.

"How do you know it's a girl? We could be having another boy."

"This better be my baby girl. Well, she damn sure enough better be or I'll push him right back in until he becomes a girl!"

Tyrelle
COME BACK TO ME

Time had really flown. My boy's wedding was right around the corner. I couldn't believe he was actually getting married in a week. I could remember when we were fresh out of college, talking about we'd never get married. Now look at us. Well, look at him because I wasn't ready for that step yet.

I needed to get my ass ready for the wedding rehearsal. I felt like being lazy right then though.

"What time will you be home?" April asked from the hallway.

"Probably round three or so. Why?"

She walked into the room. "You're not even dressed yet. Get your ass out of that bed."

"I am!"

"Well, I wanted to know because I need you to pick up my dress by five," she said.

"I'll get it on the way back from the rehearsal and drop it off before I go to the hotel for the bachelor party," I said.

"Umm, you know how I feel about that," she commented.

"What? I told you that I'm just chilling. You have nothing to worry about," I said.

"I'm not worried about you. It's those strippers I know y'all are having."

"I'm not trippin' off those hoes. I'm a family man now. I have all that I want and need right here," I said and kissed her on the forehead.

"Don't be starting anything. You know we can't do anything until my six weeks are up," she said.

"I wasn't even trying to start anything. You that damn horny?!"

"Yep!"

"Well, you need to get those fingers working and handle that," I said, laughing. "Let me get up and get ready or I'll never get out of here."

I got up and went into the bathroom.

April yelled, "I'm serious 'bout those strippers! Your ass better remember who your family is when that ass is all up in your face!"

I didn't pay her any mind. I knew who my family was and what I had at home. There was no need to mess anything up for some stripper. I washed up and got dressed.

"I'll call you when I leave the church and let you know I'm on my way," I said before I walked out the door.

I stopped and gave her a kiss goodbye. I wanted to put her mind at ease about that night because she really didn't have anything to worry about.

"Boo, I'm serious. You don't have to worry about any other woman ever taking me from you. I love you too much. You and Khalil are the best things that have ever happened to me. I'm not going anywhere."

"I know. I guess sometimes I just need to hear you say that. I love you, too, baby!" she said.

I gave my lil' man a kiss and left. I arrived at the church and, as usual, was the last one. Terry and Jeff were sitting in the back pew chatting. I didn't see Michelle around though. I joined them.

"What's up, fellas?"

"Nothing much," Jeff said.

"Late as usual, I see," Terry added.

"I know you're not talking, T. You're never on time," I replied.

Both of them bursted out laughing.

"I just walked in like five minutes ago myself," Terry said.

I laughed with them.

"So what's the holdup? Let's get this show on the road. I have other things to do today," I said.

"Chelle had to run and pick Jodi up. Her car broke down again. You'd think she'd buy a new one, with the money she makes," Jeff said.

I knew Jeff was just eager to throw her name in my face; like I was going to have some type of reaction. I was actually looking forward to seeing her. This way I could prove to Jeff that I was over her.

"How's my godson doing? You taking good care of him?" Terry asked, trying to change the subject.

"He's fine. He sleeps half the time."

"That won't last long, so I'd enjoy it while it lasts. I remember when Johnny was about three, maybe four months, he started waking up (it seemed) like every two hours. I couldn't take that shit. Oops! Excuse me, Lord. I forgot where I am," Terry said.

"Where's April? Why didn't she come?" Jeff asked.

"We didn't see any reason for her to come. She isn't in the wedding so it really doesn't make any sense for her to be here. She'll be at the wedding next week though," I said.

"Oh, I know that. She better be here," Jeff said.

I wasn't sure if he was trying to start things or what. I didn't put it past him but what I did know was he'd show his angle soon enough. Terry tried to give Jeff a look on the sly so I wouldn't see it but I caught it.

"Ay, look, for real. I know I haven't been the biggest supporter of you and April but I'm *your* biggest supporter. If she's who you want to be with, I can't do nothing but accept it and treat her like family; just like I would anyone else you'd mess with. Trying to watch your back only pushed you away and I don't ever want to do that.

"I wasn't sure of her intentions with this whole pregnancy thing but who am I to judge her and tell you who to be with. She's your girl and this is your life. If she makes you happy, then I'm happy for you. I'm sorry, dawg! I know we squashed the lil' beef between us a while ago but I never apologized and I know I needed to do that," he said.

He'd caught me off guard by what he'd just said. I'd never expected Jeff to accept her. She was nothing like Jodi and he was in love with her. Jodi was this successful and accomplished doctor and April was a plain old administrative assistant at a real estate company. I felt like breaking down into tears after hearing those heart-filled words come out of his mouth. I hugged him to show my gratitude.

"I'm glad we can finally put closure on this and move forward."

"You're my man and all this beefing over a choice you made concerning your life is silly. We're older than that. That's that lil' boy shit! I'm a grown-ass man and I need to act like it," Jeff said.

"Jeff!" Terry cut Jeff off, reminding him where he was.

"My bad. I'm just trying to let Ty know how I feel."

Michelle walked inside the church.

"Okay let's get this started. We're running late," she said.

In walked a sight I hadn't seen in a while. She had on a pair of blue jeans with brown boots, a white collared Donna Karan shirt and her leather coat. Jodi looked perfect from head to toe. Our eyes met with one another. She smiled slightly as she walked towards me.

"How are you?" she asked.

"I'm fine and yourself?" I replied.

"I can't complain."

My stomach was in knots. I couldn't remember the last time I was that nervous and I didn't even know why I was.

She continued, "I hear you had a little boy. What's his name?"

"Khalil," I replied.

"That's cute! I know you didn't come up with it," she joked.

"What are you trying to say?" I questioned.

She nudged me on the shoulder.

"You know exactly what I'm saying. Don't fake."

We both laughed.

It felt really good, being around her and talking to her again. It felt just like old times. If there was one thing I'd missed about her, it was the friendship. We were always better friends.

"Okay, people, I'm not trying to be at this all day," Michelle said.

"Well, I guess that's our cue," I said.

"Hey, I've been thinking a lot lately about things and..."

Michelle cut her off. "Come on, Jodi. We need to get started. Talk to him later."

I jumped in. "We'll talk."

She agreed.

We practiced walking down the aisle and went through the entire ceremony twice. It took almost two hours just for that. I was coming up short on time. I still had to pick up April's dress and get things ready for the bachelor party.

"One more time, everybody, and we can call it a day," Jeff said.

I thought the last time would be it since there were no mistakes. I thought wrong.

After we finished the entire ceremony for the third time, Michelle said, "Let's go through it one more time. We're going to do it double-time though, folks. I know we all have other things to do, so let's make it good."

We all took our places. Michelle stood up front, watching everything; making sure everything went smoothly. She didn't walk down the aisle or say the vows or anything since the bride didn't rehearse. Jodi and I played the bride and groom and read the vows. Her mother took her place coming down the aisle with her father.

"Okay, let's go!" Michelle said.

Mike walked down the aisle with Michelle's girlfriend Kelly, Darin walked down accompanied by Michelle's sister Tiffany, Terry and Tracy followed them, I came down after them with Jodi and in walked the ring bearer and flower girl. Lil' J was the ring bearer and Tiffany's daughter Dayja was the flower girl.

"All right now, 'Here Comes the Bride' starts to play and I walk in," Michelle said.

Michelle's mother and father walked down the aisle. Michelle stood at the altar, next to Jeff and Rev. Jackson, watching. Once they'd made it up the aisle to the altar, Rev. Jackson gave us the simulated version of the ceremony.

"Thank you all for showing patience with me. I just want everything to be perfect for our day," Michelle said once we were finally finished.

I went over to give her a hug goodbye.

"I'll see you later, sweetie," I said.

"Bye, knucklehead. Don't be having my man doing anything he shouldn't be tonight! I *know* you," she said, pointing her finger and squinting her eyes.

"Come on now," I said, walking away.

"I'll meet you at the hotel in about an hour," I said to Terry.

I made my way out the church and into the lobby. Jodi was standing there.

"Well, it was nice seeing you. I'll see you at the dinner next Thursday," I said.

"I told you I needed to talk to you," she reminded me.

"Oh, I'm sorry. I forgot all about it. Can you walk me to the car and talk at the same time? I'm in a bit of a rush. I still have some things to take care of for tonight," I said.

"Sure," she replied.

We walked out the front door.

"I've been thinking about you a lot lately and how things ended between the two of us. I was really hurt by the fact that you cheated on me again. But I think the fact that she became pregnant intensified it. I always envisioned myself having your first child; all your children really.

"I find myself lately missing you, thinking about you or wondering what you're doing. We've been through hell and beyond but my life seems empty without you. You're with April now and I've tried to respect that but I can't help but think she's happy now at my expense. I can't just sit back anymore. However, I'll respect whatever you say.

. "Basically I'm trying to say that I want to give us another chance. I want to see if we can make this work. I'm still in love with you and I always will be. I want you back in my life. I need you back in my life."

Words couldn't express how I felt. I'd envisioned this day over and over in my head a long time ago but never did I think I'd see it. My stomach was in my throat. I didn't know what to say or how to respond.

She continued, "I don't expect you to answer now. I'm sure this is a big decision for you. Take your time and think about it. I'm not going anywhere."

She hugged me and kissed me on the lips. She went back to the church and I got in my car and headed home. I replayed the conversation in my head over and over. I could remember staying up at night when we'd first broken up, praying to hear those words. Now those same words I'd once craved had put my life in an uproar.

My heart was with someone else. We had a family together. I couldn't betray her trust but I had to be true to my heart as well. I stopped and picked April's dress up. It was the only reason why I was going home, so I couldn't forget it.

I got home and made myself a quick drink. I needed it. I went upstairs with April's dress. She was lying on the bed asleep, with Khalil beside her. She looked so peaceful. I hung the dress up on the back of the door so she'd see it and left.

I went straight to the hotel where we were having the party. I wanted to throw it at the club but we were there enough as it was. Plus I didn't want to pay anyone to clean up or do it myself. We'd booked the penthouse suite at the Hyatt Regency in Crystal City, Virginia; right across the bridge.

❖ ❖ ❖ ❖

The party was off the chain. We had women everywhere and none of them had hardly anything on. The ratio had to be like three to one up in there. Jeff and Terry were having a ball. It would've been nice if I was doing the same but I couldn't. I stayed at the bar and got drunk. Jodi had ruined any chance of having fun for me earlier. All I can think about was what she'd said and what I was going to do about it.

Two or three months earlier I wouldn't have had a problem getting back with her but things had changed so much. Things were really going well between April and me and I was truly in love with her. I was so deep in thought I didn't even notice the woman standing behind me talking. She tapped me on my shoulder to get my attention.

"Hello there! Want any company? You look like you can use it," she said.

"I'm sorry but I wouldn't be much company right now. I have a lot on my plate and I wouldn't want to burden you with my problems," I replied.

She understood and walked off. Not long after she'd left Terry and Jeff walked over.

"This must be a record or something. All this pussy running around and your ass is chilling at the bar. We know you have a girl, but damn. You're not even having fun with us," Terry said.

"T said shit between you and April was getting serious, but I didn't know she had you like this. You won't even dance with these broads up in here," Jeff added.

"My head's too fucked up right now. I probably don't even remember how to dance," I said.

"Why? What's up?" Jeff asked.

"This wouldn't have anything to do with Jodi, would it? I saw her walk you to the car after the rehearsal," Terry said.

"It has everything to do with her. She basically said, in a nutshell, that she wants us to get back together. She said the fact that April got pregnant really hurt her but she's been thinking about me lately. She wants us to try and work things out," I said.

"Get the fuck out of here!" Terry said.

"This nigga lying! If that was the case, I would've known already because she would've told Chelle and Chelle would've told me," Jeff said.

I looked at them sternly. "I'm dead serious."

"So what did you say?" Terry asked.

"What could I say? I was stuck. I didn't know what to say."

"So y'all just stood there and looked at one another?" Jeff asked.

"He had to have said something 'cause she kissed him," Terry added.

Jeff looked at me, shocked.

"Get the fuck out of here!" Jeff said.

"Don't let your mind go wandering. You 'bout to sit here and get shit twisted. She told me she didn't expect me to answer her now. She wanted me to think about it. I agreed 'cause I was speechless and she kissed me goodbye. It wasn't a passionate kiss or anything like that," I said.

"What is there to think about? You're with April, right?" Jeff asked.

I wasn't in the mood for one of his little mind games or for him throwing anything in my face.

"If you're going to throw shit in my face, then I'll handle this by myself!"

"Hear me out before you start jumping out there." He paused. "I've been giving you hell about April since day one and you've ignored every word I've said. You were even willing to stay with her at the cost of our friendship. The two of you have a child together and are in a serious relationship, so why is it a problem? Okay, now Jodi wants to be with you. So what? That still doesn't change the way you feel about April. You're still in love with her. You still want to be with her."

"But things have changed. I didn't have Jodi when you were harassing me about April. She didn't want to be bothered with me. If I did have her, I would've listened to you and been with her. Now, out of the blue, she wants to be a part of my life again," I said.

"Okay, why didn't you tell her you wanted to be with her then?" Jeff asked.

"Because I'm with April and I'm not trying to hurt her. We actually have something good going, something special," I said.

"That's my point. Your mind's already made or you wouldn't have a problem with getting back with Jodi. This isn't a job when you have to decide. This is love and in love your heart makes all the decisions for you. I can hear it but you have to. Just listen to your heart, man," Jeff said.

"Damn, Jeff, that's some deep shit! I need to get a swig of what your ass is drinking," Terry said.

"What you don't understand, Jeff, is that talking to Jodi really brought back a lot of old feelings that I had and still have for her. There was a time when she was the one I wanted to spend the rest of my life with," I said.

"Look, Ty, I can't put it any better than Jeff did, but it all boils down to you. It's your decision. No matter what your decision, we'll be here for you," Terry said.

"See, look now, man. I'm ruining your party. Come on; let's have some fun. I'll figure it all out but for now, it's your bachelor party and we should be acting like it," I said.

"Naw, fuck that! You're my man and if something's wrong with you, we're going to tackle it first," Jeff said.

"Thanks but you were right. I just need to listen to my heart. So come on and let's party. Once you tie that knot, we won't hardly get to see you," I said.

"Whatever! Y'all are my niggas, married or not! Nothing will come between us!" he said.

I put my arms around the two of them. "Let's party!"

Jeff
THE WEDDING BELLS ARE RINGING

The pressure was starting to really get to me. I was getting married in one day. I couldn't believe it. I needed to talk to someone. I called Ty to see what he was up to. It felt good, being able to talk to him again. I was praying he was home.

"Hello," he said.

"Aye, what's up? You going anywhere?" I asked.

"Naw, I'm in for the night. You are getting married tomorrow, you know. I have to get up early so I won't be late for once," Ty said.

"Well, don't go to sleep just yet. I'm on my way over there," I said.

"Why? What's up?" Ty asked.

"We'll talk when I get there."

"All right!" he replied.

I went straight over. April answered the door.

"What are you doing over here this time of night? Tomorrow's your big day."

I didn't really want to hear about that. It was only making things worse.

"Yeah, I know! I need to talk to Ty about something. I won't be long though. How are you doing? We haven't really had a chance to talk since y'all have gotten together. I know I've been pretty much an asshole," I said.

"Naw, not really! I don't see it as you being an asshole; just trying to look out for your boy. I can't do anything but respect you for that," she said.

If I didn't have respect for her beforehand, I sure enough did then. She could've been a real bitch about things like I was but, instead, she tried to see things from my point of view as well.

"He's downstairs with the baby. Tell him to make him a bottle before he comes to bed," she said.

I walked down the steps to the basement.

"Let me see lil' man. I didn't really get to hold him at dinner yesterday. Your other godfather was trying to hog you," I said. "Oh, before I forget, April said don't forget to make him a bottle before you go to bed."

"Okay, so what's up?" Ty asked, getting straight to the point as usual.

"I don't know about this wedding, man. That's what's up. Everything's happening so fast. I mean, it's tomorrow! I think we need a little more time. I'm not trying to make a mistake," I said.

"I knew it. I knew that was it. Nigga, if you don't stop playing with me. You're just having cold feet. That shit will go away. It's nothing but jitters. You need to get some sleep and get ready for tomorrow. You're just nervous, that's all," Ty said.

"I thought the same thing yesterday, but now I'm not too sure. I sat at that dinner table just thinking that come Sunday I will be married. *Married!* That doesn't even sound right."

"I remember when Terry went through this. I think every man does. Go home and get some rest. That's all you need to be worrying about right now," he said.

"I'm going home and calling this thing off. That's what I need to do. We need more time; maybe another year or two. I'm not ready to be anyone's husband. What if we break up or something? I can't just say it's over and move on. We'll still be married. Then we have to get divorce lawyers and all that. I'm not trying to go through all that shit."

"Listen to you. You're not even married yet and you're already talking about divorce. If that's how you feel, then let's call it off because you shouldn't be thinking about no damn divorce right now. You should be thinking about all the good times the two of you are going to have as man and wife. Buying your first house together, having kids, and family vacations. You know, shit like that. You should be thanking the Lord for giving you such a good, loving, and caring woman. Do you know how many niggas out here would kill to be in your shoes? I know I would. Look at the shit I'm going through. Here I am in love with two damn women and wanting to do right by both, but I can't. I'm going to have to hurt one to get true to the other.

"Man, look, if there's one thing I have learned throughout all of this it's that love doesn't come cheap. It's not like it is in the movies. You find the girl, marry the girl, and live happily ever after. It takes hard work, dedication, and commitment. You have to *want* to make things work in order for them to, then you have to show the commitment and dedication to make it that way. I don't know two people that belong together more than the two of you. Y'all are going to be just fine."

Everything he said was right. I couldn't argue with not one point he'd made. It all made perfectly good sense.

"I hope you're right," I said.

"Now you go on home before Michelle starts worrying about you and we have another situation," he said.

"Can you give me a minute to chill with my godson at least? *Damn!* This is the first time I've really gotten to chill with him. You still haven't told me what you're going to do about Jodi. Have y'all even talked yet?"

"Briefly last night at dinner, but I didn't want to make things obvious. You know, with April there and all," he said.

The man was going out of his way not to hurt April but still, he couldn't see his own answer.

"So what did you say?" I asked.

"I just said that we'll talk about everything tomorrow after the wedding. There's no need to draw this thing out. I just need to go 'head and make a decision," he said.

"True!"

❖ ❖ ❖ ❖

I got up at 6:00 a.m. and Chelle was already gone. She was determined to make sure I didn't see her before the wedding. I called Jodi's house to see if she was there.

"Hel-lo," Jodi answered, still asleep.

"Good morning! Is Chelle over there?" I asked.

"You know you and your wife have lost y'all's minds, coming over here and calling me this early in the morning. Hold on. Michelle, phone!" Jodi said.

"Hello," Chelle said.

"Why are you over there?" I asked.

"You already know we're not supposed to see each other before the wedding so stop acting all brand-new."

"Damn, I could've gotten a goodbye or something. I wake up and you're not here," I said.

"I did tell your ass goodbye and kissed you," she said.

"Okay, but I was sleep so how do I know. What I do know is that you're not here now."

"I'm sorry, baby, but you know how I am about this wedding. I don't want anything to go wrong, but I promise that I'll make sure you wake up to me for the rest of our lives," she said.

"Umm, hmm," I replied.

"I'll see you later. I need to start getting ready and it's going to take a while to get Jodi out of that bed. Make sure you're at the church by 9:30 a.m., no later than 10:00 a.m.," she said.

"I will be. I'm 'bout to get me something to eat. I'll see you later."

"Bye, baby. I love you," she said.

"I love you, too," I replied and hung up the phone.

I swear even when I was mad at her, she made it so hard to stay that way. I wanted to take my ass back to sleep since I couldn't have any morningtime fun but it was too late; I was too awake then. I got up to get my wedding day started.

I arrived at the church around nine, trying to be early so I could be around to greet people as they arrived. Five minutes felt more like fifty to me. Time was creeping by and my nerves were setting in.

"How you holding up, partna?" Ty asked.

"I wish we'd get on with this. I'm ready to do this *now*. I'm tired of waiting and playing hostess," I replied.

"Last night you wanted to call everything off. Now, you want it to be over. You sure have your mind made!" Ty said sarcastically.

Terry looked at Ty like he was crazy, then he looked at me.

"Oh, I didn't tell you, T? Last night this nigga comes over my house like around midnight talking 'bout he wanted to call things off. He wasn't sure if he wanted to get married or not. You know, the same shit you did before you and Tracy got married," Ty said.

"Oh! He had jitters. Everybody goes through that sometime before their wedding," Terry said.

"I wish the nigga would just make up his mind!" Ty commented.

"How are you doing? That's good!" Terry said, greeting a wedding guest. He continued, "I went through the same thing you're going through now. At first I couldn't believe the wedding was coming so fast, then it seemed like it wasn't coming fast enough on my wedding day. Don't worry about it. Everything will happen when it's supposed to happen. Just relax, y'all will be married soon enough," Terry said.

"I'm trying; believe me. Let me go in here for a minute. I'll be back," I said.

I needed to be by myself to collect my thoughts.

❖ ❖ ❖ ❖

We all took our places, as the wedding was about to begin. I was so nervous. It was finally happening. The music began playing and my nerves were on edge. I felt like I was floating on water as I walked up the aisle towards the altar. I turned around and faced the crowd.

The church was packed. We had to open the upper balcony to fit all of our guests in the sanctuary. I could see Mike coming out of the lobby. My wedding was finally here. My mother and father walked down the aisle, hand in hand, as the music played. All attention in the church was on the center aisle as the wedding party started coming down.

Mike and Kelly walked down the aisle together like we'd practiced. As they were halfway down the aisle, Darin and Tiffany came down. Lil' J was next. He came down, holding a pillow with a replica ring on top. Terry and Tracy were next. Terry was wearing his black tux with the silver vest and bow tie. They walked down gracefully as if it was their wedding day all over again. Ty and Jodi followed behind them. Both of them had radiant smiles on their faces, lighting up the church. I couldn't help but feel a little jealous for April myself. The two of them looked like an item again. Dayja was the last of the wedding party to come down. She stole the show. You could hear the *"Awww's"* from the crowd as she strutted down the aisle in harmony.

"She's so precious," you could hear a woman from the crowd say.

Each step closer she took, the closer I was to the wedding. My heart began to beat fast. I hadn't seen Michelle all day and now it was finally time. The music stopped and "Here Comes the Bride" started to play.

The audience all stood, awaiting their first glimpse of Chelle. My nerves were at full blast. Then I saw Chelle's face as she came around the corner to come down the center aisle. She was so beautiful. She looked like an angel from heaven. Ty was right. I knew, at that very moment, that everything would be all right. I was the luckiest man in the world.

People started to take pictures as she made her way past them. The wedding photographer stood in front of her, snapping shots as she took each step closer. We didn't want to miss an expression. Tears began to trickle down my face. She stopped at the first step, still holding hands with her father. The music stopped and Rev. Jackson began the ceremony.

"Dearly beloved, we are gathered here today, in the presence of God and of this company, so that Jeffery Long and Michelle Renee Davis may be united in holy matrimony. We are here to celebrate and share in the glorious act that God is about to perform—the act by which He converts their love for one another into the holy and sacred estate of marriage.

"This relationship is an honorable and sacred one, established by our Creator for the welfare and happiness of mankind, and approved by the Apostle Paul as honorable among all men. It is designed to unite two sympathies and hopes into one; and it rests upon the mutual confidence and devotion of husband and wife.

"May it be in extreme thoughtfulness and reverence, and in dependence upon divine guidance, that you enter now into this holy relationship.

"If any man can show just cause why they may not lawfully be joined together, let them speak now or forever hold their peace."

Silence filled the church.

Rev. Jackson continued, "Being assured that your love and your choice of each other as lifelong companions are in God's will and that you have your families' blessings, I now ask, who gives this woman to be married to this man?"

"Her mother and I do," Mr. Davis said.

He placed Chelle's hand in mine and stood next to Mrs. Davis.

"You may all be seated," Rev. Jackson said.

Everyone in the audience took their seats.

Rev. Jackson continued with the ceremony. "The apostle Paul compared the relationship between husband and wife to that between Christ and the church. Marriage is a decision of two individuals to share the same type of pure, Christian love described by Paul.

"In first Corinthians, Chapter 13, verses 4 through 7, it says, love is patient; love is kind and envies no one. Love is never boastful, nor conceited, nor rude, never selfish, not quick to take offense. Love keeps no score of wrongs, does not gloat over other men's sins, but delights in the truth. There is nothing love cannot face; there is no limit to its faith, its hope, and its endurance.

"This kind of love enriches each part of life and marriage enriches love. Two lives, shared with this kind of love, can hold more fulfillment and happiness than either life alone."

He paused. "Jeffery, are you ready to enter into this marriage with Michelle, believing the love you share and your faith in each other will endure all things?"

"I am," I replied.

Rev. Jackson looked at Chelle. "Michelle, are you ready to enter into this marriage with Jeffery, believing the love you share and your faith in each other will endure all things?"

"I am," she said in a soft voice.

"We will now have the reading of the word by Nicole Brown," Rev. Jackson said. Nicole got up from her seat and walked to one of the podiums.

"Good afternoon, church. I am glad to be here for such a joyous occasion. I will be reading from the book of John, Chapter 15, verses 9 through 12.

"As the Father hath loved me, so have I loved you: continue ye in my love. If ye keep my commandments, and abide in his love, even as I have kept my Father's commandments, and abide in his love. These things have I spoken unto you, that my joy might remain in you, and that your joy might be full. This is my commandment: That ye love one another as I have loved you.

"Please turn in your Bibles to Colossians, chapter 3, verses 12 through 14.

"Put on then, as God's chosen ones, holy and beloved, compassion kindness, lowliness, meekness, and patience, forbearing one another, and, if one has a complaint against another, so you must also forgive. And above all these put on love, which binds everything together in perfect harmony.

"May the Lord give His blessing to the reading of His Word."

She walked back to her seat.

"Next, we will have a selection by Marc Duncan," Rev. Jackson said.

"When I was approached by Jeff to sing at his wedding, I was extremely shocked. I didn't expect the request. Then I started to get excited because of the chance to sing at his wedding. I then felt honored. Well, I later got a call from the two best men, Tyrelle and Terry, explaining why I was chosen for the job. A little disappointment set in. They wanted to surprise Jeff and Michelle with someone else to sing and used me as the cover-up. But once I found out who was singing, the disappointment quickly went away. Ladies and gentlemen, without further ado, courtesy of Def Soul Records, it is my pleasure to present to you Ayana, Ayinika, and Musiq Soulchild."

They all walked out from the back and the younger women in the crowd started to scream. I couldn't believe it. My boys had gone all out for me. The band started playing. I glanced over at the two of them and they were grinning from ear to ear.

The trio started to sing.

Your love, it means the world to me.
Words cannot express the joy you bring.
Your love, it moves me tenderly.
To have you by my side means everything I sing.
Your love, it has the best of me.
If I could give you more then that would be yeah.

As they continued, I started reminiscing about the first time Chelle and I had met, the first time we had made love, the long walks, backrubs, all the happy times, and all of the bad. I envisioned us having our first child together and having a life filled with love and happiness.

For the next five minutes Musiq Soulchild ripped the song. He poured his heart all through it. When they finished, I was speechless. The audience gave them a standing ovation. Once everything calmed down the group took a seat in the front row and Rev. Jackson continued with the wedding.

"We will now have the wedding vows. Both parties have written their own vows."

"I, Michelle Davis, take thee, Jeffery Long, to be my lawfully wedded husband, secure in the knowledge that you will be my constant friend, my faithful partner in life, and my one true love. On this special day, I give to you in the presence of God and these witnesses my sacred promise to stay by your side as your faithful wife, in sickness and in health, in joy and in sorrow, as well as through the good times and the bad. I promise to love you without reservation, comfort you in times of distress, encourage you to achieve all of your goals, laugh with you and cry with you, grow with you in mind and spirit, always be open and honest with you, and cherish you for as long as we both shall live."

My emotions started getting the best of me as the tears came down my face. I just looked into her eyes.

"I, Jeffery Long, take thee, Michelle Davis, to be my lawfully wedded wife, knowing in my heart that you will be my constant friend, my faithful partner in life, and my one true love. On this special day, I give to you in the presence of God and these witnesses my sacred promise to stay by your side as your faithful husband, in sickness and in health, in joy and in sorrow, as well as through good times and the bad. I promise to love you without reservation, honor and respect you, provide for your needs as best I can, protect you from harm, comfort you in times of distress, grow with you in mind and spirit, always be open and honest with you, and cherish you for as long as we both shall live."

"Let us pray. Father in Heaven, You ordained marriage for Your children, and You gave us love. We present to You Jeffery and Michelle, who come this day to be married. May the covenant of love they make be blessed with true devotion and spiritual commitment. We ask that You, God, will give them the ability to keep the covenant they have made. When selfishness shows itself, grant generosity; when mistrust is a temptation, give moral strength; when there is misunderstanding, give patience and gentleness; if suffering becomes a part of their lives, give them a strong faith and an abiding love. In Jesus' name, let us all say, amen," Rev. Jackson said.

He continued, "It is a Christian custom to exchange rings as a symbol of love. As the rings have no end, so your love should have no end. As the rings are made of gold symbolizing purity, so should your marriage have purity. As often as either of you see them, you will be reminded of this moment and the endless love you promised.

"Jeffery, what token do you give that you will perform your vows?"

Ty handed me the ring and I handed it to Rev. Jackson. Rev. Jackson looked at Chelle.

"Michelle, do you receive this ring in token of the same?"

"I do," she replied.

He gave me back the ring and I put it on her finger.

"Michelle, this ring I give to you in token and pledge of my constant faith and abiding love," I said.

Tears started to come down her face.

"Michelle, what token do you give that you will perform your vows?" Rev. Jackson asked.

She turned to get the ring from Jodi, then handed it to Rev. Jackson.

"Jeffery, do you receive this ring in token of the same?"

"I do," I replied.

He gave her the ring back and she put it on my finger.

"Jeffery, this ring I give to you in token and pledge of my constant faith and abiding love," she said.

Ty and Jodi each lit a separate candle and passed it to Chelle and me. Standing in between the two of us was a big candle, unlit.

Rev. Jackson continued, "The candle represents the joining together of two individuals to live together as one in spirit. Jeffery and Michelle, the candle yet to be lit represents the new family which is being created today. Jeffery and Michelle are leaving their families to make a new life together."

Together we both took our single candles and lit the Unity Candle, uniting the two of us as one.

"Let us pray: O thou eternal God, who art our Father and our Friend, as You have heard these words of promise just spoken, may the Holy Spirit deepen in the mind of this man and this woman the sense of the sacred and binding power of their vows. And as in Thy name these words were spoken to make these lives one, may Your rich blessings be added. Give them Your grace and guidance that they may loyally fulfill the vows they have taken. May Your joy abide with them always, that thus they may be a blessing to each other, and to those about them, finding in the blessedness of the life on earth as a sample of the happiness of Thine eternal home. Through Jesus Christ our Lord. Amen."

Chelle and I joined right hands.

"What therefore God hath joined together, let no man put asunder. Forasmuch as Jeffery and Michelle have consented together in holy matrimony, and have witnessed the same before God and this company and have pledged their love and loyalty to each other, and have declared the same by the joining and the giving of rings, I, therefore, by the authority of the District of Columbia, pronounce that they are husband and wife, in the name of the Lord Jesus Christ." He paused. "You may now kiss the bride!"

I picked Chelle's veil up off her face and kissed her. The audience applauded and took pictures.

"I now present to you, Mr. and Mrs. Jeffery Long!"

Tyrelle

LISTEN TO YOUR HEART

Their ceremony was beautiful. All of their hard work and preparation had paid off. It had even brought a tear to my eye. I didn't know how much longer I could sit next to those two at this reception, though. The two of them looking all happy and in love made me wanna throw up.

Actually it was nothing but jealousy because they looked kind of cute together. I'd caught Jodi staring at me a couple of times. I could only imagine what was going through her mind. She was expecting her answer and I hadn't the slightest idea what I was going to do or say.

I needed some fresh air. I excused myself from the table. I had to get out of there. It felt like the walls between Jodi and April were crashing in on me. Some fresh air couldn't do me anything but good. I went in the bathroom and took a deep breath.

"Get it together, Ty," I said.

I washed my face with cold water and left out the bathroom. Jodi was standing in the lobby, anxiously waiting for me. I tried to sneak past her while she had her back turned, but she caught me.

"Ty, we can't keep acting like this. It's time we talk," Jodi said.

She was right. I couldn't take it anymore. I didn't want April to walk out and see us though. I didn't want her getting any ideas.

"I know we do but can it wait until after the reception, at least?" I asked.

"I'll try," she replied.

I walked back inside the reception and Jodi went the other way. I stopped at the table where April and Khalil were sitting.

"How are you, sexy?" I asked.

"I'm enjoying myself. That was a nice ceremony. I can only hope to find the kind of love the two of them have," she said.

"I thought you already found it?" I questioned.

"Boy, hush! We're nowhere near the level the two of them are on. Hopefully, one day we'll get there though," she said.

"What time do you want to leave?" I asked.

"Why? You're ready to go already?"

"No. I thought you might've been. That's why I asked."

"Oh, well, it doesn't matter to me. Whenever you're ready, so am I. You go and enjoy yourself and share this day with your boy," she said.

I went back to the table and tried to take my mind off Jodi and the whole situation; just enjoy my man's day like April had said.

After the tossing of the bouquet and the garter belt, I started to relax. The two people who probably hated each other the most had caught each. I couldn't help but laugh. It felt like a scene right out of the movie *The Best Man*. I was actually shocked Jeff didn't purposely aim for me.

Ding Ding Ding

I tapped my glass to toast the bride and groom.

"Today has been one of the best days of my life, as I was able to share the union between Jeff and Michelle. I've grown up with Jeff from birth. Ever since that first night we spent together in my crib as babies, he has been my right-hand man. Today I'm filled with joy and sadness.

"I'm sad that you have found a love that we all search for in our lives and I haven't quite found, but yet happy that this love has found you. I can't think of anyone who deserves it more. I can remember a time when we would sit around in high school and college and profess how we would never get married. Boy, how have times changed!"

I paused, then continued, "Please excuse me. For some reason, I can't find the words I want to say. Last night I sat around thinking of exactly what I wanted to say but after watching that wedding, I'm at a loss for words. Over the years I've seen Jeff grow as a man and one thing stood out to me. I've been to I don't know how many weddings over the course of my life and I always find myself saying '*I hope they make it.*' Today that thought never entered my mind because I know the two of you will.

"Today, I saw your future and in it was happiness, encouragement, success, comfort, laughter, sadness, crying, pain but, most importantly, I saw love. I saw a love that will guide you through any turbulent times the two of you should encounter. Follow that love because, in the end, that's all you'll need. This is truly a blessed day.

"Jeff, I couldn't be any more happy for you than I am now. I've always looked at you as my brother and not my cousin. Today, my family has just gotten bigger, as I have a new sister; hopefully another godson after tonight."

Everyone started to laugh.

"On a serious note, Michelle and Jeff, I want the two of you to know that no matter what you need, you can always count on me to be there, to give you whatever I can, to help however I can. I love you guys and wish you all the best. Right now, I'm going to turn it over to the other best man."

Terry stood up.

"I don't know how I'm going to top that. Ty's always trying to outdo someone, even at a wedding," he said as everyone chuckled.

"Today I witnessed a man and woman start a new journey together as man and wife. Let me offer you this bit of advice. I've started my journey already and I'm still walking. On your road, you are going to encounter happy and sad times and good and bad times. You are going to come to a point where you feel like you can't walk anymore or start to wonder if you are even going down the right path. Just always remember no matter what turns you make or what direction you go, do it together. Together you can get through anything.

"There's no manual or book that tells you how to make your marriage work. The only thing you have is each other and the Lord. Now, I'm not one to preach about God but what I can testify to is that without Him, I wouldn't have made it through my journey as a man and I'm still making it through my journey as a husband.

"He has shown me how to enjoy and cherish the good and happy times and to learn from the bad and sad ones. So everyone raise your glasses and toast to their new journey through life together!"

Jeff and Michelle were both so moved by our speeches, they stood up and gave us hugs.

The DJ got the attention of the crowd. "It's now time for the bride and the groom to have their first dance as husband and wife. Ladies and gentlemen, singing his hit single 'Love,' here is Musiq Soulchild."

Jeff and Michelle got up from the table and walked to the center of the dance floor.

The lights were dim and the spotlight was on the two of them as they gracefully danced. The photographer caught every movement possible on film. It felt as if Musiq Soulchild was making love to the song he was singing. The crowd was hypnotized by his every word and the happy couple just danced. The music faded and Musiq Soulchild stopped singing.

He turned to Jeff and Chelle and said, "I want to thank Terry and Ty for inviting me to join the two of you on such a joyous occasion. It's not every day we get to do things like this. I was sitting around on the plane thinking of what song would be perfect to sing today. Three came to my mind. I'm going to sing this last one, especially for the two of you, and we would also like the wedding party to come up and join them."

"Sing 'L' is Gone'! That is perfect, at least for me it is," our Uncle Bobby blurted out.

Everyone who had heard that song before started laughing; others just wondered what was so funny.

"Naw, brotha, the two of us can sing about that later. I'd like the wedding party to come on up here, along with the mother and father of both the bride and the groom," Musiq Soulchild said.

The music started to play. I couldn't believe what he'd just said. Did he not know that I was partnered up with Jodi?! I wished Michelle had chosen Tiffany as her maid of honor. She stepped to me and I tried to remain calm and play it cool.

As he sang, my heart was pumping and my blood was boiling. She felt so good. I'd missed holding her close to me. It felt like we were the only ones on the dance floor, dancing in an empty room. This song was perfect for the mood. I still loved her. There was no denying that and I was sure she knew it. I probably always would love her. Musiq Soulchild finished the song.

To say it to you so I simplified and broke it down
To one, four, three – and that means I love you

We stopped dancing and looked into each other's eyes for a split moment that seemed to last an eternity.

"We need to talk," I said.

"I was going to say the same thing," she replied.

Everything was so clear to me. For a while I'd been uncertain about everything but that was no more. I couldn't please both of them so, unfortunately, I would end up doing what I was trying to avoid; hurting one of them.

Musiq Soulchild made his way to congratulate Jeff and Michelle.

"Give it up, y'all, for Musiq Soulchild. Make sure you get his new album, *AIJUSWAN-NASEING (I Just Want to Sing)*, in stores now," the DJ said.

Jodi and I slipped outside during the commotion of people trying to get his autograph.

"Look, Jodi, I love you and I always will. I can't deny it anymore. You're everything that any man would want in a woman. While I watched the wedding and listened to the vows that were made, I thought of how your love has changed me."

Her face started to light up, anticipating us getting back together.

I continued, "There was a time when the only thing I wanted in life was you and to be with you. I would've given my right foot to get you back. Now, I have you back in my life but, unfortunately, I can't get back with you. I'm with April and I can't and won't betray her trust. I love her and that's who I belong with. I'm sorry, Jodi."

I felt like I'd finally gotten the world off my back.

"I don't understand. How can you choose her over me? How can you sit here and tell me that you still love me and I'm the one you wanted to spend the rest of your life with, then tell me some shit like this?" she asked.

"I know it might not make sense to you now, but it will. When it does, then you'll understand. I'm sorry, baby. I just can't be with you. I'm in love with April," I repeated.

She shook her head. "I hope life brings you nothing but happiness, Ty. I love you," she said and kissed me on the forehead.

She walked off.

I turned around and looked out the window. I felt weird. I'd made the right decision. I just hoped that Jodi could find what she needed and deserved one day.

"Hey, stranger! Are you okay?" April asked.

I turned around.

"I could sure use a hug right now," I insinuated.

"I think I can help you with that," she said.

She walked over and hugged me.

"Where's my son?" I asked.

"With his godfather. I heard what you told Jodi and I don't know what to say."

"How 'bout nothing at all? Sometimes words can't do it so I'm going to say to you from my soul to yours—one, four, three!" I said.

She started smiling.

"I love you, too," she replied.

We kissed passionately, embarrassing one another.

"Come on, baby. You still owe me a dance," April said.

We went back inside and danced the night away.

Tyrelle

LOVE'S GAME

Dear Jodi,

I feel like I need to better explain why I said what I said at the reception. I think I at least owe you that much. Let me clear the air off the top, I still want to be with April. Throughout life we all will make mistakes because we are all human. I truly believe that the only way to prevent making the same mistakes over and over is to learn from them and correct it. The way I treated you was a big mistake. Let me be the first one to admit that. I didn't appreciate the value of your love until it was too late. Luckily though, your love changed me and turned me into a better man before you left my life. It turned me into the man I am today and should have been for you all along. I wish things could have been different. I wish I would have known the true meaning of love from the start. Things between us probably would have been different. Maybe it could have been us walking down that aisle together. Before you, I thought of love as nothing but a game. I played with it and took it for granted. Then I realized that love was only playing a game with me. It takes some of us longer in life to realize that we're not the ones playing the game but the ones getting played. I didn't realize it until just before I asked you to move in with me. I changed my ways and concentrated on only being with you and loving you but by then it was far too late. The game I thought I was playing finally played me for a final time. That's when you, of course, found out about me cheating on you with April. The one thing I have told you over and over since that dreaded day was that I was a changed man, not the one being portrayed. I still stand by that as of this day. In order for me to have changed, I have to learn from my mistakes and prevent them from recurring again. With that being said, how could or should I say can I possibly be with you? April and I are in a relationship together. She has put her trust and faith in me just as you once did. If I were to get back with you and leave her that would only prove that I have not changed. I would still be the selfless bastard that I once was. I don't know how far our relationship will go nor do I know if we will last but it's not up to me to question it. I can't shortchange it! I'm going to see things through and put everything in the hands of God. Maybe our paths and hearts will cross again but, for now, take my love and know that you have forever changed me and, for that, I will always be grateful and love you.

Tyrelle

AUTHOR BIO

Harold L. Turley II was born and raised in Washington, D.C.
An author and performance poet, he lives with his children in
Oxon Hill, Maryland. *Love's Game* is his first novel.

SNEAK PREVIEW: AN EXCERPT FROM

Azucar Moreno

BY SHELLEY HALIMA

COMING DECEMBER 2004

Mario is stuck with bartending duties for a while. You know how folks are; once they see someone with something, they want it, too. Which is what happened when people saw Chico and me sipping on margaritas that Mario made. Even though we've got beer, wine, wine coolers, Jack Daniel's, Jim Beam, Vox, and Hennessey out and available—that's not enough, they want margaritas, too. So right now Mario's blowing up the blender.

Alejandro, Dante, Chico and a couple other guys are at one of the tables playing Dominoes, while a few other guys are at another table playing cards. Other people are milling about socializing or dancing to "I Get Around" by Tupac. Rosie, Rhonda, Crystal, Odell and I are sitting together at a table.

I notice a new arrival coming late. It's our neighbor Sabrina's new boyfriend Thomas. Ugly must be taking a holiday. We've already got damn near a yard full of fine brothers and here comes another. Sabrina started dating Thomas recently and is already head over heels in love. I ain't mad at her. Thomas is a fine, tall glass of water that you want to sip slowly. He looks like a darker-skinned version of Boris Kodjoe. Not to slight my baby Mario and Alejandro who have awesome bodies, but still, compared to Thomas' sculpted frame, he makes them look like they go to the gym to look at the weights instead of lift them. Oh my.

"Here comes our crush, Rosie," I say.

She turns her head to look and she breaks out into a big smile.

"Oh, hell yeah! He know he fine, girl."

"He is hot," Rhonda says in an awed tone.

"He sure is," says Crystal, leaning forward. "Who is that?"

"That's Thomas. Sabrina's man," answers Rosie.

"Wha-ah. Hold up! Put the tape on pause!" Odell says, holding up his hand. "That's the new boyfriend y'all was talkin' about Sabrina had?"

"Yeah," I say. "Why?"

Odell purses his lips and cuts his eyes upward.

"What, Odell?" asks Rosie. "You know him or something?"

Odell crosses his arms and legs and starts humming, still looking upward.

"No way!" I exclaim. "Do not tell me you know him."

Rosie snaps her fingers at Odell. "Okay, spill it, bitch."

"Should I spill it?" Odell asks to himself, putting a finger on his chin. "No. I think I'll save that tea and spill it some other time."

"You better start talking," says Rosie.

"Yeah, Odell," Rhonda says.

"Okay, y'all done pried it out of me." He scoots his chair closer to the table. "I met him summer 'fore last when he walked up in Menjo's."

We all lean in closer to listen.

"Chile, he had e'erybody's head turning like we was in "The Exorcist." But me being the fastest sissy of the West Side, I made it to him first. I bought him some dranks and we got a little convo going. Now at the time, he was living with some crow named Delores. He said he need to have his breaks now and then to explore the other side. And honey, we ended doing some explorin' later on that night. Just a little explorin', mind you. Odell don't put out all the good china the first night. After that we hooked up wherever, whenever—at his house when nobody was home, mine when nobody was home, Rouge Park. We went strong for at least two months or so. Then I started falling in love." Looking upward, he raises his hand and makes a falling gesture. "Falling like a star from a moonlit sky."

"Oh, brother," we all grumble.

"This bitch is so dramatic," says Rosie.

"A-ny-way," he says, rolling his eyes and smacking his lips. "One night I told him how I felt and that I wanted to only be with him. Shoot, I was fixin' to leave Roberta and everythang. But you know that Negro had the nerve to say 'I can't be in no relationship with another man.'"

"What?" Rhonda says incredulously. "No, he didn't."

"Oh yes, he did, girl. Here we is laying up there in bed naked as jaybirds and he gonna say he can't be in no relationship with a man. We had been sneakin' on dates like dinner and the movies. Hell, technically we was already in a relationship. I just wanted it to be open and exclusive. Anywho, I broke it off after that, I knew how that story was gonna end—Odell, broken-hearted."

"We shouldn't be surprised I guess," I say. "These days so many people are up for any and everything." I cut my eyes to Rhonda and we exchange knowing looks.

We all look over at Thomas whose standing behind Sabrina with his arms wrapped around her. They're laughing—looking like the picture-perfect couple.

"Do you think someone should tell Sabrina?" I ask.

"No," says Rosie. "You know how she is—if you try and tell her anything about some man she's seeing, she automatically thinks you're lying and you're jealous of her. You remember how you tried to tell her when you found out that guy Clarence was married?"

I nod my head.

"She told you to stay out of her business and that you were hating on her—knowing damn well that you're not like that."

"Really?" asks Odell. "Oh, she wrong for that. If it ain't coming from somebody that be all in folks' business and be causing trouble, you need to listen."

"I know," says Rosie. "And what ended up happening? She ran into him, his wife and their two kids downtown at the African Festival. And that time Zoë tried to tell her that that other dude was a crack dealer. Sabrina said the same shit to her. It had to take him getting busted by the police for her to believe it. She's one of them females that you can't warn that the stove is hot, they gotta get burned themselves. If we tell her anything, she's not going to listen. So when she walks in on him with his dick up some man's ass—she'll find out."

"Uh-uh!" Crystal laughs.

Odell, Rhonda and I laugh also.

"You know," says Odell, running a hand across his cornrows. "I think I'll go over to Miss Sabrina and have her introduce me to her new man."

"Odell, you wouldn't!" I say.

"Wouldn't I?" he says, smiling at me. "Trick, you know me. I ain't scared to stir up some shit now and then."

"Weren't you just talking about folks being in other folks' business and causing trouble?" Rosie asks.

Odell tilts his head like he's thinking for a moment. "Yes, I did say that, didn't I?"

He gets up and sashays over to where Sabrina and Thomas are standing. All of us are looking with our mouths agape. The look that comes over Thomas' face when he sees Odell...If no one thinks black folks can go pale—Thomas is proof that they can.

ANOTHER SNEAK PREVIEW: AN EXCERPT FROM

Confessions of a Lonely Soul

BY HAROLD L. TURLEY II

COMING SOON FROM STREBOR BOOKS

CHAPTER 1
And So The Story Goes

MARCH 12, 2004, 10:30 A.M.

No one knew what to expect. No one knew what to think. All anyone could think about was the fact that I was just here talking, laughing, and joking with everyone last week. Now today we are here to bury me. Life was unpredictable and what I was about to reveal would send shock waves through everyone's heart.

My mother, accompanied by her husband, my brother, sister, and in-laws walked in the church deep in mourning. My mother dropped to her knees at the sight of my closed casket. Pictures of me filled the church. She knew she had to be strong but no parent wants to live the nightmare of outliving one of their children. On top of that, I was her first born. The oldest. Step by step brought back memory after memory. She remembered the first day she brought me home from the hospital, my first step, my first day of school, my first-grade school crush, when she caught me having sex, the day I graduated from high school, the day I graduated from Towson University, my wedding day, the first day I brought my daughter home from the agency, and her last and probably most treasured memory, my 30th birthday party. The tears started to pour down her face. She tried harder and harder to control them but the closer and closer she'd get to my casket the heavier each tear seemed and the easier they trickled down the side of her face. Finally she approached my casket and laid her arms across it and prayed.

"Dear Heavenly Father, please look after my son as he makes he journey from the flesh into the spirit. Please guide him throughout and never leave his side as you've never left mine. Look after my family, Lord, during our time of grief and give us the strength and the will to see us through. In Jesus' name I pray, Amen," she whispered as she lay on my casket.

My mother wiped the remaining tears from her eyes and sat down. After her, my brother, sister and in-laws begun to pay their respects. My family sat down and watched as the church began to fill with friends and family.

As time approached 1 p.m., the Reverend Young started the ceremony. Even in death I found a way to be late for something. The funeral should have started at 11:30 a.m. but it seemed as if the steady stream of people never stopped. The church was packed to capacity and then some. Never would I have thought I'd touch so many lives by trying to educate and expand their thinking.

Reverend Young approached the podium.

"Good afternoon, church! We are here today to celebrate the life of DeMarco Montreal Reid. Not to mourn but to celebrate the *life* of a man who devoted his time and efforts to HIV and AIDS education, awareness, and prevention. I can remember my first time hearing him speak to the congregation: he spoke on how HIV/AIDS isn't a death sentence but a new beginning, a new chapter in a different book of life. He taught us whether we were or were not positive the importance of treasuring life because it's a gift bestowed upon us from God. He'd make us laugh. He'd make us cry. But most importantly, he'd make us think about life and not to live for our future but in the present.

A lot of you are probably wondering why? Why did the Lord have to take him away from us at such an early age? If you've come today seeking an answer, it will not come from me. Go to the Lord and he'll not provide you the answer but the strength to see you through. Now I promised brother Reid I wouldn't preach today but what I will do is deliver His message. Go to Him! When you're up late at night and wondering why Marco is no longer here, call on Him! When you're lying on the couch watching TV and you think about one of the many memories Marco left you with and the depression starts to set in, go to Him! When life seems as if it has you down and the struggles of life won't let you back up, go to Him! No matter what the cause, no matter what the occasion, no matter what the question, no matter what the situation, go to Him and He will provide you the resolution. He will solve the problem! He will ALWAYS be in your corner. He ALWAYS will be on your side. Go to Him!"

Reverend Young stepped back from the podium to the sound of *amens* and *hallelujahs* throughout the church. Everyone was so caught up in her mini-sermon that no one noticed the larger overhead projection screen coming down.

"Let the church say, 'Amen!'" I yelled to the audience on film. "Cheer up! I know this is my funeral and all, but damn, my body isn't even cold and in the ground yet."

People in the crowd started to laugh. Even my mother cracked a smile as tears still frequented her face.

"Let me first apologize for not allowing anyone to say a few good things about me and speak on how I touched them and yada yada ya. No, I've always been different and I'm not going to stop now even in death. I don't want any of you crying so the ushers have instructions to escort anyone out of here they spot crying. I'm just playing but seriously, I'm in a much better place now.

"It's a little hotter down here then I thought though. Okay, lemme stop! Seriously though, it's nice up here. Me and Tupac are going to my 'Welcome to Heaven' after-party over at Nat King Cole's jazz club tonight. The drinks could be better though. All they serve is water or wine, no Remy. The wine is strong though; I'll give you that, but you know how a brotha loves him some Remy. It's all good though 'cause Jesus sure knows how to throw a party. I'm telling you. Ma, I think you are right; Jesus is a black man cause he sure can dance. Last night over at Nipsy's he started the Electric Slide line. I thought I'd fall out."

My cousin Tia burst out laughing loud enough that someone across the street could hear her clearly.

"Tia, it ain't that damn funny!" I said.

She stopped, astonished—wondering how I knew she was laughing from beyond the grave.

I continued, "It don't matter where we are or how corny the joke is, Tia will find a way to laugh as if Eddie Murphy was on stage doing his rendition of 'Saturday Night Live' or 'Delirious.'"

People in the audience started nodding their heads in agreement.

"We could be at a funeral and everyone is in there crying, but she we'll find a way to laugh about something somebody says. Hold up, we are at a funeral right now. Hmmm!"

The crowd laughed.

"But seriously, folks, Tia, your laughter is what is needed throughout the world. You have the gift to be able to see the bright spot in the darkest cloud. You never let anything get you down and always find a way to find the positive out of every situation. I love you for that."

"I love you, too, Boo," Tia replied as tears began to come down her eyes.

"I hope all of us can in a way follow Tia's example on how to deal with a crisis or a tragedy when you deal with my passing. I know some of you will miss me, mostly because I owe a lot of y'all money, but make this a happy occasion because I was able to do what the Lord placed me on this earth to do. Don't think about the fact that I won't be acting a fool at no more of the family reunions but that I was able to share so many with all of you. If all else fails, be happy that I'm up there with Tupac and Marvin Gaye cutting a rug at Club Nazareth every Tuesday and Friday."

As hard as people were laughing now, my funeral seemed more like a comedy show at a comedy club rather than a funeral at church. People were gasping for air, they were laughing so hard.

"Okay, I better stop before my mother tries to kill herself just so she can come up here with her switch. Mama, don't do it! There isn't no coming back if you do. There you go. See that smile on your face right now? That is how I want you to remember me, with that same smile. I want you to remember me as a man who'd strive to put a smile on someone's face no matter what the situation.

"I know Reverend Young has asked y'all to look toward the Lord in your time of grievance but I also want you to look toward one another as well. Be there for each other and don't judge one another's faults. We are family and without family we have nothing.

When I lost Kalia, I no longer had a desire to live. My family gave me my strength and my desire to want to keep going. Each one of you played a role in being a part of my motivation and my inspiration. Because of you, I couldn't and wouldn't allow HIV or AIDS destroy another family as it did mine."

Everyone looked around in confusion wondering what I was talking about. As far as everyone knew, no one in our family had either disease. I always told every one I lost a close friend of mine to AIDS and that is why I pushed and strived so hard to concur the disease.

"Today, it's time for the truth. I've never told a soul what I'm about to share with each of you and vowed to take it to my death bed out of respect for my wife but, one of the reasons why Kalia committed suicide was because she found out she was HIV positive."

The crowd sat there stunned at what they heard. It couldn't have been true, not Lia. She would have come to someone. She would have told somebody. She didn't.

"She decided that instead of facing the challenge of fighting this disease, she'd take the easy route. I sat up countless nights wondering why she never just came to me. Why she didn't let me help her through it because I needed her just as much as she needed me? I also think the fact that she didn't want to see me suffer knowing she gave me the virus played a role in her death as well."

"That is bullshit! Turn that shit off! I'll be damned if I sit here and listen to him lie about my daughter like that. She didn't have no AIDS. She would have come to me. If anything she killed herself because of that bastard and the problems they were having in their marriage due to him cheating. She killed herself because of that bastard!" Mr. Robinson said interrupting the tape playing.

"You call my brother a bastard again and I swear on my life I'll beat the shit out of your old ass. If my brother said he got AIDS from that bitch then that is where he got it from."

"Kenny! Watch your mouth in the Lord's house and sit your ass down. I'm not going to sit here and listen to either of you being disrespectful. Right now all of us are shocked and left with a lot of questions and finally someone is providing the answers. If you can't respect my son on his day, then please leave," my mother said.

"Phil, just calm down. We have known Marco for over ten years and have never known him to be a liar. Please, just listen to what he has to say," Mrs. Robinson said.

Everyone settled themselves down while Reverend Young rewound the tape.

It replayed, "I also think the fact that she didn't want to see me suffer knowing she gave me the virus played a role in her death as well.

"She never let me tell her that I didn't blame her though. I blamed myself. If I had been more of a husband instead of trying to further my career, then she would have never gone to another man for attention and comfort. I'll never forgive myself for the pain I caused her. All I could do was live each day for her memory and our love.

"She is my best friend, my angel. Finally I'm with her again and able to hold her."

I paused as I became choked up and tears started to come down my face at the memory of the love of my life.

"Mom, Kenny, Diamond, Mr. and Mrs. Robinson, I'm sorry I've kept this from all of you all these years, but I never wanted any of you to look at me differently. I didn't want you to look at me with sympathy rather than admiration. I never viewed this as a punishment but rather a test of my faith and determination. Luckily for me, Ma, you raised me to fight in what I believe and that I believe is what enabled me to save lives. How can that not be a blessing?" I paused.

"When Lia left me, I was left with the answer to a lot of questions. I'm not going to do that to any of you. Today, I come clean. Today, I tell the story and let all of you know what happened."

Johnson, Keith Lee
Sugar & Spice 1-59309-013-7
Pretenses 1-59309-018-8

Johnson, Rique
Love & Justice 1-59309-002-1
Whispers from a Troubled Heart 1-59309-020-X
Every Woman's Man 1-59309-036-6
Sistergirls.com 1-59309-004-8

Lee, Darrien
All That and a Bag of Chips 0-9711953-0-7
Been There, Done That 1-59309-001-3
What Goes Around Comes Around 1-59309-024-2

Luckett, Jonathan
Jasminium 1-59309-007-2
How Ya Livin' 1-59309-025-0

McKinney, Tina Brooks
All That Drama (December 2004) 1-59309-033-1

Quartay, Nane
Feenin 0-9711953-7-4

Rivers, V. Anthony
Daughter by Spirit 0-9674601-4-X
Everybody Got Issues 1-59309-003-X
Sistergirls.com 1-59309-004-8

Roberts, J. Deotis
Roots of a Black Future: Family and Church 0-9674601-6-6
Christian Beliefs 0-9674601-5-8

Stephens, Sylvester
Our Time Has Come 1-59309-026-9

Valentine, Michelle
Nyagra's Falls 0-9711953-4-X

White, A.J.
Ballad of a Ghetto Poet 1-59309-009-9

White, Franklin
Money for Good 1-59309-012-9
Potentially Yours 1-59309-027-7

Zane (Editor)
Breaking the Cycle 1-59309-021-8